Praise for Leo Hunt

Thirteen Days of Midnight

Shortlisted for the Waterstones Children's Book Prize 2016

'A self-assured debut that's as funny as it is terrifying'
Publisher's Weekly – starred review

'A truly unique plot and perfect pacing combine to immediately hook readers'
School Library Journal – starred review

'The most entertaining and original fantasy I've read in a long time' *Addicted to Media*

'A tense, compulsive, edge-of-seat read for teenagers' *Booktrust*

'A great debut. Confident and enthusiastic in its storytelling … I really loved [it]' *The Bookbag*

'Hunt manoeuvres the psychology of his readers with great skill, playing elegant tricks on the readers susceptibilities'
Books for Keeps

Eight Rivers of Shadow

'Whopping good suspense in the netherworld' *Kirkus*

'Hunt's ear for teen voices is acute – in a sub-genre overwhelmed by twinkly vampires, it is salutary to have a ballsy, convincing adolescent male voice' *The Guardian*

'Full of fantastic thrills, supernatural spills and wail-out-loud wit … .uk

Also available

Thirteen Days of Midnight

Eight Rivers of Shadow

Seven Trees of Stone

PHANTOM

ORCHARD BOOKS

First published in Great Britain in 2018 by The Watts Publishing Group

1 3 5 7 9 10 8 6 4 2

A CIP catalogue record for this book is available from the British Library.

ISBN 978 1 40834 503 0

Typeset in Minion Pro by Avon DataSet Ltd, Bidford-on-Avon, Warwickshire

Printed and bound in Great Britain by Clays Ltd, St Ives plc

The paper and board used in this book are made from wood from responsible sources.

Orchard Books
An imprint of Hachette Children's Group
Part of The Watts Publishing Group Limited
Carmelite House
50 Victoria Embankment
London EC4Y 0DZ

An Hachette UK Company
www.hachette.co.uk

www.hachettechildrens.co.uk

ORCHARD

It is the Age of Machinery, in every outward and inward sense of that word.

THOMAS CARLYLE

Young woman walking through lush green grass. Sky clear, cloudless. Her eyes radiant with curiosity. We follow her gaze, see a tornado of butterflies rising from the grasslands. The insects are all shapes and colours, swirling like rainbow smoke against boundless blue.

'We know that within every human being lies the spirit of infinite possibility.'

Close-up of her beautiful face. Her skin becomes glass. Inside her head, we see an oval shape. Sunshine yellow. It begins to stir.

'We understand your potential. We want to let your mind soar.'

The yellow object is a chrysalis, and it is hatching. A delicate yellow body is emerging. Yellow wings unfurl.

Music – strings, light and airy.

The butterfly is moving through the woman's glass face, like a swimmer through water. It is free. It is in the sky. It is joining the others and they rise, rise, rise into the blueness.

The music swells.

We follow the yellow butterfly, our butterfly, as it tumbles among many others.

'That's why, if you choose the BlissMedia Infinite package today, we're offering you unlimited metadata streaming, right to your neural-implant rig. So there's no limit on your mind's potential. Experience life. Experience adventure. Experience freedom.'

The butterfly descends from perfect blue. The woman holds out one hand. The yellow creature lands on her glass palm.

She smiles at us, unafraid, young, and radiant.

'Experience Bliss.'

part one

NOVA

Sky goes glitchy when it rains, makes the lumens ripple like they're dancing. The droplets mess up the proximity calculations and you see the logos overhead as smears of paint in water, losing their proper shapes, becoming glittering broken things. Scattered glifs, whispered dreams. *You deserve this*. A hamburger melting into a haze of light. *Try out new flavours*. A yellow butterfly emerging from a woman's face. *Experience Bliss*. Peaks of the buildings getting lost in the clouds and the shifting lumen-glow, and for a moment I imagine I could walk up the walls of these cityblocs to some other beautiful place.

No one else looks at the sky; they're focused on what's ahead. There's a whole crowd pouring out of the magrail station, dressed in rainwraps, bored faces staring behind laminated masks. Most of the people pushing past are corpsmen, low-rank workers with corp uniforms and corp implants and corp minds. Born in corp nursingblocs, live in corp housingblocs. Drink together at corp recreation nights and cry together at corp funerals. I can see a guy with a fry-stall, smell the locusts sizzling in pans under a canopy, like anyone will buy his food today if there's a chance the rain touched it. A column of moonies dressed in bright orange, carrying coiled lengths of cable, walking in unison. A squad of Metrowatch enforcers by the station gates, black armour branded with their staring eye, water glistening on their visors. A snoop prowls the air above the crowd, rotors just louder than the rain, shining its little light on one commuter's head, then another. So that's what you've got out here this morning: corpsmen, vendors, moonies, police. Everyone with somewhere to be and nothing to hide.

And then there's me.

Who am I?

When I was born – the only name I ever got given for free – I was Hanna Latch. The first time I robbed someone my name was Imelda Barlow. Last week I was Mindi Wheatman. Today, outside the magrail station in the rain, I'm Charlotte Alorda. But if you really knew me, if you saw through me, you'd call me Nova.

What I'm doing here is work, even if it looks like I'm watching the world turn. There's another city behind this one. An invisible city, without streets or buildings, a city built from code and cold light. This hidden city is the metanet: the web that links every person, every product, every machine, everything the corps value. It's all around us, data flowing through secret pathways like the corpsmen flow through the station's turnstiles. I lean against the wall and watch the crowd and listen to the whispers. I hear the snoops checking faces against active warrants; I hear the implants inside every commuter monitoring their heart rate and blood sugar and eye movements; I hear people talking to their families, downloading music, catching up on the newsfeeds – all this and more is the metanet, an infinite sea of information. This is where I do my work.

I've got digital assistants out in the crowd already, travelling unseen, prying and probing, trying to scent who's strong and who's weak, who doesn't have the right ice, who didn't update to the latest version. When my assistants find someone, I hear a chime and my optical implants highlight the target so they shine like a beacon in the rainy station concourse. Right there: today's unlucky object of my affection. One figure among countless others, ablaze with lumen-light.

I join the crowd, jostling through plastic-coated bodies. I'm running a list of programs in my head, watching their glifs fizz behind my eyelids: icebreakers and spoofers, leechers and loopers, port-jammers and proxies, ready for the day's business. Some are pre-fab; some are custom programs I made myself. All of them are illegal.

My target's up ahead. I can't see him any more, but I can see the lumen-trail he leaves behind, a thread of light in the air. The commuter concourse blends into a shopping plaza that hangs between two cityblocs, the magrail line running below us. I duck underneath a guardrail, ram through the gap between two commuters, elbowing and pushing with my gaze set blankly into the distance, like the people around me were nothing but walking cushions. I'm good at moving through crowds, and soon I've caught up to my target, a corpsman with broad shoulders and blond hair flattened down under the plastic hood of his rainwrap. I get to work.

It's pretty simple, the way it happens. Everyone's got a wristhub, the implant in your arm that lets you buy stuff.

Your wristhub talks to someone else's and you fork out that way. What I'm doing is setting up a transaction, one that goes from him to me, without his permission, no receipts and no refunds. It's called leeching. The first problem is making sure he doesn't know it's happening, which is why I need my box of tricks. The second problem is that wristhub transactions have a limited range, so I need to stay right next to him.

It's going good so far. I can see readouts in the corner of my eye: confirming the first transaction, telling his hub that it already agreed to send me the money. A snoop hovers overhead, bathing the pair of us in harsh light, but my heart doesn't miss a beat. I've got a rainwrap over my face and a nice fake ID with no criminal record, so there's no reason for security drones to take an interest. The snoop barely pauses before whirring away.

First transaction goes down smooth. It's best to carve cash out in small chunks. If you're greedy, try and drain all the byts from their account in one go, it'll get frozen and flagged and some BytBank operator will be squealing in their ear. You come away with nothing. Right now, if anyone is monitoring his payments, it looks like he bought a meal on the way to work. Second transaction goes through. He's feeling generous, bought a meal for a friend as well. We walk further, past a camp of non-econs sheltering from the rain in a disused storefront, and on to a pedestrian bridge, still pressed together, and I'm looking into the distance, face emotionless beneath my mask. Third payment goes through, more byts flowing from his account to mine. This is an excellent start to the day.

Out of nowhere he stops dead. I walk straight into his back. He's definitely realised. I keep cool. I've got location spoofers running, so there's no way for him to track where the leecher is. I brush past him, disengaging my programs. Nothing to see here.

A hand grabs my wrist, pulling me round so hard I nearly fall. I'm face to face with the corpsman, water beading on his rainwrap, dripping from his laminated chin.

'Get off me!' I yell, trying to slip away. He keeps his hand on my wrist, the tight, professional grip of a man who's used to catching people.

'Ms Alorda,' the guy says, 'you're aware unauthorised wristhub transactions are a Category Two crime.'

He's not a corpsman. He's Metrowatch. He's bait. Goes into the crowd with deliberately weak ice and waits for a leecher to bite.

'Got one,' he's saying into his hub's mic. 'Need a compliance team at my position.'

One of the big problems women have on the magrail

is gropers. It's so crowded and some revolting guys just can't resist having a feel, especially because they know you can't move away. A lot of commuter girls carry these little shockers, civilian-grade nerve disruptors. They're totally legal. You can take one through a Metrowatch checkpoint and they won't even blink.

So what I do is scream 'PERVERT!' and give him the highest dose possible, right in the gut. He yells and convulses, letting go of my wrist as his hand spasms. Corpsmen are still flowing past, nobody giving us a second look. Who can afford to be late for work? If you're fired, you're nothing. Lose your apartment, your healthcare, your whole life.

'He tried to grab me!' I yell, pushing away from the enforcer, who's twitching on the wet concrete. 'You saw! Dirty groper!'

'Watch out!' someone shouts as I bounce into them. The Metrowatch guy is trying to get back up, but his legs don't work too well yet, can't hold his weight. I'm taking stock. He led me into the middle of a bridge, making it as hard as he could for me to get away. I can see a snoop diving for us through the rain; three Metrowatch enforcers push through the crowd ahead, warning glifs on their armour strobing nosebleed red. Behind me the undercover enforcer is getting to his feet.

Trapped.

Other people, maybe they'd give up. Get taken off in cuffs. But some of the programs I run on my implants are way more illegal than unauthorised wristhub transactions. Two of my icebreakers are Category Five prohibited software, not to mention my copy of Phantom. The big corps don't care that much about someone robbing one of their workers. Once they've paid him his wage, it's his problem what happens to that money. What they do care about are the programs that break their encryptions and steal their secrets. If they arrest me and find something like that … it's over. I'll end up as a moonie, head shaved, working down in the dark until I die. Makes me shudder thinking of it. The Moth himself couldn't get me out of that kind of trouble.

Four Metrowatch enforcers. One girl on a bridge. It doesn't look good. No easy way out of this. Like I said, other people, maybe they'd give up.

But do you know what a nova is? It's when a star shines brighter than it ever has before, a blazing beacon up there in the blackness. You don't get people calling you Nova by being dull.

So I jump off the bridge.

For a moment, there's nothing beneath my feet, just me falling with the rain, the void between the cityblocs yawning wide. From an upstrata floor like this one, the fall to the ground is close to a mile.

I'm not suicidal. There is something between me and that abyss. The thing is, it's not a walkway – it's the magrail line. I hit the metal hard, the shock fizzing in my legs. The enforcers are yelling overhead, but I know they aren't keen to follow me. They won't risk their lives to catch a teenage leecher.

I've solved one problem. Now I need to get off the track before a train hits me. The magrails travel fast, almost silent, and I don't have long. I've never walked on this bit of track before, but they're all built the same. There are hatches at regular intervals, maintenance access for the moonies, which take you down to a crawl space underneath the magrail line. I just have to find one before the next train gets here.

I set off as fast as I can, looking for an orange door in the ground. Ten steps, twenty, rain still crashing down on my hood, and now there's a static feeling too, a vibration in my bones. Train coming.

I can't see any orange hatch up ahead, and I'm starting to panic, with nothing below me that's close enough to leap on to, and then my foot hits something and I nearly fall over. A handle. It's the maintenance hatch, so dirty that it's black, not orange, with the locking panel right where it should be. I press my wristhub against it. No idea how long I have. I send icebreakers shooting out into the system, invisible fingers pulling the lock apart.

Rain beats down on my back.

Should've just let them catch me.

No. Better dead than a moonie.

Static rising. Every hair on my arm standing on end now. Fizzy feeling in my stomach. Magrail's almost on me. Every breath could be the last one. Icebreakers worming through the lock.

The track is shaking beneath my feet.

Please.

The locking panel chirps, telling me to enter. I grab the handle and wrench the access hatch open, throwing myself into the crawl space below the track.

As I hit the floor, the magrail passes overhead. I clutch my head to cover my ears, pain throbbing in my hands and knees, the world shaking like I'm inside a drum.

The noise only lasts a moment, and the train is gone. Rain drips through the hatch, pooling in the dirt around me. I check my rainwrap, but it's fine, no holes. I breathe in deeply, tasting oil and chemicals and the rubbery tang that the air picks up from my mask's filter. Still alive.

The crawl space is dark, but I light my fingertorch, casting a blue glow over the grimy metal walls. My optic implants project a lumen-thread into the air, showing the way back to the station. I know the enforcers can't get a location trace on me, Phantom takes care of that, and, though there won't be such a crowd now, there's always someone around who isn't as secure as they think they are. We're behind on our payments; Patches will want more money than I got. I should try again.

No. They'll be on the alert for a young female leecher now, even though they couldn't get a proper trace on me. I've had bad luck once already. For all I know, that station is swarming with Metrowatch decoys. I have eighty byts in my leeching account, and that's not nothing.

I turn and crawl away from the magrail station, towards an engineering relay. There's an elevator there, which will take me all the way down, into the undercity. I'm going home.

It's quiet down here, nothing like the living City above me. No corpsmen, no snoops, no Metrowatch, no lumens flickering around you. The metanet is almost mute. I'm a long way from the nearest active transmitter. All I can pick up are a few threads of information, the rest of it fizzing above me, out of reach.

The City started growing upwards a long time ago. The taller the cityblocs get – the more layers of pedestrian concourses and traffic tubes and magrails that are built between them – the less sunlight reaches the lower floors. When their floor goes dark, everyone who can afford to moves upwards, and the value of the apartments they left behind drops. Eventually whole floors are abandoned, and the City has grown another layer. What you end up with is a few hundred floors of respectable, sunlit, upstrata City, and a shaded world beneath it, where people who can't afford to see natural light live. Travel a few hundred floors below *that*, and you're in the undercity.

Down here, at the very base of the cityblocs, you'll find everything nobody wants, everything they left behind: plastic packaging lying in drifts, burnt-out skycars, rotting food, piles of old furniture. Me. Doorways and walkways and lifts that don't move, broken screens and empty trains. The only machines that do function are the tangles of waste-disposal tubes, rumbling as they spew sewage and refuse into the void. Most of the people who come down to the undercity are moonies, making sure the foundations are still intact, that the cityblocs aren't going to collapse into the poisoned earth. You can see traces of their work crews as you walk around, the ration wrappers and broken tools they dropped. The other people who come into the deep darkness are the people who still live here.

I step across a pool of stagnant water, the blue radiance

of my fingertorch reflected in its surface. City mapping programs don't get updated as the lowest floors decay, so you can't rely on them to find your way around, like you would in the upper strata. You have to know the ground, know which walkways will hold your weight and which are rusted all the way through; which doorways are jammed shut and which ones can still be opened. I cross a pedestrian bridge, the decaying twin of the bridge the enforcers trapped me on, hundreds of floors above.

The area past the bridge used to be a leisurebloc, I think. The debris is so thick, it's difficult to tell. I walk softly down a long spiral staircase, my fingertorch sending jagged shadows to jitter on the wall as I move. After a long time, I can hear lapping. I push open the door at the bottom of the staircase and step into an apartment decorated with the most fashionable of undercity accessories: thigh-deep toxic water.

I'm in the deepest roots of the City, about as low as you can get. There are still floors beneath me, but they're flooded, have been for decades. The water's pure poison, thick with floating trash and sewage and this yellow-white algae that doesn't need the sun to grow. Even with my mask, the smell is strong and sour. Plastic debris moves, slow and stately, around my rainwrap's boots as I wade across the flooded room. I stop just short of a huge broken windowpane, which once would've led out into the empty space between two cityblocs. Now it opens on to a sunless sea.

I reach into the pouch at the front of my rainwrap and pull out one of the raft capsules Patches gave me. Military equipment, something he saved from the war. It's a green plastic pill, but you don't want to swallow it. Once the pill gets wet, it grows, expanding into a plastic boat within minutes. I peel away the non-reactive outer coating and dip it in the water. There's a hissing sound and it starts to unfurl, growing and warping, and soon it's an oval green raft. I climb in. The boat was built to carry a soldier, someone in body armour with a hunchback of weapons and gear, so I fit with room to spare. I peel the paddle from the raft's floor and sail my boat through the wide broken window, away from the side of the citybloc, out into the open water.

The slow current takes me through an old shopping concourse, the abandoned floors of the blocs looming over me, my fingertorch only lighting little snatches of their grey ruin. I see places where the walls have started to crumble and moonies have done repair work, put in new beams to stop the whole citybloc collapsing. Power cables hang overhead, laden with fat white bats. Some sleeping, some flapping and squeaking when my light reveals them.

Not much further now. The current pulls me closer to home. I see lamps moving on a floor above me, maybe scavengers. There's no reason for them to trouble me, but I kill my torch just in case, sailing in pitch-blackness until they're out of sight.

I lie back and look up through my rainwrap's clear mask at the darkness above. Somewhere up there people are living, working, going through their routines for the corps, looking through the same windows every day at the same rain. Not me. I fell through the cracks in the world and survived, found something else down here. The black spaces beneath their feet are my open sky.

The air's getting warmer now, and I know I'm near the Gut. I can see our sign, the green glif Patches painted on the wall by our dock. I paddle over and pull myself and the raft out of the water. I leave it on the concrete bank, white algae clinging to the underside. You need special powder to make these rafts shrink back to pill size, and it takes about a day, a real pain if you're in a hurry. I think that's why the securicorps stopped using them. We've got a big tub of the shrink-powder back in the Gut. I've just got to remember to come back out here.

I climb a staircase full of plastic trash that hisses

weightlessly as I wade through it, and cross a pedestrian bridge over a chasm between two ruined blocs. A torrent of waste water falling past me, my ears filled with ceaseless white noise as it greets the dark lake below. It's growing warmer as I get closer to home. I'm starting to sweat under my rainwrap hood. I'm safe from the rain here, so I open the fastenings by my neck and let the mask hang open, breathe unfiltered air. There's a doorway marked again with our glif, third from the right, and I duck into it, finding myself in a doom-black hallway lined with derelict apartments. I know the route now. Down two floors, take a hard left. I walk slowly, keeping my ears open.

Halfway down the hall I hear a soft noise at my back, like a quiet cough. That's what I was listening for. I whirl round, fingertorch lighting the space behind me in ghastly blue.

The hall is packed with skinny white animals, hunched over like beggars. My torchlight shines on their eyeless faces, the pale, damp tongues dangling out of the end of their snouts. They were waiting inside the empty apartments, and they snuck out behind me as I passed. That cough's like an alarm, about the loudest sound they ever make unless they're fighting. I know this pack; it's Cromwell's crew, and I can see him at the front, pulpy warts all over his muzzle.

There's more life down here than you'd think, and blind dogs are top of the food chain. They're a bit like the dogs people used to keep as pets, but they're not tame any more. They changed in the darkness, became misshapen and wild. Ade says they're not natural, insists they got genomed by a corp and released on purpose to thin the underdwellers out, make sure nobody wants to squat down here. There could be something in that.

Blind dogs hunt in pitch-black, or as close as they can get, and they can hear your heartbeat from miles away. They're climbers too; I've seen them go up walls that look smooth as glass, toes finding cracks you'd never know were there. They're not so brave on their own, but watch that change when they're in a pack, and there's no hope for you if you corner one by accident. They'll fight in a frenzy if you trap them with no way out, or if they think their children are in danger. Everyone who lives down here's had close calls. Right now they're testing me, waiting to see what I'll do.

My heartbeat's not too fast, which is good. If they think you're scared, it gets them excited. I get the shrieker out of my rainwrap pouch and bring it to my lips.

When I blow into it, the pack start coughing in unison, stamping at the ground. Human ears can't hear the noise the shrieker makes, but to blind dogs it sounds like a shuttlejet breaking the sound barrier inside their skulls. I blow again, taking a step towards them, and the pack backs away, coughing and slurping. Cromwell yawns at me, showing the speckled black inside of his jaws. I give him a third blast and he turns round and runs back into their apartment, his family vanishing with him.

Moments later and you'd never know they were there at all. When I'm sure they've gone, I turn and hurry along the corridor, down two flights of stairs, hard left across a dark, empty landing, and through our secret door.

We call it the Gut because it's built around an old geothermal conduit, part of the system that powers the whole of the City. It's warm and shakes when pressure gets released, makes a sound like your belly growling after a day of no food. Patches has lived down here for years now and never been cleared out, which is pretty solid for an undercity squat. Walls are concrete, covered over in chipped purple paint. There's carpets hanging off them too, big foreign carpets with whirling patterns and galaxies of holes burned through by cigarettes. I take a right, push through a curtain of plastic beads, and I'm in Patches' workshop.

It's a dim, crowded room, hung with junk he's fixing. He's good at that; likes it when the kids bring him stuff they've found in the undercity's huge rubbish dumps, the older the better. One wall is taken up by obsolete monitors, teleputers, bits of hardware from back before people had implants, when we used to look at screens and all the tech was still outside our bodies. On one rack I see a broken snoop; solar panels off a military satellite from the Water Wars; the engine from a skycar, a black, greasy mass of tubes and valves like a burnt heart, leaking coolant on to a sheet. The side tables are laden with machinery I can't put a name to, coils of wire lying limp next to molten fluxes of plastic that look like a daydream made solid. Patches collects broken things.

The man himself is sitting at his workbench, tinkering with his left hand. Got the synthskin pulled back so you can see metal underneath. Tin mug of coffee steaming beside him, lamp casting a glossy sheen on the ruin of his head. Half a cigar tucked behind his ear. Work shirt that's green beneath decades of oil and dirt. He hears me come in and looks up.

Calling Patches ugly would be flattering him. He looks like two different people got torn apart and someone tried to make a new person with the remains, in the dark, using their bad hand. His skull's bumpy as an asteroid, with one wet human eye and a white synthetic one that whispers in the socket as it tracks you around. There's no hair on his head, no eyebrows or beard, not even a short, curly bunch poking out of his nose. His lower jaw is flesh-coloured plastic, his neck mottled with burn scars. His left arm is synthetic up to the elbow, and both feet are gone, replaced by metal leg braces he undoes when it's time to bunk down. When he walks, it's in lurches, side to side, keeping himself upright with a cane. I've never seen him without his shirt and I don't want to.

'What're you working on?' I ask.

'Index finger,' he says 'Getting involuntary flex.'

He tightens a tiny screw in the palm of his metal hand.

How Patches got like this is he was in the war, decades before I was born, the final Water War when the American Empire collapsed. He worked for a military corp, flew an exosuit for them. Way Patches tells it, he was first in and last out, tip of the spear, didn't know what fear was. Thought he'd live for ever. Then he came to the day his luck ran out. He survived the crash, but wished he hadn't and the enemy took what was left of him into one of their detentionblocs. He won't tell me what that was like, except he had both his eyes and hands when he went in.

The people he was fighting lost the war. He got released and his old employer released him too; he couldn't fight for them any more and didn't want to anyway. He came to the City and got as much surgery as he could with the money he had saved up, and then he sank, came down to the undercity where there's no daylight and no laws and nobody to ask who you are or where you came from. He was the one who founded the Gut. If you're a kid and you can leech for him, earn for him, there's a bed and a meal here.

'You're back early,' he says.

'Got tagged,' I say. 'Thought I'd head below. Let things cool off.'

He puts his screwdriver down. 'Again?'

'What d'you mean, again?'

'Means again. Last month—'

'Last month's last month! They didn't make me then, didn't make me now either! Metrowatch had bait out. I leeched on to him by mistake. I got away, no heat.'

'You're not careful enough,' he says.

'I am careful!' I snap, remembering the noise the magrail made as it went over me. I nearly died on the tracks this morning. But he doesn't need to know about that.

'They only have to catch you once,' he says. 'And then what would I do, eh? What's Patches going to do without your help, Nova? You know I can't walk well any more. You know how things are. We already lost good people. I need everyone bringing in a solid earning right now, and you're my best. We can't have you going away.'

'They didn't catch me. I jolted him in the stomach; everyone thought he was a groper. I got away, and I still got his byts too.'

'You kept the cash from a lure?' he asks. Patches can't move his face too well, but he's trying to scowl. 'You brought us money with a trace on it? I know you aren't that stupid, Nova.'

Feel a burning in my face. Hot shame. Of course there's a trace on the money. I took it from a Metrowatch enforcer. We can't spend it. I should've wiped it hours ago.

'Sorry,' I say. 'Didn't think. I'll get rid of it.'

Patches puts his hand, his warm human one, on my shoulder. Feels good, like I'm not alone down here. But there's still the shame, sharp-toothed and sour, gnawing me. I can't afford to make mistakes. We might be squatting in the undercity, no rent to a housingcorp, but we've still got costs: tools, coffee, water filters, pay a gang to keep the other gangs off us. And I need the latest software, need icebreakers and spoofers and leaked securicorp data to keep myself in business as a leecher, and nobody in Nightmarket gives out gifts. Nothing in the City's free, and I just brought home eighty byts with a trace on them. Today's a big hollow zero.

'You get rid of that money fast as you can,' he says. 'And it puts us short. It's no good, Nova, no good at all for a morning's work. This isn't what I keep you around for, is it?'

'I know,' I say. 'I'll fix it, I will. I'll get us more. I'll go back up—'

'Don't know about that,' Patches says, shaking his head. 'Luck's not with you, it's not with you. I think you stay here for today. Let the world turn, eh? Got work needs doing down here, as it happens. Ade's coming by for collection, so you're going to be the one tells him we can't pay this week.'

'We didn't pay him last week either.'

'I know,' Patches says with a grimace. 'We didn't. But he likes you. You're his friend. So you're going to keep him sweet so he keeps his father sweet. Right?'

'Ade likes me,' I say, 'but he's not gonna be put off much longer. They'll come down here and start—'

'I know!' Patches says, raising his voice. He gestures sharply with his left arm, forgetting he's working on it, and then winces and rests it back down on the work desk. His index finger starts flexing, rotor making a high whine as the finger curls right round and presses into his palm. He grips it with his human hand and pulls the finger back into position.

'That hurt?' I ask.

He shakes his head, but I know it does. His arm's old and it never gets serviced, not by a proper technician, just by him peeling the synthskin off and poking about with his own greasy tools. They put Patches back together, but they did it as cheap as they could and now he's coming apart again. A good cybernetics surgeon could fix it, give him a new arm, freshen up his implants, but that kind of surgery costs more byts than he could ever save, even if he had twice the kids leeching for him. So he keeps going, running the Gut, pretending like his muscles aren't slowly shutting down, like he isn't getting worse nerve damage every day. Three years ago, when we first met, he could still walk pretty well, went upstrata to do business sometimes, but now he barely leaves the Gut. In the past month, he's rarely even out of this workshop, too painful to hobble down to the hygienebloc we've got on the lowest level.

Neither of us wants to talk about it. We look past his shaking limbs and whinging rotors, look past the fact that I do more and more of the jobs that used to be his, organising work timetables and servicing the machinery that keeps the squat running.

'So what do I tell Ade?' I ask.

'Who cares? Stall him, Nova. You're good with him – he likes you.'

'Right,' I say. Ade does like me, and I like him, as far as other people go, but he won't like what I tell him at all. He's got his dad to answer to, and he can't keep letting us off. Truth is, I can't afford bad days like this. The second-best leecher got caught about a month back, and some of the other kids left soon after. It scared them. We're not pulling in anything like the money we used to.

The walls around us rumble as a discharge goes off in the geothermal generator. Patches' tools rattle in their tray. I realise my stomach's growling a bit too.

'Any food going?' I ask.

'Come home empty-handed and you're wanting fed?' Patches says, looking back down at his finger. His synthetic eye makes soft whirring sounds as it focuses on his work.

I take that as my cue to leave, down the hallway and into the kitchen. It's the same size as Patches' workshop, a mirror image, with the same vents and pipes on the ceiling, lit by the same white fluoro strips. Don't know what this room was before it was our squat. Patches installed cooking units, a freezer, a sink that empties back into our water tanks. Padlock on the drinking-water spigot. We can filter water about six times, but who knows how safe it really is? Damp rags hanging from pipes, dirty metal plates, some empty bottles of synthbeer. There is food going: I can see a tray of fried insects, two left, big agricorp locusts splayed out in a grave of white sugar. I pick one of them up, bite off the head and thorax. Nice crunch to it.

There's a boy asleep under the table. Mistook him for a pile of rags before. All I can see of him is dark hair and a snatch of forehead, rest is all wrapped up. No idea who that is. Kids are in and out of the Gut all the time, anyone with nowhere else to go. Patches won't turn you away, not if you have something to give him. Boy under the table smells rough; makes me think he's been in those clothes a long time.

I suck the last sugar granules off my fingers, then head down another corridor, this one sweltering hot and lined with power conduits. I climb a short-runged ladder and push through the hatch into my room. Easy to miss, this place. Exactly how I like it. If I drop the hatch closed and put my furniture on top of it, there's no way you can get in after me. Space is tight up here, so I've got a hammock hung between two pipes. Walls are bare metal streaked with rust, hung with a round, dusty mirror. Floor I've piled up with rugs and stuff, make it kinder on bare feet.

One storage locker for clothes, another for tech. What more do you need?

I peel my rainwrap away from my body, then pull off my boots; tuck them away in the corner of my room. I roll up the sleeve of my jacket, exposing my wristhub's access ports. Then I open up the tech box and bring out my baby: my assembly terminal. Unlike the junk in Patches' workshop, this thing's brand new. It's a Bliss Inc. Assembly and Syntax Unit, Chrysalis 3 model. Lost count of how many drunks and commuters I had to leech from to afford this on the black market. It's a bright yellow, egg-shaped case, stamped with the Bliss Inc. logo, their butterfly. You can hold it in one hand, but it's heavy, dense with clever engineering.

I unfurl an infovein and plug it into my wrist's port, linking the Chrysalis 3 to my nerves. I feel the bright rush of the metanet; see glifs bubbling in the corners of my eyes.

Your implants can do a lot of things, but they're powered by your body's energy, and that has its limits. If all you need to do is run simple programs, like most people, then that's more than enough. Your optical implants will show you anything you want to see; aural implants mean you never have to live a single moment without a personalised soundtrack. Whole world of information right there for you. But, if you want to alter programs or build your own, you need an assembly terminal.

I close my eyes and let myself sink into assembly space. It's a white room lined with half-finished programs, formations of glifs spinning around me like galaxies. I reach for one and haptic feedback in my hands makes the program feel solid.

This one's an icebreaker I'm working on. When you're talking about the metanet, ice isn't frozen water. It means ICE: Information Concealment and Encryption. Everyone and everything that belongs to the corps is covered in layers of ice; it stops hackers accessing their data, altering their permissions and protocols … everything I want to do, in other words.

Dealing with basic, consumer-quality ice is like opening a lock on a door; with the right key or enough force, you can get inside. High-grade corp ice is different. It builds intricate labyrinths that only the cleverest, luckiest people can navigate. The hackers who do make it through sometimes share the routes with everyone else, and then anyone can break that brand of ice, until the corps realise it's been compromised and they have their icemakers build something new, and the cycle starts again. They want to lock things down, control them, shut us out; we want to find a way in.

So that's the metanet: corps on the inside, all the money and all the power, hoarding their information in citadels of light, ringed with the thickest, strongest ice you can imagine. And outside there's us: hungry ghosts, prowling the darkness, sneaking in through cracks to take what we can.

There are other things you need besides icebreakers if you want to be a hacker, even just a street-running leecher like me. If you want implants and a subscription to the metanet, you have to be registered with the corps who made your implants, full name and real-time location and everything, and that's no good if you're going to break the law. They can track you down whenever they like. So what I have is a program that makes me into a ghost. It's called Phantom. Anytime someone tries to find out who I am, Phantom gives them a different name. Anytime Metrowatch put a trace on me, Phantom throws them off, gives them a million different trails. It's the first tool any hacker gets hold of, and the most important. Without a copy of Phantom, you won't live very long.

The person who built Phantom was a hacker called the Moth. He's a legend. Nobody knows who he is, but every hacker's got a story about the Moth. People say the Moth can make BytBank accounts appear out of thin air, create money whenever he feels like it. People say the Moth was the one who crashed the database of the biggest healthcorp in the world, erased millions of people's medical debt. When there was a blackout on one of the prison isles in the Pacific and more than a hundred anticorp fighters escaped, everyone reckoned it had to be the Moth who wrote the code that crippled the power plants. Whenever there's a really big database crack, whenever there's some unbreakable ice finally broken, whenever a corp gets hit with a proper gut punch, that's the word you hear on the hacker chatfeeds, over and over: *Moth*, *Moth*, *Moth*.

Some people say that the real Moth's long dead; that the corps got to him and turned him into a moonie; or that it's a group of people working under one name. The Moth's a hacker god, whoever they are or were, because Phantom's never been broken. It's the ultimate digital disguise, a mask that shifts shape every time someone looks at it. There's only two rules: one is you can't tell upstrata people about Phantom. It's for hackers and underdwellers only, not for rich kids to use as a fake ID to go to bars. The second rule is that if you get caught, it won't save you. The minute someone from a securicorp arrests you, Phantom vanishes from your implants, like it was never there.

What I really want is to learn enough about coding to make something like Phantom, have the name Nova on every hacker's lips. I'm good at programming, better than most of the zeroes posting their crap for people to marvel at. I want to be just like the Moth, but it's tough; not as if there are guides out there that'll teach you to work like that. I've tried to look at the source code of Phantom, me and a thousand others, but you can't get anything out of it. When you load it up into assembly space, all you'll see is a super-dense blob of darkness; nothing you can understand.

All the same, I want to try. You'll never learn if you don't fail sometimes. I push the rest of my programs aside, scattering them into the edges of the work area, and summon Phantom. It doesn't buzz and sing and glitter like the other programs I own. Instead it oozes into view, hangs in the air like some shifty thought you forgot about before it was fully formed.

I put one hand on it and my fingers pass straight through. It's tough because Phantom doesn't even fight you trying to look at it, not the way others do. The corp-made programs will resist, wall you out, throw up these labyrinths of light and colour, but there's always a way in once you know the logic. They fight and fight until there's nowhere left for them to go, and then they break and they're yours. Phantom doesn't fight you. It just flows around you like water, eluding your grip.

And standing there in assembly space, one hand in the program, I have a thought. When I break into corp programs, I attack them the way they defend themselves, with the same logic and rules, with icebreakers that are inverted mirrors of the corp ice they unlock. But Phantom wasn't built by someone from a corp, doesn't have their logic. It's still a program, built from info-glifs and metadata, but it has different rules.

So what I do is wait. I stand in assembly space with both hands resting on Phantom, fingers drifting into the boundaries of the shadow construct. And then I stay perfectly still, like there's an animal I'm trying to tame. I don't know what I think will happen, but I'm playing the program at its own game, trying to break it without force. I think of myself like Cromwell and his family, hunting in the pitch-black for a heartbeat.

And then, under my right hand's little finger, I find something. A soft chime, something I almost feel rather than hear. I move my finger gently upwards and pull a strand of the black stuff out with it, a famished thread of darkness. I put it close to my eyes and see it's a line of code, info-glifs arranged into dense, crazy columns. I don't think I've ever been so excited in my life. Nobody's done this; nobody has ever got close to seeing how Phantom works. Even if I don't understand what I'm looking at right now, I can learn. I won't just be Nova the leech, Nova the street kid; I'll be *Nova,* the girl who learned from the Moth. I try to magnify one of the glifs from the thread I've pulled and find I can't. They aren't obeying my instructions. The thread has gone taut, like something's pulling it back.

I'm a little afraid, and I never have been in assembly space before. Nothing here can hurt me; this is my terminal, my programs, my rules. I can log out whenever I want. But that doesn't change the fact I've got this black string stuck to me, and now it's pulling me, taking my hand into the centre of the Phantom program. I'm sunk to my elbow in rippling black shadow.

There's another chime and the force releases. My hand's right at the core, and I feel haptic feedback shivering as something touches my hand. There's no longer any force keeping me stuck to Phantom, so I draw my hand back to see what this new sensation is.

Part of the darkness comes away with me, sitting wetly on my wrist. It's like the Bliss butterfly stamped on my terminal, but, instead of sunshine yellow, the creature is midnight black, traced with silver. I pulled a black moth out of the middle of Phantom. A moth made by the Moth.

Is this some kind of test? It's not really alive, of course. You can make metanet constructs look like whatever you want, but this moth doesn't seem to be an art piece. It's more than that.

The moth construct flutters up in front of my face. Fractal patterns of light flood from its wings and back, making this amazing shape. Is this how you control Phantom? This strange web of glifs that I don't recognise, shimmering, silent, looming over me? I feel like it's looking at me, like there's something really alive in there, that it's more than just a script or a program, like this thing unfolding around me is something's mind and it can see me.

Who—

And at that moment, when I know I'm about to understand what's truly inside Phantom, I feel a hand shaking me, and the proximity alert goes off. There's someone in my room.

5

I exit assembly space with a roaring rush and gasp, but it's only Ade in my room, shaking my shoulder. One moment I'm looking at the silver threads the black moth was weaving, the next I'm looking up at his stupid, grinning face, can feel that I'm lying on my back with pillows piled up behind my head.

'Nova,' he's saying, '*Novaaaa*. Log out.'

'Idiot! This was important! Don't get me out of it like that!' I snap. I dive back into assembly space, but the moth construct is gone. Whatever was happening, Ade broke it. I feel a cold wrench of disappointment, like when someone wakes you up from the best dream you ever had. I was sure someone was about to speak to me, tell me something that really mattered.

What if I never see that moth again? Was it just an accident? Was it a genuine dream, my neurones misfiring, some weird malfunction of my assembly terminal? How did any of this happen?

'—chill out,' he's saying when I come back into the room.

'You … That was so important! I've never seen anything like that!'

'Patches said you'd be up here,' he says. 'When I saw you, I got worried, sis. Sounded like you were getting hurt or something. You were whimpering.'

'It didn't hurt. I really thought I had something. I saw—' I stop myself. I'm not sure exactly what I saw, but I don't think I want to tell anyone about it yet.

'Well, whatever. You looked like you needed a break, sis.'

I check the time on my wristhub. He's not wrong. I spent hours in assembly space, trying to unpick Phantom's secrets, and didn't notice. My stomach hurts, my bladder is whinging, my tongue's dry, and I've got a prickly feeling behind my eyes. It's like a hangover without drinking. Corp programmers have immersion rigs that let them stay in assembly space longer: the machines feed them and let them go to the toilet and stuff without logging out. I'm not that lucky.

Ade's got some water for me, plastic squeeze bottle. I suck it down, infovein still ported into my wrist. The water tastes of the recycling filters.

'You're still a pest,' I say when I finish it. 'Seriously, you ruined something really great.'

'Dunno how you get so into it, sis,' Ade says. 'It's mad boring. Absolute null.'

'It's work you need half a brain for,' I say. 'That's why you don't like it.'

He laughs, showing his neon-green teeth. They're nano-treated, glow from inside like chunks of lumen. Ade eats every second day, but he's always got the money for some stupid cosmetic treatment, whatever's the latest thing with the gangs. His head's shaved and video-tattoos flare over his white scalp, chequerboards of blue and yellow, then a pattern of red skulls and daggers, glifs spelling out *Danger, don't touch, I won't back down.* He's wearing a combat visor to shield his eyes, bright yellow trousers, a hot pink bulletproof jacket. Handgun in a holster under one armpit. I steal from people subtly, with webs of lies and deception, reaching into their bank accounts with invisible hands. Ade sticks a gun under their chin and asks if they want to pay him or die. He's probably the best friend I've made down here.

'So what's news?' he asks.

'Not much. Tried to leech on to Metrowatch bait, had to go back under.'

'Got you with the decoy, huh? Mad unlucky.'

I shrug.

'They tag you?'

'Nah,' I say. 'I stuck his guts with my shocker and jumped off the bridge.'

Ade laughs again. 'Stuck his guts! Wish I saw that, for sure. For a sunsider, you have a mad heart, Nova.'

That's what he always tells me. That I have a mad heart. Maybe he's right. He would know, if anyone did; Ade's got about the maddest heart of anyone I ever met.

Unlike me, Ade Akram was born down here, in the black belly of the City. He says he went the first ten years of his life before he ever saw sunlight, and he's got the bleached, translucent skin of a real underdweller. He doesn't even like the sun, can't look at it without his tinted visor. He's spent his whole life in Nightmarket, the parasite city beneath the City, anything you can imagine for sale down in the darkness. I met Ade on one of my first trips there, a couple of years ago. He was fist-fighting a man twice his size outside a café that I later found out was a gang front.

Ade was losing, but there was something fascinating to me about his energy, how he kept laughing and jumping back up from every punch and kick. Like the world was a joke and only he got it. I'd never seen someone take a beating like that, spring back up so many times to face an opponent they had no chance of overcoming. Eventually the huge guy laid Ade out for the tenth time and he couldn't get back up, just lay in the gutter with blood leaking from his grin. The big man went back inside. Everyone else was pretending they didn't see Ade, but I didn't know to ignore gang business then. I went right over. I gave him some water from my flask, helped him get to his feet. I felt like, if anyone can bounce back from that kind of hurt and still be smiling, I want to know more about them. I want to know how to do that too. Turned out to be a smart move for a lot of reasons, because the big guy beating Ade up was his father, and Ade's family is a gangster dynasty. People know the name Akram in Nightmarket. They know the name very well. Ade's become our connect to the gangs, makes sure everyone in the Gut is straight with those people.

Thing is, right now, we're not.

Ade sits down on the floor of my room. Pulls his gun out of the holster and starts spinning it on his finger.

'What's news with you?' I ask, feigning casual cheerfulness, watching the pistol twirl. Gunmetal shining in the light of my lamp.

'Not much, sis,' he says airily. 'Got money, got space to sleep tonight, got a pile of people want me dead. They'll not get me though.'

'So look,' I say, 'about the tribute …'

'Ah, don't do this, Nova.'

'Do what?'

'Don't have that tone in your voice, sis. Not a good sound.'

'Look, I don't like this either.'

'No, I'm the one don't like it,' he says, holstering his gun. 'Come down here, bring you water even, and you got nothing for me *again*? Come on. My dad, what's he gonna say when I come back empty? He'll say to me, Ade, you're going too soft on them in the Gut there. You're going too soft on the cripple and his pack of leechers because Nova's your friend. I'll get a beating, and then they're gonna come down here and take whatever they can get. Maybe flatline one of you to make a point. Nasty business.'

'We don't have the tribute,' I say. 'It's Patches, not me. I can't help it.'

'I need something.' His video-tattoos flash crimson over his forehead. Guns and bombs. 'What about that thing?' he says, pointing at my Chrysalis 3.

'No way. I need this, Ade. For my work.'

For a moment, his face looks hard and I think he's going to demand the terminal, but then he shrugs and smiles.

'So what is it then, sis?' he asks me. 'Reckon I can stall them another week, but I'll catch a beating, for sure. Make it worth my while.' He smiles in a flirty way, but I just laugh and push my hand at his face, sending the idea away. Hardest part of our friendship has been convincing him that I don't want to be with him or any of his gang mates. Three years and he still can't quite let it go.

I run through the contents of my room in my mind, until I think of something I can spare. I open my tech box, and take out a chip-case. I flip it open and show them to Ade, who cracks a luminous grin. There's a row of six information chips inside, all about the size of a fingernail.

'Partycrasher?' he asks. I nod.

'This is Eclipse,' I tell him. 'I've been working on it myself. Side project.'

Partycrashers are programs that change your brain chemistry by making your implants malfunction. It's basically a computer virus, but a really fun one, something that can make your troubles go away or keep you dancing all night. They come on read-only infochips, one-time use, so you have to keep buying them if you like your first taste. Using them is a mega violation of the terms of service you sign when you get your implants, but nobody really cares. I've been messing around with this one for a while now, learning how the code works. They earn good money if you make one people like.

'Hype,' Ade says, 'very hype.' He picks one of the infochips out of the case and looks it over. 'You're making this yourself?'

'Starting to. I'm modifying the base code.'

'This'll work, sis,' he says, replacing the chip. 'This'll definitely work.'

'And you'll talk to your captain? We'll have everything next week.'

Ade waves his hand. 'Yeah, yeah. Hype. So are you coming to crash with me, or what? Take this for a test run?'

What I want to do is dive back into assembly space, try and find that moth construct again, but I can see Ade's got it into his head that we're going to spend time together, that this is part of the price. I should be glad, I suppose. Our problem's solved, for now at least. What we'll do when next week comes around I don't know. We're way in the hole with Ade's dad now.

'Let's go,' I say, standing up. I move over to my tech locker and put the Chrysalis 3 back inside, hiding the lock mechanism from Ade with my body so he doesn't get a look at the combination. He is a friend, like I said, but assembly terminals sell for serious money. I've lived in the undercity three years; I know how it works. People look out for themselves.

'You're gonna crash dressed like that, sis?' he asks. 'They'll laugh you right outta there.'

I'm still wearing my work colours: a weak greyish-blue that makes me look like a low-ranking corpswoman. Down in the undercity, people wear the brightest stuff they can find, the more glowing accessories the better. Up above, the only bright colour you wear is your corp's logo, and if you're an exec you won't even wear that. For my leeching I have to fit in with the crowd, but if I roll up at some undercity dancepit dressed like this, it's going to look like I got lost.

Fortunately, my leeching outfit has some tricks it can pull. This whole get-up's made from chameleon cloth; can mimic and store thousands of different shades and patterns. Best thing I've ever stolen. I access the menu via my implants, telling the cloth to cycle between primary colours every five seconds. Way better. The fabric doesn't change all at once, so it's like waves of colour flowing over my body, starting from the head and working down to my toes. I spread my arms out for Ade's approval, bright gory red running down the sleeves, replacing the grey.

'Better?' I ask.

'Was hoping you'd have to get changed,' Ade says with a leer.

'In your dreams. Look, get out a minute. I need to do my face.'

He sighs in exaggerated disappointment, but I give him a proper hard look and he leaves. I get my party paint and stuff out and sit down in front of the mirror.

My hair's black and cut pretty short, slicked back, again to disguise me as a corpswoman. I don't have time to do much with it – I unslick it from my scalp as best I can, and run my fingers through until it's a mess of inky spikes. For make-up, I line my lips poisonous blue, and smear red iridescent paint in a bar across my eyes. Lastly, I slip on a trashed pair of orange Sneeks. You can tell I got ready quickly, but it'll do.

I let the hatch to my bedroom slam shut above my

head, and I head back through the Gut to the kitchen. The boy under the table is still here, though how he can sleep through this I've got no idea. Ade's crew, all of them strapped up and kitted out, are making themselves at home. My stomach lurches when I see the other gang boys. Ade was ready to take our tribute by force if we didn't hand over what he wanted. Patches needs to figure a way out of this. I hide my dismay with a smile. I gave them the partycrashers – they should be happy for now.

Myshka and Rue are Ade's cousins and cronies, who he bullies or rewards, depending on his mood. They look exactly like him: pale, no hair, scalps flaring with video-tattoos, eyes hidden by combat visors. They're wearing bright clashing colours and patterns, chequerboard trousers and searing pink jackets and boots that glow green in the dark. There's a pair of gang girls here as well, with their heads shaved and tattooed up like the guys' are, except for a patch of hair right at the crown, which they bleach and grow down really long. One of them's wearing stutterjeans that disappear every other time you blink, so you get these frames where she's not wearing any trousers at all. I stare for a second longer than I should and then snatch my gaze away. Keep my face blank.

'Nova!' Ade says. 'This is Quell and Molli.'

The girls look at me with real hard eyes. I look back. They don't think much of my unshaven head, but I know they're jealous of the chameleon cloth. A wave of summer sky blue makes its way down my body, followed by a harsh yellow.

'Hey,' I say. They nod.

'Ade says you made this stuff?' Myshka asks me. 'It good?'

'I made it,' I say. 'Of course it's good.'

Ade laughs. 'Yeah, see? That's my girl. Mad heart, like I always say.'

He hands out the infochips. I hold mine in the palm of my left hand: a sliver of black metal, so light you can barely feel that it's there.

Rue whoops. 'Eclipse!' he yells. 'No sun! Mad fun!'

'Mad fun!' Myshka echoes. The gang girls don't yell, just dilate their access ports and slide the infochips in, looking as bored as they did when I walked in.

I do the same.

WARNING.

A synthetic voice, coming from my aural implants.

This program is not recognised as originating from a registered software publisher and loading it will be a violation of your terms of service. This program may be harmful or malicious.

This isn't news to me. I made the thing. I gesture towards the Ignore glif.

Are you sure you want to proceed? You do so at your own risk. Bliss Incorporated are not liable for nerve damage, brain injury, or death in the event of implant malfunction.

Ignore. Load program.

The voice cuts out. I hear that spiel ten times a day, the amount of illegal stuff I run. We're all standing in the kitchen, looking at our wrists. My hub is reading the data from the partycrasher, sending it to my neural implants. Eclipse is travelling the wires inside my flesh, visiting my brain, worming into my ears and eyes, sparkling in my fingers and tongue.

I take a deep breath in. Breathe quicksilver back out. The air ripens with static, like a bad signal. Lights dim. Eclipse. Apocalypse. End of the line. Silver veins in my arm. I look at the shorter gang girl and see her face turn to glass, glitch-glass, like a broken lumen, with black wings unfurling inside her face—

Ade's bent over me. He's laughing. Gleaming neon teeth.

'Hey, get off the floor.'

He pulls me up. I don't remember falling down. There are other people around us, but I can't recognise them.

Their voices sound metallic. Why was I lying down?

'Is she OK?' an echoing metal voice asks.

I think I made this too strong.

'I'm not OK,' I tell them. 'I'm Nova.'

And then I explode.

Silver heat in my head. Pressure pulsing behind my eyes. Is someone knocking? Yeah, that's someone knocking. There's a web covering my face, which turns out to be my hammock. I peel myself away from the plastic. My chameleon cloth is still cycling through red and blue and yellow, making my eyes hurt worse. I ask it to mimic the ambient colours instead: rusty brown and grey. I tip out of my hammock and down on to the floor, crawl until I can stand upright again.

What happened last night? Eclipse happened.

I remember flashes of the dancepit, sweating ceiling, Ade's teeth glowing in the darkness. Did he pull a gun on someone? It's hazy. At least I made it home. No injuries as far as I can tell, which is an improvement on most of my nights out with Ade. Clearly still some work needed on Eclipse, to try and smooth out some of these after-effects. My face is smeared with red paint, like I've been crying blood. There's another sharp knock on the hatch in my floor. I kneel down and pull it open.

Patches' ruined face stares up at me. White eye, pale areas of scar tissue on his cheeks. He's got his hand fixed at least, synthskin hanging loose over the metal fingers.

'You are here then,' he says.

I point to my face. 'I was out,' I say. 'Went with Ade. I had to keep him off our backs.'

'How selfless of you. Saving our hides by going out partycrashing. A true hero. Did you leave a boat up by the waterway?'

I forgot about that. I need to shrink it down.

'Yeah,' I say. 'I'll go with the powder—'

'Not now,' Patches says. 'We've got business.'

'Money business?'

'Looks that way. Eat first. Then we'll talk.'

Eating sounds good. Money sounds even better. We can't put Ade off another week. I climb down the ladder and follow Patches as he limps to the kitchen, leaning heavily on his cane. There's a stranger, a blond-haired guy, sitting at the table with a coffee. His face is soft and creasy, and when he smiles most of his teeth are missing. He's dressed like a moonie, dirty orange utility shirt and trousers, standard-issue work boots that are worn and grey, but he isn't one. Moonies don't smile. He must've got the clothes from a municipal worker who died down here. Patches doesn't introduce him. He picks up a squeeze-can of liquid protein, grown in our pseudowomb, and squirts it on to the hotplate. The kitchen fills with the smell of cooking meat. I realise how hungry I am. I haven't eaten since the locust yesterday, and that was hardly a meal. I pour coffee into a plastic mug.

'So,' Patches says, flipping the patty of meat with his synthetic hand, no worries about touching the hotplate with that, 'this guy says he's got work for us. For you, in fact.'

'Yeah?' I say. I look the stranger up and down again. He comes off as an absolute bottom-feeder, kind of drifter who's too dumb to scam or hustle and too cowardly to stick people up. A guy who picks through garbage piles to find a meal. 'What kind of work?'

The drifter looks me over. 'Not me,' he says. His voice is hoarse and quiet.

'What do you mean?' I ask.

'Our friend,' Patches says, 'represents a third party. Someone who can't be here themselves.'

'Right,' I say. This doesn't make much sense so far. I'm not much of a hacker, not yet. I'm doing my best to learn, but I'm really just a street-leecher. I rob corpsmen who don't have their personal ice up to date. I'm not the kind of name someone would hire for a job. And how did they know where I live? The Gut's not easy to find. Why not contact me through the metanet?

'Came to me, a vision,' the drifter says, staring through my face to some invisible point beyond. 'Said I come down here to you.'

I give Patches a hard look. He's got too much of a soft spot for guys like this, you ask me. Don't know why. Way too ready to listen to any crazy with one foot in the grave who shows up at our door. Drifter's brainstem is probably collapsing and he thinks he has some message for us. This doesn't seem like promising work.

'Show her the box,' Patches says to the drifter. The guy takes something out of his coat and lays it on the table. It's just a grey bit of tech, terminal core or a syntax driver. It looks useless, broken down, like everything else about this guy.

'Impressive,' I say, with all the sarcasm I can muster.

My head still hurts. 'Looks cutting-edge.'

'Before your time,' Patches tells me. He scoops the patty off the stove and on to a plate. 'It's a military field resonator. Used them in the war.'

'So?'

'Message is in there,' the drifter tells me. He pulls up his sleeve, and I see he's got a wristhub. He was part of the system at one point then. Used to be an upstanding consumer.

'Not here,' Patches says to him sharply. 'My workshop.'

I take the plate Patches hands to me, meat patty and a side of algae paste, then with that and my coffee I follow them into the workshop. The drifter sits down in a chair and puts the old field resonator on the desk in front of him. He dilates the access port on his wristhub and connects himself to the resonator using an infovein.

'What's this resonator do?' I ask Patches.

'Communicator,' he says. 'High-density encrypted transmissions. I haven't seen one in twenty years.'

'Where'd he get one?'

'They're obsolete. Might have found it in the trash. But I don't think so.'

I inspect the resonator. It still looks like garbage to me. It doesn't seem to be doing anything, no lights or lumen display. The drifter is lying back in the chair, eyes open, but it looks like he's asleep.

'So he's receiving signals?'

'Suppose so,' Patches says.

'Can he hear us? Who is this guy, Patches? Why did you wake me up for this?'

'He said there's a job for you. Said there's lots of byts in it, which we need. Doesn't know who he's speaking for. But he knew my old unit call sign from the war, and he had this X15 field resonator, like I haven't seen in decades. So I figure he's a front for something real. Could be bad, could be good. But I don't think we ignore this.'

I take a bite of my patty. I'm so hungry I don't mind the charred taste of the outside. Patches leaves these on the hotplate way too long. I smear some algae paste over the meat and bolt the rest down. The drifter hasn't moved. He's lying completely still in the chair.

'Is he brain-dead?' I ask. 'Seriously, he just died in here.'

'The resonator is transmitting,' Patches says.

'He's just fried himself. Is he even breathing?'

The guy doesn't move. The parts of Patches' face that still work properly are frowning.

I touch the drifter. I can't feel his pulse. He really has just died in Patches' workshop.

'You woke me up for this? So now we have to dump him—'

The drifter takes a huge gasp of air. I don't like to admit I'm shaken up, but I scream. Jump away from him.

His head tracks me as I move. The eyes aren't blinking, but he's alive.

'Who do I address?' the drifter asks me. 'Answer, if you hear me.'

'Nova,' I say. 'And Patches.'

'Hanna,' the drifter says. 'Hanna Latch and Captain Michael Niven.'

'How do you know that?' I ask him. Nobody knows our real names. Phantom makes sure of that. Is this corp stuff? Can't be though. Securicorps wouldn't go through all this runaround to get you. They just blow the front door off and shoot anything that moves.

'I know a great deal,' the drifter says. 'It's my life's work to know as much as I can.'

'Who are you?' Patches asks the drifter. 'Who's speaking to us now?'

It took me a moment, but I've worked out what's happening. The drifter has no ice, no security on his neural implants at all. He's allowed someone else, another user, remote access to his nervous system.

Usually this kind of exploit is used by hackers to see through someone else's eyes: eyejacking. Lets you turn anyone into a spy camera.

What's happening now is different: full access to the nervous system, complete control. It's called puppeteering. This is god-level hacking, proper black magic. I've never seen it done before. It takes an absolute torrent of information transfers for it to work, and we've barely got a scrap of a metanet connection down here, which must explain the military transmitter – high-volume encrypted streaming. The drifter is just a courier, a human speaker system.

'I am known as the Moth,' the drifter's head tells us.

I look at Patches, and see he's staring at the drifter with a stone-serious expression, cigar smoking in one hand. I burst out laughing. I can't help it.

'Yeah,' I say, 'sure you are. Obviously the most wanted hacker in the world is talking to us. There's no other explanation. You take this idiot seriously, Patches?'

'He knew my real name,' Patches says quietly. 'My old rank.'

The drifter's head looks at me gravely.

'Prove you're the Moth,' I say.

'I already have,' the drifter's head says. 'I maintain the Phantom program, which you use to conceal your identity. Yesterday you found an avatar inside my program while you were trying to uncover the source code. I am the only person who knows what you saw inside Phantom – a black moth, with silver fractals in the wings. I know other things about you as well. I know your true name, Hanna Latch. I know every false identity my program has ever supplied you with. Mostly recently you were caught leeching from a Metrowatch enforcer. The false name my program supplied their records with was Charlotte Alorda. There is now a warrant out for Ms Alorda's arrest, but we both know this trail leads nowhere.'

'Other ways you could know all that,' I say, but I don't see how. I didn't tell anybody about the black moth construct I saw inside Phantom, not even Patches. I remember how I felt like something was looking back at me. And how else would they know the exact fake name I was using yesterday?

I realise this is real. The most famous hacker in history is speaking to us. He's looking right at me, while I have a face smeared with iridescent paint, a nest of dirty, post-crash hair. And I've been rude to him, laughed at him. I'm amazed he's still talking.

'What is this about?' Patches asks the drifter's head.

'I have work for you, Nova,' the head says. 'It will not

be easy work. But you will be well paid.'

'How much?' I ask.

'Forty thousand byts now. More if you complete the job to my satisfaction. There may be a great deal of profit in this enterprise.'

Forty K to start ... that's a better payday than leeching at the magrail station, for sure. That's way better.

'What do you want for that?' I ask.

'In one week, an interview process begins. The CEO of Bliss Incorporated, Grale Inselberg, is hiring a new personal assistant. Three candidates from hundreds have passed the initial stages of screening. Now they will be meeting the CEO face to face within the Bliss Inc. spire. One of those candidates is you. You will take on the identity of a young corpswoman, Kirsten Cosset. Your task is to pass the interview process and become the CEO's new assistant. If you succeed, you will receive another forty thousand byts, delivered to whatever account you choose, and your next set of instructions.'

'*Grale?*' I ask it. 'The CEO of *Bliss*? Seriously?'

'I am quite serious,' the drifter's head replies. 'We have a rare opportunity to compromise the highest level of the world's largest corp.'

'Why Nova?' Patches asks.

'As I explained, she uncovered a kind of alarm within

one of my pieces of software, the program you call Phantom. This alarm is designed to reveal individuals who are especially adept at manipulating metanet programs. Individuals I might profitably collaborate with. Nova is one of very few to trigger this particular alarm. Certainly she is the youngest.'

I feel a warm wash of pride. The youngest ever.

'There is more. Physical infiltrations like this require certain characteristics. Charm, courage, the ability to improvise. Nova, you already impersonate a corporate worker every day. You were born in their system. You do not resemble an underdweller. You understand the system, but you live outside of it.'

'Still don't understand why you want me,' I say. 'I'm just a leecher. Don't you have other people you work with? Proper anticorp hackers?'

'I don't have many friends,' the head says. 'I never work with the same person twice. It's the only way I've kept myself alive. If you refuse my offer, you will never hear from me again.'

I bite my lip. My instinct, first reaction is to say no. This plan is madness. I'm a thief, not a spy. I can pretend to be a corpswoman well enough to blend in on a packed train. Becoming Kirsten Cosset and infiltrating one of the biggest corps on the planet, becoming the personal assistant to an exec … a chief exec even, Grale Inselberg. It's a fantasy.

But then I think of that payout. How long am I going to keep leeching commuters at the station? How long before I get caught? I'm good, but nobody gets away with it forever. They nearly got me yesterday. I nearly got hit by that train. I'm sixteen now. When I think about being twenty-six, I can't imagine how I'd get there. If this works, then I can quit leeching, running around nearly getting tagged by Metrowatch decoys and jumping on to magrail tracks and always worrying where our next byts are coming from. I could invest in some real equipment, take the time to properly teach myself metanet assembly and syntax, instead of nibbling around the edges like I have been. I could learn things, make something, really do work that's good, not having to worry about Patches getting at me for money every day.

And more than that. There's a voice inside me that's excited, that craves this like a fire burning in my stomach How many times have I wanted people to know me? To know who Nova is, talk about me like they talk about the Moth? To be something more than a forgotten person who fell out of the sunlight when her parents died.

If I say no, the Moth will vanish. I'll never hear from him again. I'm sure of that. If I say yes, everything will change. The life I have now won't be the life I have for ever.

You don't get people calling you Nova by being dull. Like on the bridge yesterday, I've only really got one choice. I decide to leap.

'I'm interested,' I tell the Moth.

'Excellent. If you examine the bottom of the field resonator you'll see a set of co-ordinates. They'll give you a set point in the City. If you're there in exactly twenty-four hours, alone, I will take that as accepting this job. You will receive your first payment and your first contact. If you miss the time window, you will never hear from me again.'

There's a pause, and then the drifter takes another of those gasping breaths, like he's surfacing from deep underwater. He blinks and moves his head and I can tell the Moth's left his body. The gestures are totally different.

'Got what you need?' he asks us. Seems like he doesn't remember anything that happened while the Moth had control of his flesh.

'We did,' Patches says.

'Good,' the drifter says. 'You gonna pay me?'

Patches snorts. 'Pay you for what? Doing the job you already got paid for?'

'I need something, man. Just some water. It's hard out there.'

Patches puts a hand on the field resonator, leaning over the drifter, standing so the guy can see Patches' pistol holster. 'You can fill a flask with water,' he says to the drifter. 'Then you're gone, right? We're keeping this –' he taps the resonator – 'and you were never down here. You forget we spoke. You don't know my name, you don't know my face. Understand?'

'Don't worry,' the drifter says. 'I forgot you already.'

The guy unplugs himself from the resonator and stands up, shrugging his shoulders. Patches follows him out of the workshop, leaning heavily on his walking stick. As he leaves, he turns back to me and his ruined face cracks into a rare smile. He mouths *forty thousand byts* to me. That'll cover our debt to Ade's family easily, and that's just the upfront payment. One less problem in our lives. But it's brought a whole lot more with it. Now that I've made the leap, I can't believe I did it.

Impersonate a corpswoman, Kirsten Cosset. Go for a job interview inside the Bliss Inc. headquarters. Get close to Grale Inselberg, who nobody's seen in public for years. It sounds impossible, but the Moth said he had been working on this for a long time. They've got a plan. I just have to do what they say.

I turn the resonator over. Scratched into the casing I see a string of numbers, just where the Moth said they'd be, giving me a point in the municipal grid. It's somewhere above us, I know that much. What'll happen when I get there, I can't imagine. Will I meet the Moth in person? That seems unlikely. Maybe some other associate, someone who knows more than that drifter did?

Twenty-four hours, and I'll find out.

Early next morning I head to the closest transport nexus and pay a few byts to take an elevator a hundred floors up. When I step out, the pedestrian concourse is crowded and shabby. This neighbourhood hasn't gone under yet, might not for years, but it's only a matter of time. Sunlight, strata, status: it's all above you, inching out of reach. For now, there's still legit corp franchises in this shopping district; Metrowatch enforcers patrolling with rifles slung on their backs; lumens capering above the walkways, juggling their products and barking slogans.

Sunlight still shines on this floor of the City, but faintly, and the shadows are deep and rich.

I head for the location marked by the co-ordinates the Moth gave me. I wonder if he can see me as I walk. Wherever you go in the City, there are a million eyes on you. There's cameras skulking in every corner and a web of transmitters built into the cement of every wall, speaking to my implants, monitoring when I'm hungry or thirsty so they can get the lumens to show me food and drink, sensing my stress and joy and pain, feeding it all back into their customer-research databases. The metanet carries all this information; I'm in there like a ghost, a little package of consumer data. The Moth must be somewhere in there too.

I find myself in an autocafé, dim and steamy, the ceiling veined with conveyor tracks, a lumen-menu floating above the counter. The menu's glifs are cheap and badly programmed, distorting when I move my head too fast, unable to adapt to a rapid change of perspective. I order a coffee and a side dish; swipe my wristhub on the payment strip. This makes sense as a meeting point. Autocafés are unstaffed. Sometimes you have a manager in the back booth to make sure the machinery runs smooth. I can't see anyone in the booth today. Short of murder, nobody much cares what I do here.

A table and chair pop up from the floor panels. They'll be here for an hour, and then they'll vanish when the time's gone. Everything's smooth metal and plastic, wipe-clean materials that never get wiped clean. My chameleon cloth matches the ambient colours, dirty whites and faded greys. The ceiling-mounted conveyor brings my coffee and the bowl of salty roasted mealworms. The other customers are sad people, forgettable faces and colourless clothes, nursing glasses of synthbeer. A group of non-econs, all women, are lying on the dirty floor, jackets folded under their heads, trying to sleep.

This is the point the Moth directed me to. I still have ten minutes to go before the time they specified.

I watch the front window for a while, people passing outside, uneasy shapes beyond the glass. Everything looks cheap and rough, on the verge of falling apart. I can see a bunch of TiniTels, lumen-signs outside their doors showing how many coffin-sized rooms are still available. Gaming halls, tanning salons, a dozen more autocafés like this one. Nowhere that encourages you to stay for long. We're close to a skyport, and most of the pedestrians are shuttlecrew, dressed in bulbous flight suits. A work detail of moonies goes past in lockstep, followed by a street vendor with a wheeled cart laden with good-luck charms. Here walks a shifty pale man who I'd bet is a gang courier. There I see a pair of round-faced children, snug inside an automated pram that follows their mother.

I wasn't born down in the undercity, and if you know enough about genoming you can tell. They spent good money on me, and I look like I belong upstrata, a proper City girl, which helps with the leeching. I have great eyesight, a nice genomed face that corpsmen trust. I might not live for centuries, like people say execs can, but if I stay out of trouble I'll live a long time, and age well too. You can tell someone cared about me when I was born. It's written in my cells. I was loved.

My parents died in a car crash, which is an old-fashioned way to die. Most people don't know it can happen any more. Nobody drives. You just jump in your car and tell it where you want to go. The algorithm is a careful driver, reacts faster than a human can, so it's rare that anyone gets hurt. But every system has flaws.

So here's something most people don't know about their car: sometimes it will kill you. When an accident is unavoidable, your car will try to harm the least amount of people, even if the evasive manoeuvre kills the passenger. There's a points system, deep down in the code, which measures how valuable each life in the equation is. The car assigns one point for adults, five points for minors, ten for newborns, and no points for anyone with a terminal illness or a serious criminal conviction. If you're just a regular person, and you find yourself hurtling head-on towards another car with a child inside, your own car will swerve into a wall and kill you, to save the child. It's one point vs five. You lose.

What happened to my parents was unlikely. There was a drunk man walking near a traffic tube. The tube was meant to be sealed, but the rain covering was partly lifted, for maintenance. The wind blew his hat off, and it landed inside the tube. He climbed out of the pedestrian concourse and down into the tube to get it back. My parents' car came round the corner at full speed. Only a split second for the car to react. No time to brake. It should have run him down, but instead it swerved into a barrier, and they both died instantly.

Why?

The man's father was a high-up exec in a healthcorp, and was paying thousands of byts a year to the corp that built the cars, so that he and his family had special weight in the system. This was a secret subscription they offered for execs. The son was worth one hundred points. My parents were worth two. They needed ten newborns in the car with them to stay alive, but they only had one, and I was at daycare.

There was a corpcourt case. The exec's son was found

negligent and fined. The fine was two days worth of earnings for his father. The transportcorp that maintained the traffic tubes was found negligent and fined. The fine was seventy seconds worth of the corp's yearly profits. The corp that made my parents' car was found not liable, because the small print in the consumer contract explained that your vehicle might murder you under certain circumstances, and they had accepted these terms with purchase. The contract was hundreds of thousands of glifs long. I don't think my parents read it.

My mum's family lived a long way away, and she hadn't spoken to them in years. They didn't respond to any messages about her death. My dad's parents were dead. There wasn't anybody else. I inherited my parents' BytBank accounts, and the compensation from the healthcorp, and the compensation from the transportcorp. I was just over a year old. As part of the compensation deal, the healthcorp, where the exec whose son killed my parents worked, agreed to let me live in one of their careblocs, on a floor for sick children and orphans. So that's where I grew up.

I taste the coffee, which is bitter, and run my tongue over my teeth. Thinking about my parents has put me in a black mood. I want to go somewhere, walk in the City, leave those memories and thoughts behind in this horrible autocafé, but I have to stay put. I'm nervous, more nervous than I ever get while I'm out leeching. I hate just sitting here. What if I misread the co-ordinates? What if something went wrong and the Moth doesn't show? I don't even know what I'm supposed to be looking out for. Another person? Some kind of metanet message?

The conveyor system rattles overhead again, and the mechanical arm deposits a small tub of sweetener on my table. I stare at it, confused. I didn't order this. Another glitch in this stupid, broken-down world.

Then I realise.

I take the tub in one hand and twist the top off, looking out of the window as I do so. I dip one finger into the powdered sweetener, and fish around until I find what I'm looking for. An infochip, buried in the condiment. I pull it out, brush it off on my sleeve. It's dull grey. Nondescript. This must be the contact from the Moth.

I look around the autocafé as casually as I can, but nobody's interested in what I'm doing. I slide the chip into my hub's access port. There's a soft ping in my ear, and I see there are two files in the chip. My implants create a visual of them on the table, a pair of lumens glowing beside my food. One is the transfer code for a bank transaction. It looks safe and regular, a white rectangle with a reassuring golden BytBank stripe running through the middle. All happy and legit. No problems there. I tap the transfer-lumen and it sings a jolly, jingly song and money floods into my account. Leaves me breathless. Forty thousand byts. I just became the richest person sitting in this autocafé, perhaps on this whole shabby floor. For once, I'll need to watch out for leechers.

The other program is clearly something the Moth made himself. It's tar-black, spiky-looking, rotating on the greasy tabletop. When I ask my file categoriser to identify the program, it comes back as a blank. No data, no way of knowing what it is.

I came this far. I can hardly back out now, after I took the money. That would be suicidal. I select the strange black program and order my implants to run it.

WARNING. This program is not recognised as originating from a registered—

I gesture for Ignore.

Are you sure you want to proceed? You do so at your own—

I hit Ignore again. The oily black program loads on to my neural implants.

For a few minutes, nothing happens. The program is in my directory, I can see that it's running, but trying to find out what it's doing still gives no data. I sit and watch the window, drink my sour coffee. The Moth's inscrutable code races through my body like dark blood.

Hello, Nova.

I start. Somehow I wasn't expecting the voice. It seems to come from behind my left shoulder, although of course it's coming through my aural implants. The Moth.

'Hello,' I say quietly.

Now we have a secure channel.

The voice is different to the voice of the drifter that the Moth hijacked, of course, but I still feel it's not his real voice. It's a synthesised voice, with no trace of gender or accent. Every syllable is precise and cold.

'This can't be traced?'

As long as you follow my instructions, you're safe. No security personnel will tag you; nobody will flag your accounts. You're under my protection.

I feel a prickle of joy at this. If I pull this off, I'll be famous, no doubt. Other hackers will speak about Nova. The girl who got to Grale.

What do you know about Bliss Incorporated? the Moth asks.

'Big corp. They make neural implants. They made mine. They've made almost everyone's.'

Indeed. The most profitable corp in the world. They produce neural implant hardware and the software to

run on it. Targeted advertising, media sales, data gathering. They take a cut from almost every transaction on the metanet. And who knows what else they're making in that grand spire?

'So what exactly are we hitting?' I whisper.

Grale heads her own department within Bliss Inc. It is known as Human Futures. I need something from inside this department. So far my efforts have been fruitless. I need an inside plant to gain access. That would be you, in your capacity as Grale's assistant.

'Human Futures?'

Do not say those words out loud. You are surrounded by microphones.

I look around the autocafé. I realise the Moth is right: anyone in here with implants has a mic built into them. Even if the people themselves aren't listening, someone else could be. Securicorps filter through passive data every second of every day, looking for key phrases.

'Sorry,' I whisper.

Nova. To succeed in this task for me, you will need to be many things. Careful is one. Careful always. Smart, resourceful, calm: all necessary traits. Can I count on you?

'Yes,' I say, without thinking twice.

Good. I am a meticulous planner, but chance will

always have a role. They say small actions can have a larger impact than anyone dreamed. No one can foresee every outcome. The butterfly flaps its wings, and a storm brews on the other side of the world. Perhaps one could say the same of a moth's wing. You and I, we are both small. But if we breach Human Futures, and steal what is concealed there, then our actions may change the world profoundly. You are with me now, Nova. You are important to me.

I start to say something else, ask what the Moth is talking about, what he thinks Grale's working on, but the hacker keeps talking, cold, synthesised voice murmuring in my left ear.

The urgent thing that we must do is alter your body. The security scans before you meet with Grale will be biological as well as electronic, far more invasive than a standard Metrowatch checkpoint. Your irises and fingerprints will already be on record, from your time in the carebloc as a child. These must be altered. We need a faceshaper. You will find one in the barter district you know as Nightmarket. His name is Dr Kiyagi. He will know you are coming. Tell him the Moth rises.

A ping as information is transferred to my implants: information about Kiyagi, and confirmation of my appointment with Bliss Inc. Very soon.

I will leave. There is much to prepare.

The hacker's presence is gone, leaving me sitting in the autocafé alone, cold coffee dregs in a cup by my wrist. Forty thousand byts in my account. I feel excitement, feel important. The sadness that was in my gut before has faded.

I stand and push away from the table. I leave the autocafé, leave the losers to nurse their synthbeers and sleep on the floor. I cross the dim street, stand at the guardrail, and look down. I see a chasm, traffic tubes and plazas and walkways clinging to the sides of the cityblocs, and beneath them all is darkness. I watch the people moving along their pathways, rushing this way and that, the crowd a seething shape that means nothing. Everyone down there busy and hungry and scrambling for cash. Anonymous, tiny figures, forgotten even before they're dead.

One day they're all going to know my name.

Nightmarket is ripe with lanterns. Some electric, some guttering gas-flame. Some, the ones I like least, are filled with luminous worms, blind prisoners writhing over the curved walls of their cells. The air is still and humid, heavy with steam and smoke. I can smell cooking fat, tobacco, bleach, cheap sickly perfume. Metal seems to sweat. It's as crowded as a magrail station at rush hour, but Nightmarket is this busy every minute of the day. Ade is ahead of me, bulling his way through the throng. I follow as closely as I can. I've been up here plenty of times, only way to get the latest icebreakers, but this place still makes me nervous. I keep one hand on my nerve disruptor, hidden under my jacket. Don't go to market alone, that's our rule in the Gut.

Nightmarket is the liveliest part of the undercity. It swells like a gaudy cyst beneath the lawless skin of the darkness, danger and pleasure fused into one, the place where anything is possible and everything is for sale. Metrowatch don't set foot here, and gangs battle to rule the streets and tax the vendors.

The people pressed around me are underdwellers, just like Ade, born in the darkness. Pale skin and sensitive eyes, with mutation and disease leaving their marks on flesh. Children with six fingers or flat noses or strange shrunken skulls, their front teeth sticking out at right angles. Adults clawing at patches of red rawness on their necks, the first symptom of rainwater poisoning. No voice below a yell, prices repeated like mantras. Old women wrapped in rags, hunched over stoves. Young women half dressed with video-tattoos flaring on their thighs. Long painted fingernails, long cigarettes. Men with closed doors for eyes and guns displayed in their belts.

We pass a tank of blue crabs with their claws tied shut, then a stall hung with blind dogs, dead and skinned, ready for the cooking pot. Pans of sizzling locusts. Racks of cheap sandals. Rummage bins full of bootleg software, infochips in sealed bags. Barbers, acupuncturists, fortune-tellers. Water-mongers blowing their whistles and shaking flasks of whatever they're passing for clean. Little boys running through the crowd, thin and laughing, barefoot. Big mob of gang guys sitting in a café, playing dominoes. They call out in greeting to Ade as he passes. Music thumping from a dozen different speaker systems, real music that you hear in the air rather than download into your nerves; lots of people down here don't have functioning implants. My chameleon cloth mimics the hues of drug bars lit by flickering blue neon, love hotels pulsing passion pink. We pass a dozen doorways you could walk into and never walk out of again. Dark, sweaty shapes draped over couches or lying on the floor. Off-duty thieves lounging in grimy alcoves. Streets made of glimpses. Night never ends down here, but if you fall asleep you won't wake up.

'This is it, sis,' Ade calls.

'You're sure?'

'Only one Kiyagi in Nightmarket.'

I follow him into a doorway anyone would've missed, no sign, down narrow stairs and through a beaded curtain. This place doesn't look promising. The faceshaper's clinic is just as dark and humid and cramped as the street outside. There's no peace from the yelling, the water-mongers' whistles, the *thump thump thump* of music from the gang cafés. A young woman is sitting behind a desk, with her legs up on the chair opposite her. A cigarette is burning in a pink ashtray. She has an infovein trailing into her wrist, and seems to be watching some immersive lumenfeed.

'Hey!' Ade says. 'Looking for the shaper.'

'Not here,' she says. There's clearly another door that will take us deeper into the clinic, but she's blocking it with her legs.

'So where is he?'

She doesn't answer. Someone outside in the street screams, like in real pain, but the music doesn't stop.

I can see Ade's getting angry, but I don't want him to get rough with anyone. I catch him by the arm.

'Don't,' I say.

'What we even here for anyway, sis?' he asks.

'Can't say,' I reply. 'Job.'

'Don't seem like your sort of job.'

'We'll find out.' I don't know what to do now. The Moth told me to come here, but he's been silent ever since. Was there something I'm forgetting?

Wait.

I lean over the girl and snap my fingers in front of her

face. She turns to look at me, angry.

'Listen,' I say. '*The Moth rises.* Understand?'

She doesn't say anything. Instead she picks up the pink ashtray and smacks it down on the desk a few times, making a racket. Then she gets back to whatever she was looking at before. I don't know if that was a good response or not. If this doesn't work, I have no idea what I'll do. I stand with Ade in the tiny room, sweat running down the sides of my face.

'Did you say "moth" to her?' Ade asks.

'I can't talk about it, Ade,' I reply.

'You mean like, *the Moth*, sis? The one they say can crack anything?'

'Yeah,' I say. 'That Moth. But you can't tell anyone.'

'This what you was working on yesterday? When I found you all wired up in your room?'

I nod. Ade whistles.

'You should've said something, sis! That's mad stuff.'

'You can't tell anyone. Any. *One*. Understand?'

'Yeah,' he says, 'hype. I got you, sis.'

Footsteps. A tall, strange man appears in the doorway that the woman is blocking. He's wearing a medical worker's gown, but every bit of his exposed skin crawls with colour. He's covered in video-tattoos, and what they show is a shoal of glowing fish, long orange and black carp that glide across his flesh. He raises one hand and says something that I don't understand. A moment later my aural implants catch up.

Old friend Ade, new friend Nova. Welcome.

'Dr Kiyagi?'

Yes. It is a pleasure to meet you. Our mutual friend told me to expect a young woman, but they did not say how charming she was.

'Thanks,' I say. His sentences are much shorter in his native language. My implants keep translating long after the faceshaper finishes speaking.

Follow me, please.

His sullen receptionist – perhaps his daughter, they look alike – moves her legs to let me past. As Ade follows, Dr Kiyagi raises one hand.

The client's instructions do not include you, valued friend.

'Said I'd sit in with her,' Ade says.

I cannot indulge this. The client was very clear.

'I'll meet you when I'm done?' I ask him. 'Please? You know who's making the calls here. Don't cross them.'

Ade snorts. He actually looks jealous. Ever since we met, he's been the one with the important, scary connections, his dad and brothers and uncles. Akram might be a big name down here, but I've finally got an even more impressive connection, a name people know far beyond the lightless slums of the undercity. I can't deny the thrill of finally seeing my contacts open doors Ade can't follow me through.

'Back here in two hours,' he says, dismissing us, like he's giving me permission to leave him. 'Otherwise you walk out of Nightmarket on your own. Can't babysit you all day, sis.'

Many apologies, old friend, Kiyagi says, bowing to Ade. *Send my fondest regards to your family.*

I follow Kiyagi down another narrow flight of metal stairs, into his low-ceilinged surgery. He closes the heavy hatch door behind us, and the din of Nightmarket finally fades. The dominant sound here is the sloppy mumble of churning fluid, intercut with the ticking of antique machinery. The room smells of cigarettes and disinfectant. The lights are weak and green, his surgery awash with shadow. My chameleon cloth turns dull mucusy shades in response. Kiyagi gestures to a reclining chair.

Please.

I sit. As I do, I realise with a nasty shock that the far wall is lined with faces. They're held behind greasy glass, suspended in a cloudy liquid, but even through this dimness they're clearly human faces, skin stretched out on racks. Old, lined faces, young, smooth faces, faces dark-skinned and light. Their mouths and eyelids are closed, as if asleep.

'Are you … ?' I gesture to the faces.

Not today. It is not required. But if ever your face is no good. If the corps have your face in their memory banks. You know where I am. I can make you new again.

The faceshaper pulls over his tray of tools.

I believe the client has already explained what I will do. Your irises and fingerprints must change. They cannot match your birth records, but must convince also. They cannot appear counterfeit.

'Is that easy?'

No. But I am very good at what I do. That is why the client chooses Kiyagi.

'Do you … know the Moth?'

I know enough to know we should both be silent.

'All right,' I say. Dr Kiyagi adjusts the tool he's holding, a hooked instrument with a tiny laser light at the tip. The video-tattooed fish pass over his face, swimming just under his skin. His eyes are very dark, almost black.

The faceshaper seems to be thinking.

The job you do is dangerous? You must be hidden?

'Something like that.'

He puts his tool down and draws out another tray.

Holds it up to me. A selection of teeth, laid out against velvet black.

Very secret. Very safe.

'What do they do?'

Kiyagi removes one of the teeth, a molar, from the tray. He presses an almost invisible protrusion on the side of the tooth, and the crown opens up, revealing that the thing is hollow. He lets me look at the space inside.

No X-ray, no bioscan. Hide what you want. Infochip, or poison perhaps? Who can say? Your secret.

'Did the client ask for this?'

No. But they are newly shipped in, and it seemed you could be intrigued.

I think about it. He's upselling me, trying to get more on the bill, but it does genuinely seem useful. You could keep a blank infochip inside the fake tooth. If the Moth wants me stealing data from Grale, it would be good to have a way of hiding it, so even if they search my implant memory drives they can't find anything.

'How much?'

For this? One thousand byts.

I laugh without joy, a barter laugh. 'What's your real price? You know who I'm working for.'

Out of respect for our mutual friend, I can sell at seven hundred. No lower.

'All right,' I tell the faceshaper. I gave most of the money to Patches already, but I still have nine thousand byts on my account. There's some other stuff I need to buy before the job, but this seems like a good investment.

Exquisite. Kiyagi beams, his teeth dull green in the surgery's unearthly light. He pulls latex gloves over his hands, and picks up his hooked tool. *Then let us proceed. Be calm and be still, please.*

The faceshaper leans over me, holding one of my eyes open. I take a deep breath. He lowers the laser's strobing point to my iris.

9

Commuter magrail, early morning. Corpsmen mumbling work memos, staring through each other, looking at private lumen windows. Many wear the Bliss Inc. butterfly on their lapels. I'm sitting by the door. My chameleon cloth is set to a muted blue-grey, and I have black boots on my feet. No rain forecast, but my wrap is bundled up inside my bag anyway. My hair's slicked down like a corpswoman's, my irises reshaped by Kiyagi, my face expressionless.

I made other preparations: tanning, several sessions,

to get rid of my undercity paleness, a dead giveaway. I removed, at the Moth's request, all of the illegal programs from my implants, everything except Phantom and the other nameless program he gave me. As a precaution, I loaded some of my custom programs into an infochip, which I stored inside my new hollow tooth. If I desperately need an icebreaker, I only have to open the tooth up and load the programs back into my implants. At Patches' insistence, I gave the rest of the money from the first payment to him. In case I don't come back.

Please note that the next station is now a Security Five area, the train's voice says in my ear. *I repeat: the next station is a Security Five area. A compliance zone will be in effect. It will not be possible to leave the train at the next station.*

We're heading for the heart of the City, the corp-nucleus. The metanet is different, quieter on the surface, seething with activity below that. I feel like I'm skimming over a frozen ocean, with whispering fathoms of information moving just out of reach. What I'm sensing are the corps' mainframes, supercomputers guarded by the most complex, expensive ice you can imagine.

No need to worry, the Moth's synthetic voice whispers.

'You're sure?'

The information they're acting on has nothing to do

with us. I monitor all Metrowatch chatter. You're safe.

The train passes through a tunnel in the core of a citybloc and then we're out again into the early sunlight. Traffic pulses through glass-wrapped tubes below us, silvered blood in a transparent vein. Above us I see pedestrian walkways, snoops flying in formation, promo-lumens fighting for prominence in the sky. It's dizzying and for a moment I feel like I'm about to fall out of myself.

We stop at the next station, but the doors don't open. On the platform every corpsman is lying motionless on the pale concrete in their work clothes, with their hands clasped behind their heads. Metrowatch enforcers in black armour are moving between them, scanning faces and checking IDs.

As I said. Fruitless sweeps. Who knows what they thought they saw?

I stare straight ahead, try to keep calm. I'm Nova. I'm careful, collected, uncatchable. Everything the Moth set me up with has been cutting-edge. I'm far beyond these enforcers. They could point their scanners right at me and they wouldn't find anything.

There's a jolt and the magrail pulls away, leaving the corpsmen lying on the platform. I breathe out. This isn't even the hard part. We're at the centre of corpworld. I can't start panicking just because I saw a few enforcers. There'll be plenty of security where I'm going.

The corpspires come into view as we leave the next station. The cityblocs have thinned out, making way for even larger buildings, the gleaming strongholds of the corps. Every mirrored metre of the spires is designed to remind you who rules the world, how small you are and how easily they could crush you. The Metrowatch Control Centre, a great pyramid of black glass, marked with an unblinking lumen eye. The Municipal Works building, shining in the new sun, their orange hand logo opening and closing in greeting. I see the spires of other corps too: the BytBank building, OasisCare, KFM Engineering, SportSneeks, the Lethe Beverages group, the Rahman-Obach Syndicate, dozens more. Towering metanet broadcast arrays and server farms that guzzle oceans of supercoolant. Power written in glass and steel.

And, as huge as they are, the Bliss Inc. building overshadows them all.

The Bliss spire is a shard of brightness stuck into the City's grey flesh, branded with a yellow lumen butterfly. The pinnacle is lost in cloud. I can feel the weight of the building in the metanet as well; feel the rush of data flowing into this brilliant blade. Of all neural-implant rigs installed in the last five years, 88 per cent were made by Bliss, or are running some variant of their software packages. That's billions of implant rigs worldwide, each one sending its data back to the Bliss spire: heart rates, nutrition information, the length of time a user looked at one advert lumen or another. Purchase history, purchase future. Projected profits generated by each user in a lifetime. Tidal waves of information, unimaginable.

Next stop: Bliss Incorporated. This station is for employees and visitors to the Bliss Inc. premises only. You must have a valid pass to exit at this station.

It would be better, the Moth says, ***if I left you here. Direct communication during this phase of the operation would be unwise. Metanet signals within the corpspire are heavily monitored. It should be easy to find your way to Grale. If your interview is successful, I will contact you again. If you are caught ... I cannot protect you. Do you understand?***

'Yes,' I whisper. This is it. I drum my fingers on my work bag.

I can sense that you're nervous.

'Who wouldn't be?'

You have the makings of a great operative. I did not choose you on a whim. You are with me. I have every faith in you.

The Bliss spire is rushing towards us, no longer a

shining splinter on the horizon, but a mirrored colossus, looming above the magrail track. In the time it takes me to draw a deep breath, it blots out the sun, and the train hurtles on through the spire's shadow. No turning back now.

I breathe in and out, trying to calm myself. The Moth's presence fades away, but the words remain. He chose me. He's protecting me. I can do this job. I'll walk in there and convince everyone. The Moth has faith in me.

And what if he's wrong? What if they know? Where will they grab me? The train station? Will they wait until I'm waiting for the interview, tap me on the shoulder, take me to some windowless room? If I fail, the Moth can't save me. He said so himself.

The magrail comes to a halt. The doors open. This is it. The corpsmen surge out of the doors, nobody saying a word to one another. I'm still sitting down. I have to do this. I already took the Moth's money. Patches will have started spending it. I can't go back. I can only go on.

I leap to my feet before my faltering heart can stop me and rush out of the doors. They slam shut behind me, like a trap. The magrail moves off. I breathe in again and follow the crowd.

The Bliss spire station is cleaner than the downstrata stations I go leeching in, sleek yellow flooring and spotless grey walls. The corpsmen are moving with a purpose, and I tag on to the end of their queue. We climb an escalator and then we're hurrying through a maze of rounded tunnels, everyone rushing as fast as they can without actually running, quick, percussive steps, hundreds of pairs of shiny work shoes hitting the floor in unison. Nobody pays any attention to me.

We come to a halt in front of the ticket barriers, slipping through the turnstiles one by one, holding out our wristhubs to the scanners to pay. In most magrail stations, you'd be at the exit now, but instead we go up another set of escalators, and now we're in a large, windowless atrium, a security checkpoint. Metrowatch enforcers control the room, wearing dark combat jackets and heavy boots. No helmets and no guns, just nerve disruptors in their belts. Bliss don't want their employees feeling too threatened on a morning commute, I guess. The guns will be kept in the back office, along with the riot gas and heavy armour. Some of the Bliss corpsmen know the enforcers, and they're gossiping to pass the time as we wait. They're all used to this. I keep my face blank, eyes fixed on the scanners ahead.

I feel a questioning info-beam passing over me, and an enforcer is walking over, a tall, broad-shouldered guy. Strong jaw, looks like he spends a lot of time checking himself out in the mirror. He smiles warmly, his teeth even and white, but the eye on his uniform stares at me the whole time.

'Morning, miss. You're a visitor?'

'Yeah,' I say, forcing myself to smile back. My heart goes faster. Is he about to ask me to come with him? Does he know? Are they watching for me? Hustled into the back room, maybe into a skycar. Flown off to the black pyramid, Metrowatch Control Centre, taken to the interrogation floors …

'What department of Bliss do you have an appointment with?' he asks.

'Human Futures. I have an interview at 9.45,' I say. My skin prickles under his gaze like it's electrically charged. I force myself to stand as still as possible.

His eyes flick to the right of my face for a moment. He's checking a schedule, bringing up some lumen-list.

I swallow, my tongue dry and enormous in my mouth. Any moment now he's going to put his hand on my arm and ask me to follow him. Into the detentionbloc. I don't think I'll break immediately, but they'll get what they want to know in the end.

I smile at him. It feels like a rictus on a corpse. He must know. I'm so transparent; I'm such a terrible actor. He's just toying with me.

Thud thud thud in my chest.

He smiles back and nods at something.

'What's your interview about?' the enforcer asks. The line moves forward and he moves along beside me. I can feel sweat on my forehead now. Hoping my make-up doesn't run.

'It didn't tell you?' I ask. Liar, liar, liar. The eye logo on his uniform boring into me. He can see. He knows.

'I don't have the clearance,' he says. 'Human Futures, that's top-secret stuff. Research and development.'

'You're not telling me anything new,' I say, willing him to move on to the next person, but he doesn't.

'Oh yeah? I heard it's all sealed off up there. They tell you that? Nobody goes in or out but the CEO. Can't even get a metanet signal up there, I heard. How weird's that?'

The enforcer holds my gaze, smiling. I realise, with a delirious rush of relief, he's not thinking about arresting me at all. I mean, maybe he is thinking about pushing me up against the wall, but not because I'm a criminal.

I smile, still feeling the sweat sitting sticky on my brow. Hoping he can't see it. 'It's kind of exec-level stuff. If you don't have clearance, I can't say anything.'

'Oh yeah?' He laughs. 'You're a bit mysterious, aren't you, Kirsten? I have this feeling about you, like you keep yourself hidden a bit.'

He definitely got that from some guide on picking up women. He probably has a voice in his ear right now, a metanet program feeding him lines.

'You ask so many questions of all the visitors?' I ask him.

'Only the gorgeous ones.'

I burst out laughing. I have to. A minute ago I thought this was it, that I was about to get taken to the depths of some corp detentionbloc. I thought this guy was the end of me, and now he's giving me canned lines from some pick-up feed. I can't believe this is real.

He's grinning still, if a little awkwardly.

'It's a bit early in the day for this,' I tell him. I realise this might actually be a good thing. If he's talking to me, none of the other enforcers are going to come over.

'Just a compliment,' the enforcer says. 'Life's too short not to say what's on your mind, you know? I could be gone tomorrow. My life's on the line.'

'Dangerous station, this one?' I put my bag on to a conveyor belt and send it through the scanners. Nothing to find in there, just my rainwrap, hair oil, make-up.

'Could be,' he says. 'I mean, there's bad people out there. They might take a shot at Bliss. Terrorists and that. Dangerous people, anticorp, anti-everything. You don't know who they are. Look just like you or me, half of them.'

We're in front of the security scanner now. I step into it, and my body's flooded with exotic wavelengths of light, picking out every circuit of my implants, tracing the boundaries of my skeleton, my organs, my fake tooth, recording every pore and mole and eyelash in my face. The Nova Atlas, a complete guide to my body, stored away in some encrypted memory core.

'They could be right next to you,' I say. 'It's a scary thought.'

He nods. 'Exactly! I have to be on guard.' Whether Kiyagi's hollow tooth passed the test or not, I have no idea: the young enforcer doesn't seem interested in the results of the scan. I'm walking, slowly but surely, away from the security checkpoint. I realise, with a flush of joy, that I've actually done it. One step closer to success.

'I'm glad they've got guys like you looking out,' I say.

'Hey,' he says, 'if you need something, just chat me, yeah? I know people. I'm a good friend to have.'

'I might not get this job,' I say. 'You might never see me again.'

'Nah,' the enforcer says. There's people lined up behind the scanner but he's blocking it, back turned to them, still grinning at me. 'You've got it. I can tell. You look like a winner. But let me know, yeah? We can celebrate.'

'Sure,' I say. I turn and walk down the hallway to an elevator. I hear a ping in my ear and see a new request in the corner of my eye, a contact: JAY. I grimace. Give a guy a securicorp uniform and he thinks it's open season, I swear. Blast the bad guys and get the girls, just like in his actionfeeds. I ignore the request. A short elevator ride later and I'm in the Bliss Inc. atrium.

The space is enormous, a cavernous room with curving glass walls supported by a lattice of steel beams. Morning sunlight streams in, dazzling me when it hits the shiny white floor. A snoop drifts through the air, rotors purring. There are elevator tubes all over the lobby, taking people up into the corpspire's higher reaches. Set in the middle of the atrium is a fountain, shooting out fans of crystal-clear water. Hovering above the fountain is an enormous lumen, a flotilla of bright yellow butterflies that move as one, forming the Bliss logo as they fly. For a moment, I imagine a pair of black wings flying among them, black lined with silver. A moth in plain sight, a little dark flaw in the perfect sunshine yellow of the logo-lumen. The thought makes me smile.

So now where do I go?

Hiii, comes a voice in my ear. *My name's Blanca. So super to meet you!*

A lumen-woman insinuates herself in front of me.

She's dressed head to toe in Bliss yellow. Her face is golden like evening sunlight, her eyes pools of liquid gold too, and more butterflies crawl sleepily in her long hair. A corpsman walks through her and for a moment her body occupies the same space as his, and the two images fight for dominance in my eye. I blink a few times and she goes back to normal.

I am a metanetwork-based adaptive language entity, and I'm the receptionist here at Bliss Incorporated, the lumen-woman tells me. *Please try to speak to me clearly so I can I help you this morning. We're very glad you decided to visit, by the way! We value all our guests so much! If you're looking for BlissMusic, take guest elevator one. If you're visiting BlissMovie, that's guest elevator two. BlissPlay is guest elevator three. For BlissFriends, take guest elevator four. If you want BlissSport, you can just stroll yourself on over to guest—*

'Kirsten Cosset. I have a 9.45 appointment with Grale Inselberg.'

I heard you say 'appointment' with 'Grale Inselberg'. Is that correct?

'Yeah.'

Great! If you follow me, I'll show you the elevator you need.

The lumen receptionist turns and walks off through

the crowd, leaving a golden trail on the ground behind her. I follow, swerving round columns of corpsmen queuing up for their elevators. The lumen leads me past the fountain, litres of clear water rippling in a shallow pool. I think about how hard it is to get clean water in the undercity. Running this fountain for an hour probably uses more water than the Gut does in a week.

Here we are, the lumen receptionist, Blanca, tells me. *If you scan your wristhub on the access panel, the elevator should know where to take you. Glad I could help you today, Kirsten. If you need anything while you're here, just say Blanca, OK? And I'll come and help you out.*

As the doors close, I wonder again if this is a trap. Maybe they know. My fear's twitching around inside my skull like an insect under a glass, but I have to keep calm. Can't let anything show on my face. They'll have cameras in here for sure. I brought a stress bracelet, the kind of thing young corpswomen play with on the train, and I'm palming the beads back and forth. That'll look normal at least. I'm here for a big job interview. It's not strange for me to be stressed.

The elevator moves, carrying me into execworld, the land beyond the clouds, where leechers never go. The pinnacle of the spire.

The elevator is a fast one, and I move swiftly through the strata of the Bliss corpspire. I rise past floor upon floor of low-rank corpsmen lying slack and blind in immersion rigs, infoveins snaking into their wrists, their hands grasping as they manipulate assembly space. Supervisors stalk raised gantries, and automated refreshment trolleys zoom around on rails. On another floor they're filming scenes for a VR show, something for BlissMovie, actors wearing silver motion-capture suits, gesturing and talking on an enormous empty stage the colour of a clear sky. I see a velodrome, a whole floor dedicated to cycling, Bliss employees in yellow gym gear racing each other on bicycles. The floor above this is treadmills, exercise equipment, corpsmen sweating in front of full-length mirrors. Some sort of recreation area. Above it I see what look like apartments. I know the corpsmen who live in the spire full time are favoured, considered higher grade than anyone who commutes. The fact they spend every waking moment at work is a small price to pay for that kind of status.

I climb further upstrata, past floors that are shielded with tinted glass. These are the exec levels. Management. The metanet up here is dense with secrets. I can detect a million channels of communication, but they're all heavily iced and monitored, a web of whispers.

Soon I'm higher than every other bloc and spire in the City. I've never been so far upstrata before. The only thing above me is air traffic, private skycars and the hard yellow flare of a shuttlejet taking off. The City below me is a mosaic of blocs. I've never seen it from this angle before. Never looked down on everything. I've lived my whole life in a maze of walkways and chasms, clinging to the edges of those enormous grey structures. What's strange is how flat it looks from up here. Everything, the difference between up- and downstrata floors, looks smaller.

As suddenly as the elevator ride started, it comes to a halt. I'm let out into a hallway: pale grey walls, and sweet perfume in the air. If you're already treating the air for pollutants, you might as well make it smell nice, I guess. The strangest thing up here, though, is the silence of the metanet in the floors above us. It's not the quiet of the exec levels, where I could tell there was heavily encrypted communication happening. The silence above us is the complete absence of any metanet communication at all, which inside a corpspire makes no sense at all.

I remember what the enforcer told me, down in the station. He'd heard Human Futures was insulated from the metanet. That's difficult to do, but, if you built the walls the right way, I guess it's possible. Question is, why? What kind of work must Grale be doing that she has to cut them off from the outside world so completely? I see now why the Moth needs someone like me, inside the spire. No hacker, even the most skilled hacker to ever live, can breach Human Futures if it's built like that.

There's a trail of lumen-light on the floor and I follow it into a reception room. There are two other girls in here, a pair of sleek corpswomen. One is dressed in black, with slicked-back hair and an expensive-looking bag on her lap. The model of a high-achieving young exec. The other girl looks very different, and for a moment I'm taken aback. She's wearing neon-pink trousers and a chequerboard jacket, the kind of clothes undercity people wear. Her hair's shaved at the sides and nano-treated, shifting through vibrant shades of peach and orange. She even has a video-tattoo on her hand. She's dressed like one of Ade's gang girl friends, but she's fit and healthy-looking, like a proper upstrata person, and she's waiting for a job interview with the CEO of Bliss Inc. Strange. Both of the girls are staring at me, I realise.

As they look me over, I feel a fresh wave of fear. Jay was just some gym addict with a Metrowatch contract, too busy thinking about what was between his legs to see what was in front of him. These girls won't be fooled so easily. They can see already that I'm not like them: their outfits must cost thousands of byts, and I'm wearing cheap greys, dressed like the people they're used to ordering around. Their skin is tanned from living up at the top of the City; mine's tanned from a few sessions on a sunbed. Their faces are sculpted by the top surgeons. I had some faceshaper from Nightmarket poke around in my eyes with a laser. They must sense that I don't belong here.

Don't freeze. Don't look scared. Just walk towards them.

'*Hiii*,' the girl dressed up like an undercity ganger says.

'My name's Esme! What's yours? Did you come far?'

'Kirsten Cosset. I live in the City,' I tell her, sitting down.

'Oh well, of course you do,' she says. 'I meant what part are you from?'

What she means is, what strata am I from, how high up in my bloc do I live.

'Floor 231,' I tell Esme, quickly checking the fake address the Moth gave me.

'Oh,' she says, 'that sounds so cosy! That's really nice. I'm Pinnacle 4. We used to be Pinnacle 2, but it's got so competitive recently. They added a pair of floors above us last year and Father just couldn't get in ahead of the other buyers. Mother was livid. I mean, people notice something like that. They do talk.'

'Oh yeah,' I say. 'I bet.'

Pinnacle 4 means an exec apartment at the very summit of one of the City's housingblocs. I've never met someone with a pinnacle address before. Esme is god-strata, a corp princess. Her outfit makes more sense to me now. Up close, I can see her clothes aren't quite what Ade's friends would wear. It's like someone looked at pictures of undercity gangs, and made an outfit that's ten times more expensive, to sell to upstrata kids who want to look edgy. Esme's so important, so sure of her place in the sun, that she can afford to be daring. She can dress undercity, even to an interview with Grale, because she knows she'll never be mistaken for someone who actually lives there. It's just a costume. She can take it off whenever she wants.

'So how did you hear about this position?' Esme asks me. The video-tattoo on the back of her hand is the glif that means *Love*. I can't see Ade or Rue ever getting that one, to be honest.

'I had a tip-off,' I tell her. 'Insider info. Just felt like it was for me.'

'You've done *so* well to make it this far,' she tells me. 'I think it's awesome they reached so far downstrata to find candidates. There's so much passion and talent below exec level and we don't make enough use of it.'

'Well, you know what the bad thing about being at the top is?' I say. 'There's people below you, and they might be even more driven than you are. You can't get too comfortable.'

'That is so true actually,' the other girl says. 'My assistant in my old job, she was kind of, like, downstrata, and she was so *hungry*. It was scary. She worked harder than three people put together.'

I think about the undercity, about people picking through piles of rubbish in darkness, looking for stuff they can eat or sell. I think of the fever-warm, frantic streets of Nightmarket. I think about Ade and his crew, putting the gun to strangers for anything they can get. I think about the packs of blind dogs crawling through cracks in the bottom of our world, listening for heartbeats in the silence.

'Yeah,' I say. 'People are definitely hungry.'

'Can you believe we're going to meet Grale Inselberg?' Esme asks.

'I know,' I say. 'She's such an idol to me.'

Grale's a hard person to find information on. Public record goes like this: she's been the CEO of Bliss Inc. for fifty-five years, taking over the position when her father, the previous CEO, died. That's all you get. Even by chief-exec standards, she's cloistered and wary. Only people she mixes with socially are other top execs, pinnacle people, and that's rare. Grale is subject to a Category Five privacy-screen, so no visual record of her can be distributed. In any recording that features her, Grale's face will be blurred out with static, and her voice is distorted and masked. The Moth gave me a leaked image that dates from decades ago, and she looks … normal, I suppose. Just a blonde corpswoman with tired blue eyes.

'What she's done with her father's company has been amazing,' Esme says. 'Everyone calls her a genius.

So *not* a conformist. Have you seen her speak at the World Corp Summit?'

'No,' I say.

'Oh, of course! You won't have the privacy clearance, right? Father has clearance so I can watch all of her talks. She's an incredible speaker. So … precise. And she thinks about more than just her company. She talks about humanity, like the whole thing, and where we're going in the next century. She's got so much intellectual energy. I wish she spoke like that more.'

'Wow,' I say. 'Lucky you.'

Whatever Esme's about to brag about next, we'll never know, because there's a chime, and the lumen receptionist, Blanca, appears in the middle of the room.

Hello, ladies! If you'd like to follow me, she tells us, *they're ready for the advanced security check. How exciting!*

We gather ourselves and follow the lumen. Even the pretence of friendship is sucked out of the room. This is the real thing now. There's nothing but tension.

The next room is filled by Grale's security detail, seven armed men. Four guards are posted at the corners of the room, wearing charcoal grey armour with yellow butterflies blazing on their breasts. Two more Bliss security personnel are sitting on the far side of a silver bench, which is covered in scanning tech. Behind them stands a tall, commanding corpsman. He wears white, head to toe. His combat jacket is white, his shirt is white, his trousers and his boots and his gun's grip are all white. His hands are covered by pure white gloves. His face is pale; the only colour on his body is his rust-brown hair. He looks unearthly, a cross between a soldier and a surgeon.

'If you could take a seat, please,' the corpsman in white says, in a voice that tells you there's no choice but to obey. We smile nervously at him. He looks young, but the kind of young that comes from gene therapy. His forehead is lined by frowning. He's powerfully built, broad shoulders and thick muscular arms, and his eyes are synthetic, pupil-less and colourless. Military-grade implants. He doesn't work for Bliss; the logo on his jacket is one I don't recognise, a silver person with wings. His presence in the metanet is one of the strangest I've ever felt. Wall upon wall of impenetrable dark ice, the most advanced personal-information security available. He must be from a securicorp, some outside contractor.

So this is the real test. Not the scanners at the station, not the elevator in the lobby. If there's something wrong with my clearance, my body, the programs I'm running on my implants, this is where it comes out. These are the men who'll find it.

One of the junior security people smiles thinly at me. Sweat prickles again on my brow. The palms of my hands feel too hot. I rest them on my legs, try to tell myself I'm carved out of cool stone. No pressure can crack me. I'm cold, unbreakable, emotionless.

'Please don't be nervous,' the corpsman in white tells us. 'This is totally routine. The CEO is subject to extreme security protocols. The unfortunate reality of the world today is that remarkable women like Ms Inselberg are not safe. Although I know that nobody in this room means her any harm, we need to be certain that you are who your ID says you are, and that nobody has compromised or altered your body's implants. You may not even be aware that this has happened. Modern anticorp hackers have developed some very sophisticated techniques. So we need to be sure.'

'Of course,' Esme says.

'If you can go first, please,' the corpsman in white asks me.

Too late to get out now. Just have to trust in the Moth. I sit where he's showing me, on the left-hand seat by the silver bench, opposite one of the Bliss employees. The corpsman in white stands behind the Bliss man, looking down at me. His synthetic eyes are incredible when you look at them up close. They're colourless, but the light hitting them plays off a thousand tiny circuits, creating circles of rainbow light where his pupils would be. I can see microscopic movements as they focus on my face.

'Quite a sight, aren't they?' he asks me.

'Yes,' I say. 'I've never seen implants like that before.'

'They let me see beyond the normal spectrum. Infrared, ultraviolet, low light … I don't miss much.'

As he speaks, he gestures for me to press my palms against the silver bench. I do as he says and a flush of heat spreads over them. Fingerprint scanning. Dr Kiyagi did a good job, so far as I know. Certainly the Bliss guard seems happy with the result. He scans my face, paying special attention to my eyes, again with no problems. Next he attaches an infovein to my wristhub, and I feel a pack of hunter programs enter my implants, searching through every file. I hear a high ping in my ear as each drive is accessed. The Moth knew this would happen. The programs he gave me appear harmless under scrutiny. The hunters don't find anything.

'Are you nervous?' the Bliss guard asks me.

'A bit. Why?'

'Your heart rate's quite high,' he says.

'I just, you know … I really want this job,' I tell him. 'This is a big day for me.'

The guard seems to be checking something with his

own database, and then he nods and removes the vein from my wristhub.

'OK,' he says. 'That's it. You're cleared to meet with the CEO.'

It's Esme's turn now. I watch as she sits down opposite a Bliss guard and has her palms scanned, her eyes examined, but, when it comes time for the audit of her implants, there's some kind of problem. The junior security guy runs the check again, and then gestures to the corpsman in white, who checks the readout himself, and then shakes his head.

'What's the matter?' Esme asks them.

'Miss, there seems to be an abnormality,' the Bliss guard says.

'What do you mean?' Esme asks him.

'With your implants, miss. The results from the scan are abnormal.'

Esme narrows her eyes. 'That's absolutely not possible. What are you implying?'

'I'm sorry, but the safety of the CEO is paramount. I can't clear you to meet her.'

'Do you know who my father is?' she hisses.

'Whoever he is,' the corpsman in white cuts in, leaning down so she's looking right into his colourless eyes, 'he doesn't scare me. My name is Campbell Reid. I'm a

Systems Auditor for the Archangel Corporation. If your daddy is as important as you want us to think he is, then you'll know what that means.'

Archangel. That's corporate intelligence and counter-infiltration. Top-level network security company, operatives with infinite access. If hackers are the metanet's disease, then Archangel Auditors are the white blood cells; at least, that's how the corps tell it. I've heard the name, of course – whispers on the hacker chatfeeds – but I've never seen one of their Auditors in real life before. I'm guessing this guy is assigned to Grale full-time, to protect her from people like me.

Esme says nothing. Her face crumples, like she's on the verge of tears.

'You don't need to worry,' the Auditor, Campbell, tells her, changing from stern to kindly at the sight of her distress. 'Nine times out of ten you downloaded something harmless and got a malicious program as a ride-along, without knowing it. Legally you wouldn't be liable. But you can't be alone in a room with the CEO until we clear that up.'

I don't know if I believe him. Who knows what they really found? I have this sense, crazily, that our scans got mixed up. That what they should've read from my implants; all of the dark, weird signals and

Moth-authored software got put into her readout somehow. Maybe that's part of what the Moth did to get me through this. If that's the case, Esme's in deep trouble.

'If you'll just come with me,' Campbell says, taking her by the arm of her checked jacket and walking her to a side door, 'we can run some more tests, see if we can't work this out.'

Esme vanishes with the Archangel Auditor. I decide I'll live with that. They can't make someone from Pinnacle 4 disappear. She'll get through it.

'Kirsten Cosset,' one of the Bliss guards says to me, 'Grale's expecting you now. She doesn't like to be kept waiting. Go through.'

The third candidate, whose name I never caught, is still standing by the door we came through. She looks petrified, like she wants to leave right now. If someone like Esme could be compromised, a perfect pinnacle specimen like her, then couldn't any of us? How do you even know if you're clear?

And, of course, the real infiltrator is right here. Me, Nova, under the eyes of an *Archangel Auditor*, and he didn't catch me. For one moment, the fear that's been in my stomach ever since I walked into the spire drains away. I'm uncatchable, untouchable, invisible, immortal.

'Thank you,' I say, and I give the guard a big smile. I

turn and walk through the double doors to Grale's office. It's only as I'm stepping through them that something occurs to me: I'm about to sit down for a job interview with one of the richest, most powerful women in the world, and I have no idea what I'm going to say to her.

The far wall of Grale's office is made from glass. We're so high that the sky's advertising lumens are below us, a flickering carpet of light and motion drawn over the City. The people with pinnacle addresses look like underdwellers from this high in a corpspire. Suddenly I feel less sure that Esme's family connections can keep her safe. A person who lives in a strata this far above everyone else makes their own rules.

Grale's desk is a crescent of dark metal. It's covered in objects I don't recognise, rectangular sheets of some thin pale material. Some of the sheets are loose and others are bound together between thicker coverings. Grale sits in a high-backed chair, bent over her work. She's holding a silver tool, like a stylus, and is making small black marks on one of the sheets; not glifs, but some weird language I can't read. I can see other strange objects too. There's a machine made of glass and gold that pulses softly with sound. I see a tray full of sand, with stones placed in it, and a tiny rake to shape the sand with. A jug, half filled with water. A glass with lip marks on the rim, the only blemish I can see in the whole room.

'Speak,' Grale says, still making marks with her stylus. Her voice is soft.

'I'm here for the interview,' I say.

Grale Inselberg looks at me for the first time. I look back. I see someone who doesn't sleep much, an old corpswoman with a stark, hard face. She's far more striking in real life than in the old picture I saw. Her face is all angles, strong jaw and long, sharp nose. Ash-blonde hair slicked way back, lying close to her skull. Pale blue eyes and a crooked mouth that looks like she could be about to smile. She's wearing a suit of pure toneless black, a material that absorbs every ray of light that touches it, like a skin of shadow. Fuligin cloth, it's called. Only execs wear it. A golden brooch is pinned to the fuligin suit's lapel, shaped like a butterfly. No other jewellery, not even earrings. Short fingernails, elegant hands, and no wristhub that I can see, which is strange. Maybe she has a non-standard hub configuration. I guess when you're CEO of Bliss Inc., you can do things like that.

She looks me up and down, pale gaze travelling from my shiny corpshoes to my slicked corphair. Again I have the horrible idea that she must see through me, the way I felt with the enforcer and the girls in the waiting room and the Archangel Auditor. To this woman, this powerful, strange woman, I must scream that I don't belong here. Undercity trash. Orphan from the carebloc. Get her out of my sight. She has no business in this office. But I stand before her, and she says nothing, seems to be waiting for something else to happen, and then with a hot rush I remember. I'm supposed to bow. You bow when you meet chief execs. Everyone knows that.

I quickly bow as low as I can, mumbling 'sorry' to my feet. When I stand up straight, Grale still hasn't moved. I meet her eyes.

'Who are you?' she asks me, a weird question. All she has to do is ask my implants for ID. But I've had nothing from her, not even a passive invitation to share data. As far as metanet presence goes, Grale's body doesn't exist.

She has no trace of input or output. She's like the Human Futures department above us. Totally silent.

'Kirsten Cosset,' I say. 'It's an honour to meet you.'

'Ah, I see,' Grale replies, looking at one of her sheets, 'Kirsten, of course ...'

She starts to say something else, but I can't concentrate. I'm too shocked. I just realised something crazy: Grale Inselberg doesn't have neural implants. That's why she has no metanet signal and no wristhub. She's not part of the network, never has been.

I've met people without implants before, of course. If you don't get them installed within the first twenty months of life, the rejection rate skyrockets, and that can be really dangerous, as in permanent brain damage. So that puts some adults off. Some people do have them installed, but get cut off from metanet service because they can't pay their subscription, like that drifter who came to us with a message from the Moth. I've always pitied people who have to live without implants, the same way you'd pity someone who couldn't walk or couldn't see. Imagine living without the lumens, without newsfeeds, without instantchat. No games, no shopping, no partycrashing; apartments on upstrata floors won't even rent to someone without implants and a line of BytBank credit on their wristhub. The only people who go without are tiny babies and people who've dropped out of society completely.

Add one to that list: the CEO of the biggest neural-implant corporation in the world.

Grale snaps her fingers.

'You're not listening to me,' she says.

I open my mouth to speak.

'No,' she says. 'Don't try and lie to me. I'm extremely perceptive. It's something I pride myself on. The bow we can look past, but I will not be ignored.'

'I'm sorry. Won't happen again.'

'If you're that easily distracted, then I doubt it. Where did you go, just then?'

'You don't have neural implants,' I say. This isn't how I expected the interview to go, but I don't see any point lying about it.

Grale smiles properly for the first time.

'What makes you so sure?' she asks me.

'I'm not totally sure. Maybe you have some way of hiding the signals that I don't know about. You're not supposed to be able to turn your implants off, but maybe you have a way of doing that too. You're an exec: I'm sure you have tools other people don't. But that doesn't explain why you don't have a wristhub.'

'Good so far,' Grale says. 'What if I say you're right?

How do you feel about that? Have you ever met someone without neural implants before?'

I try to imagine Kirsten Cosset, the girl I'm supposed to be. She lives on floor two hundred and something, way upstrata. It's probably never occurred to her that anyone would live without implants.

'No. It's like meeting someone with half their head missing. I don't understand how you can live.'

'So you see me as deformed? Interesting.'

'I—'

'Don't deny it,' she says, effortlessly cutting over me, despite her soft voice. 'Say what you really mean. I cannot abide people who tell me what they think I want to hear. What you said, your first impression, is what you think of me. You see me as a cripple, half a person. That is fantastic. It means our marketing works, doesn't it?'

'Yes,' I say.

'After all, humanity survived for millennia without neural implants. Even a century ago, the idea was a bizarre novelty, outside of military research programs. And now the product we sell is so widely accepted that to go without is seen as a deformity.'

'Do you think you're deformed?' I ask her.

Her expression sours. 'Of course not. Just as I was starting to think you might be suitable … Take a moment to consider. Why do you think I chose this?'

When I think about it clearly, I do know.

'It's the ultimate ice,' I say. 'Complete protection. You can't be hacked because there's no metanet connection to your body.'

Grale nods. 'Exactly,' she says. 'The nasty truth is that there is no ice we or any other software developer can manufacture that can't be breached. Either by hackers and dissidents, or, more commonly, by other corps. The metanet is designed foremost as a system of information exchange, so you must assume any information stored there can be accessed, by an intruder talented and persistent enough. My work, my thoughts, cannot.'

'But how do you … ?' I can't finish the sentence. The question is too large.

'How do I work? How do I live? I'm not completely cut off, of course. I have chosen intermediaries that connect me with the metanet. If I hire you as my assistant, one of those intermediaries will be you. You will communicate on my behalf, access corporate data, essentially represent me within the net.'

'What if I'm hacked?' I ask.

Grale takes a sip of water. I kind of need the bathroom, I realise, watching her drink. I don't know if it's nervousness or what, but I suddenly really need to go.

'Then we deal with the problem,' she says.

'Is that what happened to your last assistant?' I ask, trying to ignore the sensation.

Silence. In the huge windows behind her, I can see there's rain moving in across the City, clouds that look yellow and purple in the sunshine, like membranes full of bruises. So the forecast was wrong. I wonder if Grale has ever walked outside in the rain, worn a wrap, felt the toxic water running over her latex face guard. Maybe she never leaves this building.

She's looking at me hard, like she's trying to decide on something.

'What is it that you think we do here?' Grale asks me.

I hesitate and my implants fill the gap, whispering in my ear.

Bliss Incorporated is the world's largest manufacturer of neural implants, with a customer base—

'You manufacture and produce software content for neural implants,' I say. 'The customer base is more than five billion. You also run media departments like BlissMusic, BlissPlay, and BlissSport, which produce more than a million downloadable datapacks daily—'

'Yes,' she replies. 'That's what it says when you search for public data about my company. Anyone could find that paragraph of information and parrot it via their implants, which is what you just did. I asked what *you* think we do here. What our purpose here at Bliss is.'

'To make as much money as you can?'

'Our shareholders and board would agree with that, certainly.'

I feel a twinge in my bladder, insistent. I shuffle my feet. What is up with that?

'But you don't agree?' I ask.

'My opinion on this has changed over the years. Today, for me, our revenue is not the most important part of Bliss Incorporated,' Grale replies. 'It is undeniably necessary. My work cannot be done without the money earned from sales of our implant hardware, our core software, and our media-content divisions. But these things are only the foundations of the work we do here. The department of Bliss that I personally head is called Human Futures. This is our long-term research and development wing.'

'I heard about that,' I say, because she's paused, and is looking for a response.

'Have you?' She narrows her eyes. 'The position as advertised makes no mention of the existence of that department. I'm only telling you now because you've been thoroughly screened. Where did you hear that name?'

'I, uh ...' I think quickly. Best to go as close to the

truth as possible. 'Security guy in the station. Said it was a big secret.'

'Did he?' Grale keeps her pale blue eyes on me, then seems to relax. 'People do talk, I suppose. The department's blanked out on security floor plans. No surprise that some employees speculate. Well. It's in Human Futures that we're looking for the next neural implant. I don't mean that we're trying to develop an improved form of the neural implant, necessarily. What I mean is that we're searching for the next invention that will have as great an impact on humanity, the species, as the nerve-augmentation system my father invented.'

A sharper stab inside me, a feeling I can't ignore. I seem to have gone from not needing the bathroom to about to explode, like there's a boiling rock jammed inside me. I grimace. This doesn't feel right at all.

'Many inventions have improved upon our natural physical abilities,' Grale continues. She sounds like she's slipping into autopilot, has given a version of this lecture to a whole bunch of people before me. 'The axe, the wheel, the combustion engine. Fewer improve or radically enhance our mental abilities, change how we're able to *think* about the world around us, rather than how we're able to alter it. The invention of written language, of zero ... it's these innovations that I'm especially interested in. If we—'

I can't focus on what the CEO is saying to me. I feel like something inside me is about to burst. I have this image of myself pissing all over her white floor like a baby, staining the grey legs of my suit … She'd never hire me. I'll blow the whole thing, never get access to whatever it is they're making in Human Futures…

'You're not listening,' Grale snaps. 'Again. Is something wrong with you, Kirsten? You looked very promising in your preliminary report, but I'm finding you troublingly unfocused in the flesh. Why can't you concentrate?'

I have one leg clamped across the other even though I'm standing up. All my muscles are tensed. Where did this come from?

'I need the bathroom,' I say, and it comes out like a strained hiss.

'Clearly,' Grale replies. She glares at me, and then looks back at her desk, like I've let her down. 'I think this has lasted long enough, honestly. I am not impressed. Interview over, you can go. There's a bathroom to your left. Use that. I don't want you exploding on your way out.'

As the words leave her mouth, I'm moving, almost running for the door she pointed out on the left-hand wall of her office, a doorway barely visible as a thinly sketched rectangle of grey. I push on it and the panel of wall swings open, revealing an exec bathroom, tiled in shining white, mirrored and chromed, with a toilet stall in the far corner that I'm pulled to like there was a rope tied around my neck. I can't believe how bad I need to piss, didn't know it could feel this awful. I burst into the toilet stall and—

The feeling stops.

There's nothing. I don't need to go at all.

What's happening?

My legs give way and I fall to my knees, facing the toilet. It's like something invisible is forcing me down. I feel muscles convulsing in my thighs. I try to stand back up, but I can't.

My left arm reaches out without me wanting to move it and thrusts itself down the toilet, submerging to the elbow in cold toilet water. I try to grab it with my right arm and pull it out, but I can't move my right arm either. I can't move any part of my body. I'm stuck in here, watching, as I reach deeper into the toilet and my fingers find a package, hidden there in the pipe, stuck to the U-bend with glue strips.

I try to access the metanet, sending thought commands to my implant system, the only thing my shipwrecked mind can do, but nothing works. There's some enormous data download happening, taking up all my bandwidth, blocking out every other transmission. Sinister glifs flash before my eyes, symbols of nerve damage, system failure. Even my chameleon cloth is malfunctioning, strobing through patterns and colours faster than my eye can follow. I'm being hacked, I realise. Eyejacked, puppeteered, the worst-case scenario. Whoever it is has total access to my nerves, my muscles, every part of me. There's a screeching tone in my ears, alerting me to an intrusion, but it's far too late.

I'm really afraid now, more frightened than I've ever been. Because it's the Moth doing this, it must be.

I accepted their program, in the autocafé. A black moth burrowing into a girl's glass skull. *You're under my protection.* Under your control is what you meant.

The Moth tied a noose for me and I put my head right into it. I want to scream, but I can't: my mouth won't move.

My hand comes back out of the toilet with the package: something heavy and black, wrapped watertight in plastic. I stand up, fighting every movement my body makes and making no difference, a passenger in my own flesh. I try to scream again as my hands tear open the packaging, revealing a small snub pistol, a stubby, ugly machine. Silence. Even my voice has been taken. My last words will be, 'I need the bathroom.' Pathetic. Good for nothing except being used by someone else. I thought I was so clever.

I turn and move back out of the cubicle, seeing myself reflected in the mirrored walls, a nightmare gallery of clones, each one with a dripping wet arm and a snub pistol and her eyes jammed wide open with fear. My hijacked body opens the bathroom door clumsily, with a bang as the snub smacks against the wall.

Grale looks up. Her irritation at the noise turns to shock as she sees the weapon in my hand, the strobing, crazy colours of my chameleon cloth, every muscle in my body shaking as I fight the Moth for control of my own flesh. My finger tightens on the trigger.

The snub pistol barks, the noise far louder than such a tiny gun should make. A white flower blooming in the glass behind Grale's desk.

Grale throws herself out of her high-backed chair. I don't know if I hit her or not. I'm dead, I'm already dead, there's no way they let you live after something like this.

I fire a second time, the snub kicking in my hand, but the Moth keeps my fingers clenched tight. My ears are ringing. The hacker marches me forward, walking around the side of the desk. Grale's scrambling underneath, using the dark metal for protection.

I start to crouch down.

Noise behind me, a man's voice shouting.

Grale is trapped. I look into her pale eyes, my vision swimming with tears. At least the hacker can't block my tear ducts. I still have one thing left.

'Fight it,' Grale says to me, a hoarse whisper. 'Fight it, Kirsten. Your finger. Concentrate on the finger.'

I focus everything into the trigger finger. These are my nerves. The pressure is unbearable. Grale stares at me, nowhere left to run, as I focus all my willpower on the finger of my right hand.

It trembles. I can't fight any more. I'm about to pull the trigger.

Something hits the back of my head.

I'm knocked to the ground. The gun barks once, and then someone stands on that hand.

There's a sharp pain in my neck, a shard of ice slipping into my veins.

'Disconnect her!' Grale's screaming. 'We need her alive! *Disconnect!*'

Everything switches off.

part two

Critical system errors detected.

Cold, clipped voice. Synthetic.

Shapes forming against a white background.

Assessing optic-implant function. Assessing aural-implant function.

A rank of yellow triangles. A second rank of red squares. A third of blue circles. They sit there, doing nothing. I can't feel my body, can't reach out my hand to touch them. What happened to me? I have memories of people screaming, a spreading crack in glass.

'Can she hear us?' another voice, a woman, asks. This voice is a real person. I want to move my head to look for them, but I can't.

Do I still exist?

The triangles seem to leap at me, and now they're three-dimensional: a rank of sunshine-yellow pyramids. They rotate on their axes. The squares become blood-coloured cubes; the circles ripen into blue spheres. Little smooth planets. As these shapes rotate, they start to sing to me. The triangles have high voices, like young girls. The squares have lower voices, and then the blue planets have deep bass voices, like big, jolly fathers. They spin and sing, spin and sing.

'Unlikely,' a different person says. 'She's suffered extensive neural trauma.'

'Will she die?'

'It's still possible. The puppeteering virus was meant to kill her.'

'I want her alive. Make sure she's watched, Campbell. I'm putting her under your protection.'

The choir of coloured shapes dissolves.

Cut to black.

Assessing haptic-implant function.

I wake as my left hand is bathed in cold, like I've dunked it into ice water. I'd wince, but I can't move. Then heat spreads through my right hand. For a moment, it burns there, like an ember held in my palm, and then fades away.

Stillness. I can't see anything. I can hear an air-conditioning unit.

I think I'm alone, in whatever room they've got me in.

My mind feels clearer, and with a bright rush the

memories come back to me: the mirrored exec bathroom, the way it felt as the virus took control of my body. I remember pulling the gun from its plastic packet, watching my hands move while silently screaming for them to stop. My nightmare reflections. Gunshots. Grale's pale eyes staring up at me.

Assessing gustatory-implant function.

A sweet taste sweeps through my mouth as I realise: it was all a set-up. The Moth used me, and threw me away, left me for dead. He never thought I was smart. It was the opposite. He knew I was hungry for whatever he gave me. Knew I'd load his programs on to my implants without question. That's why he chose me. I lie there, listening to the noise of the air conditioning. The sweet taste fades, and is replaced by intense bitterness.

Time passes strangely. Below the neck I can't move at all. There are no straps, no restraints, but there are infoveins running into all my wristhub's ports, and my yellow-gowned body is a stranger's.

Sometimes I sleep and wake and only a few moments have passed. Sometimes I sleep for what seems like days. Sometimes I have strange, looping dreams of walking into the mirrored bathroom, pulling the gun from its hiding place. Sometimes I dream of black moths unfurling in a night sky. Sometimes I dream of Dr Kiyagi peeling away my face and storing it in green liquid, of watching from behind glass as my faceless body murders pleading phantoms. Sometimes in my dreams Grale's guards shoot me dead and I wake up, sweating an imprint of my body into the sheets, unable to scream. Sometimes my room fills with white-coated figures, speaking of neural trauma in passionless voices, running tests that make my body convulse. Sometimes I'm given mushy food by a shaven-headed woman, a moonie nurse. She feeds me with absent patience, carefully placing each dollop of paste into my dry, mute mouth.

The room I'm in is just large enough for the bed, a plastic chair, a sink and mirror in the far corner. White walls, white sheets, white strip lights. There's a closed door opposite me. Sometimes I hear voices beyond it, but nobody's been in for a while. The only regular sounds are my own breathing, and the noise of the sheets when I turn my head.

Nothing hurts. The mattress beneath me is soft and yielding. They must have me on a dose, a tranquilliser or whatever, but I can't find it in me to worry about that.

The drug takes me out of my present self. The Moth, Human Futures, Grale: none of it's my business any more. There's nothing I can do. I feel drowsy and comfortable, and my mind starts to drift.

I grew up in a sterile room like this one, filled with the same fug of disinfectant, from when the girl who slept above me would throw up on herself in the night. She had something wrong with her stomach from drinking rainwater. I can't remember her name, but I remember the sour smell of the vomit and disinfectant mixed together, and I remember her sickly, blotchy face. I hated her; the kind of loathing that's made even worse by knowing the person can't help what they're doing, so you're the bad one for hating them. Don't know where she went, into a corp or out on the streets or what. So many kids went through that place.

It was part of a bigger carebloc, full of people who couldn't look after themselves. We had people with nerve damage on the floor above us, injured moonies on the floor below. We were all scared of the moonies: everyone used to say, if they touched you, you'd go like they were, empty-headed and bald and sleepwalkerish, but I always thought the nerve-damage people were scarier. I used to see one being wheeled around who couldn't move at all, but I looked right into his eyes once and I could still see someone alive in there. That scared me so badly, and now that's me, lying here, paralysed, and I can barely bring myself to care.

I slept in a room about the same size as this one, with three other girls, all of us stacked in sleeping alcoves in the wall, and everything I had fitted in one box. The carebloc was pale green. The floors and the walls and the chairs were pale green, and our sheets and our toothbrushes and our towels and the cheap plastic slippers – like something you'd shower in, but we wore them all day – those were pale green as well. I hate looking at that shade of green now. They weren't good years. The healthcorp that ran the carebloc made money from you being there, but they didn't make money from you being happy there.

We had school four days a week, but the teachers were lumen people, not real, just these figments like Blanca that gave their lessons from automatic scripts. They couldn't tell if you were listening to them or not. As long as you were in your seat, you were at school. Almost everything was about how to get work with a corp anyway. We had to do physical aptitude tests, personality quizzes, logic problems, all kinds of stuff to get the corp recruiters into our heads. What they were recruiting for was called Pre-Employment. The corps will sponsor your schooling and training, and, when you turn sixteen, you belong to them, for as long as they need you. Every few months, they'd come to the carebloc and pick some of us out. I never got chosen. Years later, when I lived with Patches and had got good at hacking, I went into their database and looked at my results. It's stupid, but I wanted to know why nobody chose me. It said I had a bad personality fit for the workplace. *Stubborn, independent, aggressive. Low compliance, low value.*

By the time I was thirteen, there was no money left. The byts from my parents' settlements were gone. There wasn't a corp that wanted me, so no Pre-Employment programme. No more payments for the healthcorp, so no sleeping alcove for Nova. They let me go the day after my birthday. I went out into the City, and there was a thunderstorm. I didn't have a rainwrap so I had to stay in a covered concourse and I couldn't leave. Lots of people walked past me. I knew I was greyed out, that they couldn't see my face. You can choose to block non-econs as part of your service options. Your optical implants get rid of them, so all you see is static over their skin, and your aural implants will make sure their voices don't sound like anything human, so there's no point in them begging. They're easy to walk past.

The second day I sat in a plaza. It was high enough for

some sunlight to still hit it. I didn't know if I was allowed to sit there or not. There were some enforcers patrolling, but none of them spoke to me. Everyone acted like I wasn't there. Sometimes a snoop would come down and buzz around me until I moved out of the plaza, but it never followed me too far, and I'd go back in and sit down again. Mostly nobody cared about me. I felt like the City would keep doing what it did every second I was alive and when I died nothing would slow down even for an instant. I hadn't eaten or drunk since I left the carebloc. I watched a woman eating and when she left some food on the table and a half-finished can of Lethe soda, I hurried over.

I was eating the crust of her sandwich when I knew someone was looking at me. I thought they were going to stop me eating so I shoved the whole thing in my mouth as fast as I could. He was standing over me and when he spoke I couldn't answer him at first.

He asked where I lived.

He was young, a corpsman. I think he wouldn't have been much older than I am now. Barely a man. I don't remember his face, but I remember I thought he was handsome. He was wearing a grey suit and an orange brooch shaped like a hand on his lapel. He had very light hair. The sun caught it and made it look like there was lumen-flame all around his head.

He asked again if I lived anywhere. He must've known I didn't. He knew I was non-econ, could see I was wearing the uniform from the carebloc, pale green clothes and plastic slippers. I realise now he'd been watching me for a while.

He asked if I was hungry. I said yes. He said he knew a way I could eat all the time. Wouldn't worry about being hungry. He asked if I knew anything about the Municipal Works Corporation. I said I'd seen moonies and they'd lived below me and I was scared of them. He said there wasn't anything to be afraid of. Said it was a good choice for someone in my position, and it wasn't just for people who'd done something wrong. He said the City needed people who kept it going, and that's what municipals did, and didn't I think that was good?

He said if I signed up they'd do the operation the same day and I wouldn't have to worry any more. If you're a municipal, you can't worry about anything, because they only think about their work. He said if I signed up with them for ten years it would pass like I was asleep, and when they let me go and reversed the operation I'd get paid.

I asked how much.

He said it was enough for a real life. He said if I agreed

to let them use my body for hazardous work the pay was even better.

I thought about being twenty-three. Ten years asleep wouldn't seem like any time at all. I'd be a grown-up. I wouldn't be hungry. I could be something else.

He said we could do the contracts now – it didn't take long. That I wouldn't have to worry about anything and they'd take care of me.

Another voice said, touch her and I'll cut that hand off.

We both looked around. I thought we were in trouble. The person who'd spoken was an old man, with one horrible white synthetic eye and plastic for his jaw. His skin was mottled and burnt-looking and he was hunched over, but I could tell he used to be strong. He was leaning on a walking crutch.

The young corpsman told him to go away.

The burnt man asked him how many people the Municipal Works Corp had released from service last year.

The corpsman said he didn't have that information right then.

The burnt man asked what manual work a little girl would be doing for them exactly. He asked if there was some other reason they wanted to make me a brain-dead husk.

The corpsman said he didn't know what was being implied.

The burnt man pushed his long coat aside to show he had a gun and said, If you don't leave her alone, I'll shoot you. I'm a good shot. Metrowatch might get me, but you'll still be trying to stuff your guts back in, won't you?

The corpsman walked away really fast, saying the guy was crazy and he was going to have us arrested.

The burnt man asked me if I thought they'd ever let me go. He asked who was going to make them? He asked if I thought my family would do it?

I said I didn't have one.

Sign up with them, he told me, watching the corpsman walk away, and that's it. You're a moonie forever. They put needles in your head and make you compliant. You're just a body. They cut everything else out. You'd be working till you drop, doing anything they tell you, and they'd never pay you a single byt. He asked if I wanted that.

I said no.

Don't talk to people like that, he said. Don't talk to anyone from any corp, and don't get arrested either because that's where you'll end up. Little girl like you too. Wish I had shot him.

I thought that the burnt man looked horrible, but maybe it was the other man, the young, handsome one, who was really the horrible one. He'd kept looking me in the eyes for a really long time while he was talking and trying to seem kind, but he hadn't managed to. This crippled, burnt man mostly looked at the ground, but I didn't feel like he was trying too hard to make me believe him. I thought he meant what he said.

He asked my name.

I said Hanna.

He asked if I had somewhere to go.

I said no.

The burnt man looked around. Most people were finishing their lunches. Heading back inside their officeblocs. I already knew I couldn't be one of them, and I didn't know what I could be. The burnt man said he knew a place I could sleep for a night, but it was pretty far below us. He asked if I minded being in the dark and I said I didn't.

There was more, of course, but that was the start of it. How I met Patches, came down to the Gut with him. Learned how to code and hack, how to be a leecher, how to get ahead. Learned to look after myself. Left Hanna Latch sitting in that plaza and became Nova instead.

Look where that got me. Lying paralysed in another

carebloc. I didn't get anywhere at all. I'm back where I started.

My mouth's dried out. I lick around my teeth, trying to spread the moisture.

And of course the thing is, it wasn't by chance that Patches found me that day, although I didn't understand that for a while. He knew the plaza was right next to a carebloc. He was doing the same thing the young corpsman from Municipal Works was doing, same thing the Moth was doing too. He was looking for kids like me.

I come awake and there's a lumen standing on my pillow. A woman with golden skin and butterflies crawling in her hair.

Hiii, Blanca says. She's only a few centimetres tall, right next to my eye. *I hope you're feeling good today. I'm here to tell you that you've been given a clean bill of health! We were all so worried, but you pulled through! Isn't that fantastic?*

'I can walk?' I ask. It's the first time I can remember speaking in forever. My voice sounds croaky and thin.

You can do anything you want! As long as you stick to the designated Employee Recuperation Areas.

'I can leave the room?'

As I said, Ms Latch, you can do anything you like. The day is yours. It's just before noon, and I believe they're serving food right now in the Sunburst Atrium. I can direct you there if you'd like?

I see that the infoveins running into my wristhub are gone. I can move my body. I sit up, Blanca smoothly flowing across the room and growing to normal size as I do so. I flex my fingers and toes, clench every muscle I can think of, making sure it all works. How many days has it been, paralysed and dreaming in this room? Just my sleepy, sick mind floating inside its shell, like the butterfly in those Bliss adverts.

I do a run-through of my implant systems: my programs deleted or shuttered off, my accounts frozen, access to the global metanet suspended. It's like coming back into your bedroom and finding everything open and empty. Someone's been through me and cleared me out. Hardly a surprise. Luckily I still have a few local network permissions, which is what's letting me speak to Blanca, and I still have my fake tooth. It worked perfectly. Every scan has missed it, just as the faceshaper promised. With local metanet access and my icebreakers,

I can cause a lot of trouble.

I roll on to my front, hiding my face in my pillow. Lumen people are just images and can't actually see you, but there must be a camera somewhere in the room. I reach inside my mouth, activate the fake tooth, like Kiyagi showed me, and pull out the infochip. I slip it into the access port of my wristhub, and hear a ping in my ear. There they are: my icebreakers, shining like tiny diamonds in the pink dimness behind my eyelids. I copy them on to my implants from the chip, and then hide it back inside my tooth. I roll over again, hoping it looked natural. Blanca is standing by my door, broad smile on her golden face, still waiting for a verbal response.

'Yeah,' I say to the lumen receptionist. 'That's fine. The atrium is good.'

Super! Please follow me.

Blanca melts into a thread of golden light that streaks away from me, out through my closed door.

I ease myself off the bed. My leg muscles are trembly and I nearly fall, but I brace myself against the wall and stay upright. The slippers are just like the ones from the carebloc where I grew up, except they're bright Bliss yellow to match my gown, not green. I put them on.

I need to get out of here. Blanca didn't say anything about what punishment was coming for me, but the fact she called me by my birth surname, Latch, is a vivid reminder that they now know exactly who I am and where I came from. Not to mention the Moth won't be happy I survived the virus either. I don't know how I'm going to get out of the spire, or what I'll do once I make it outside, but I have to take one step at a time. The first step will be reaching the Sunburst Atrium without falling over.

I make some faltering progress to the door of my room, which opens out into a white hallway. It really is a mirror of the place I grew up, with the same doors and light fittings. Everything's polished and bleached and disinfected. Even the ceilings look like they get a scrub-down every night. A pair of moonies goes past, wearing white, pushing a trolley stacked with medicine.

I follow the thread of lumen light down the hallway, past rows and rows of identical doors, and then down some stairs and I come out into a big, open plaza, with another fountain in it, a yellow lumen butterfly fluttering above it. The Sunburst Atrium, I assume. It's warm and the air is perfumed with something sweet and calming. There's clean white light being piped in through apertures in the ceiling. The plaza is furnished with round tables and soft chairs, and people dressed like me, in yellow medical gowns and slippers, are enjoying cold drinks and plates of food that isn't mushed-up invalid slop.

I thread between the tables, feeling steadier on my feet the further I walk, looking around for an exit door. I see the glif for an elevator at the far side of the atrium, but it's behind a red lumen barrier marked with a different pair of glifs – *NO PATIENTS*.

There's a single guard in a booth, watching the barrier. He doesn't seem especially sharp, and I assume the carebloc isn't where they post their elite enforcers, but if I walk up to the elevator dressed in patients' clothes, he will stop me. I need to wait for an opportunity.

I sit at one of the dining tables, with a view of the guard and the elevator. I want to see who goes in and out.

Unfortunately, my table-mates are interested in me.

'Good morning!' the corpswoman opposite me says.

I briefly look at her: narrow face, neat brown hair, anxious. I nod and refocus my attention on the elevator.

'Well, I suppose it should be more like good afternoon! My name's Mallory,' she says.

'And I'm Kit,' the corpsman beside me says. 'Don't you want to get yourself some lunch?'

'I already ate,' I say.

There's a beat of silence.

'I could get you some orange juice if you like?' Mallory says. They're both looking at me with desperation, eager for a response. What's wrong with them?

If I ignore them now, it's just going to look rude and weird. They'll probably remember me, and that's bad. I decide it's better to humour them, try and act more natural.

'I'm Kirsten,' I say.

'Oh, how funny,' Kit says. 'We're both Ks.'

'Yeah,' I say. Does he have brain damage or something? 'We sure are.'

'What division are you with?' Mallory asks me. 'I work for Customer Outreach, and Kit was – is – a sound designer for BlissPlay.'

'I work with Grale,' I tell her. They start, as though I'd pulled out a weapon.

'I am so sorry!' Mallory gushes. They both bow, quickly touching their foreheads to the tabletop.

'We had no way of knowing!' Kit says. 'We all look alike in these medical clothes.'

'We would never have … *so* sorry. We're only E-7s! We didn't know you were so senior, please—'

'It's all right,' I say, assuming a forgiving pose. 'None of us seem to have any rank here.'

They're looking at me with expressions of awe and fear. If you're an outsider it's hard to understand how hierarchical and rigid corp life is, with strata as clearly defined as in the City itself. Someone like Mallory might have worked in a sub-department of Bliss since she was my age without meeting anyone who'd so much as spoken to Grale Inselberg. To find that they're sitting at a table with one of her staff, even a sickly staff member stripped of her privileges, seems to intoxicate them.

Watching the looks on their faces, I think of the litter of blind dogs me and Ade found one time, nesting in a burnt-out car, fawning over their mama, crawling across her white body like grubs. Their subservience revolts me, but I realise I can use it. My status is ingrained. They will obey me. It doesn't seem to occur to them that I might be lying about my connection to the CEO. Perhaps nobody would dare.

'I'm her personal assistant,' I say, to drive the point home. 'I work with her very closely.'

'I did hear that she was on this floor the other day, don't you remember, Kit? We were all shut in our rooms ...'

'She was visiting me,' I say, dimly remembering her voice speaking from my bedside.

'What's she like?' Mallory asks me.

Pale eyes full of fear. A white flower blooming in the glass behind her desk.

'Stern,' I say. 'She's a tough person.'

Mallory nods. It seems to please her.

'Can you get a message to her?' Kit asks.

'I don't have metanet access,' I reply.

'We don't either,' Mallory says. 'A hacker tried to get through my ice, so I reported it to my supervisor and he sent me here. It's been six months. Six months!'

So that explains why they were so eager to talk in the first place. No metanet, no feeds, no games, no chat, no lumens. They're cradle-to-grave corpsmen; they've probably never gone longer than five minutes without the metanet since they were born. No wonder they're like this. Desperate for anything new, anyone to talk to.

'All that happened was I opened the wrong file transfer,' Kit says. 'A mistake! It looked exactly like a legitimate transfer. How could I have known? And then some thug from Information Security said I'd been compromised, and I was sent here, without even being able to go back to my apartment and get some things. It's been nine weeks now! I cannot get a straight answer from them. And there's no access to my chat, my mailbox. I can't even request face-to-face with a supervisor, I don't know if I still have my job ...'

'I got hacked,' I say. 'Pretty badly. I could've died.'

'There are people who've been on this ward for *years*,'

Mallory tells me. 'Years! If we're being punished, couldn't they say so?'

'Grale's just cautious,' I say. 'She gets spooked about hackers.'

'Well, of course,' Kit says, suddenly realising he's not in line with what I'm saying, 'there have to be security measures – none of us question that …'

Someone came out of the elevator and I'm craning my neck to see. It's a doctor, female, with her white coat draped over one arm. The room is very warm. I watch her closely as she crosses the *NO PATIENTS* barrier and moves through the large atrium, stopping by one table of patients to speak to them.

'Kit, Mallory,' I say, an idea forming in my mind, 'I need to get out of this ward. There's been a misunderstanding. If I can just speak to Grale …'

'Yes, please!' Kit says, and his eagerness to obey is written in the wild, hungry expression on his face. 'Can you tell Grale about our cases?'

I look him right in the eye. 'Kit, if I can get into that elevator, I'll go straight to the CEO. I'll tell her everything about you and Mallory, how you did nothing wrong. She listens to me.'

The doctor has left her coat on the back of a chair. She's deep in conversation with the patients.

'We'll do anything,' Kit says.

'Create a distraction,' I tell them. 'Whatever it takes to get that doctor –' I nod over at the other table – 'to pay attention to you.'

'Like what?' he asks.

'I don't know,' I say sharply, giving him the same glare Grale aimed at me during my interview. 'Improvise, Kit. Something they'd do on the actionfeeds. Pretend to have a fit. Make a lot of noise. Whatever it is, I need that doctor and the guard looking over at you.'

'Don't forget our names,' Mallory whispers. 'Mallory Welch from Customer Outreach. Kit Gallford from BlissPlay.'

'Of course not,' I say, holding her gaze. I'm going to escape into the undercity and forget Mallory and Kit ever existed.

'Augh!' Kit suddenly shouts. 'Aaaaugh! AAAAA!'

He's clutching at his throat, waving a big hand in the air.

'Oh no!' Mallory yells. 'Oh dear!'

Nobody's winning a prize for acting here, but it'll do. I move away from the table, leaving behind my slippers, which are no good for running. Warm tiles against my bare feet. My legs feel much steadier now. Everyone's looking over at them, the guard in his booth included.

'Doctor!' Mallory screams. 'Please!'

'AAUUGH!'

The doctor stands up, frowning, and heads for our table. I slip past her, heading for the coat she forgot. One step, two steps, three steps, and I'm there, picking up the coat as quickly as I can, keeping it bundled up under my arm for now. Kit is still screaming and the doctor is trying to calm him and Mallory down long enough to find out what's happening. I duck behind a pillar, throw the coat over my shoulders so it covers my yellow patient's gown. As disguises go, this one will hardly stand more than a glance, but sometimes that's all you need.

I slip through the red *NO PATIENTS* lumen. The guard is still looking over at Kit. No alarm seems to have triggered.

I press my wristhub against the elevator control panel, standing casually, as though I'm not thinking about anything at all. My icebreakers leap into the mechanism, unravelling the permissions and protocols, turning NO into YES. It's not a difficult program to break; I don't think anyone ever expects a major intrusion into a medical ward's elevator control panel.

Almost as soon as I started, the job is done. The elevator opens. Perfect.

And then, as I step into it, a voice cries out behind me. 'Hey!'

I look around. Caught? The guard's still looking at the pandemonium that Mallory, Kit, and the female doctor are cooking up – Kit seems to be trying to wrestle himself out of his own clothes, he really went for it, the doctor's trying to stop him – but someone's coming down the hallway. I see a pair of moonies pushing a cart of medical supplies, and another doctor, this one older and male.

'Can you hold that?' the guy calls to me.

So what can I do? If I act guilty and duck inside, he'll realise I'm not supposed to be here. I hold the doors for him.

'Thank you so much,' the doctor says to me, stepping inside.

'No problem,' I say, keeping the moonies' cart between us so he won't see my bare feet. He doesn't seem to have noticed anything wrong. The doors close.

The problem now is that I have no idea where we are in the Bliss spire. We could be at the summit or deep down in the belly of the place. The only exit I know of is the main atrium where I came in, and I don't know if I can make this elevator go there.

We start to descend. There are no windows. All I have around me are steel walls, and rough tiling under my bare feet. The moonies are staring straight ahead, waiting for the door to open.

Hiii, Blanca the lumen receptionist says, appearing in front of me. Her golden face looks anxious. *You don't seem to have the right ID to be in this area. I'm going to have to ask you to report to the nearest security personnel.*

I gesture to block the lumen transmission, but she doesn't vanish.

That is not a valid response. I don't want to be rude, Hanna, but you're a guest at Bliss and there are some places we don't allow our guests to go. I've alerted a compliance team and they'll be arriving at your location shortly. Please kneel down and put your hands on your head.

I should've thought this through. I forgot that I'm not using Phantom any more; they have a location trace on me. Stupid. This was a waste of time. They're going to catch me and take me somewhere that's even harder to escape from.

Since you don't want to listen to my instructions, the compliance team now have authorisation for lethal force. Everyone at Bliss Inc. is so very sorry it had to be this way!

The elevator comes to a stop. The doctor looks at me, confused.

'Is something wrong?' he asks me.

'Beats me,' I say, heart racing. I see there's a tray of

sharp scalpels on the medical trolley. I quickly palm one, hold it like Ade showed me. I'm not going to make this easy.

The doors slide open and I see a man dressed all in white. Rust-brown hair, a broad face lined by frowning. Colourless, synthetic eyes look me up and down.

The doctor's face pales to match his coat.

'Not here for you,' Campbell, the Archangel Auditor, says to him. He gestures at me with one white-gloved hand. Smirks. 'Now, I'm in the middle of a break from my tiring job, having a lovely chocolate croissant, and suddenly I'm hearing ten different alarms go off inside my head because you've breached Medical. So I have to abandon my snack and catch you, because you think putting a stolen coat on and getting into a lift counts as an escape plan. Do you have anything to say, Kirsten? Or should I call you Hanna?'

He takes a step towards me and I rush him, strike at his face with the scalpel. There's static roaring in my ears. Heart pounding. I can't deal with his smile, like my life is just this little amusement to him, my escape just that trivial. I want to hurt him.

The Auditor reacts faster than I ever dreamed a person could move, clamping one hand around my neck and the other around the arm that holds the scalpel. He disarms me with contemptuous ease and lifts me off the ground, slamming me into the wall. Holds me there, my feet dangling, the hand at my throat just tight enough that I know he could kill me if he wanted. Again I sense the bulk of his presence in the metanet, like a dark fortress of ice. He's overwhelming.

I stare into his colourless eyes, my anger bubbling like boiling water.

'Please,' Campbell sighs.

I try to knee him between the legs, but he blocks it, and knocks my head against the wall until I see flashes of white light and go limp.

'Are we finished?' he asks. 'You wouldn't have gone far. You don't have a floor map, and this elevator doesn't take you anywhere close to an exit. The spire is a big place.'

'Had to try,' I rasp.

'Well, you tried. It failed. Here we are. Grale wants to see you.'

6

High up in the spire again. I can feel the metanet silence overhead, Human Futures, like a strange, looming cloud. The room we enter is weird. There's a pool of water – safe, clean water, more than I've ever seen. Who knows how much that costs, to keep a whole pool filled like that? I've heard people say execs can go swimming and stuff, but it's only now I fully believe it.

Grale is stretched out on a recliner at the edge of the water. She's not dressed to go swimming. She's wearing her fuligin suit, cloth absorbing all light that touches it, with a high-necked black pullover beneath the jacket. Golden butterfly brooch at her lapel. She's looking at one of those bundles of sheets I saw on her desk, with a pitcher of orange juice on a table beside her. That and the golden butterfly are the only spots of colour in the room. Everything else is black, white or transparent – the floor, the water, the glass, the table. Even the sky outside the window is silvery-white, weak sun hidden behind clouds.

Grale looks up as Campbell brings me over. She's sitting there like she's the reason for everything existing. Like she doesn't have to do a thing and the world brings her what she wants. Campbell bows, but I don't.

'She broke out of the medical containment wing,' the Auditor says.

'And then where were you intending to go?' Grale asks me.

'Don't know.'

'We can track your movements very easily. Your location-masking programs have been removed.'

'I know.'

'So why do it?' Grale asks.

'Because I don't want to stay here.'

'Hanna,' she says, 'do you think the Moth leaves loose ends? How safe do you think you are out there?'

'Not safe here,' I say. 'The Moth already got in, didn't

they? Got at both of us.'

'Quite,' Grale says. 'But I can assure you, my personal quarters are the safest place for you in the City. I'm your only option right now.'

'Option for what?' I ask.

'Campbell, give us some privacy, please?' Grale asks.

He frowns. 'Grale, she's already tried to shoot you dead. She tried to kill me when I detained her.'

'I'm not in danger.'

'I fail to see why you need to speak to her at all. She was a pawn for the Moth, nothing more. She is of no use. You hire me to uncover the source of these intrusions, and then prevent me from doing anything that might actually help us catch the Moth. I am a Systems Auditor. I need full access to the Bliss systems. I need access to Human Futures.'

'No. I have made my position on this clear. I will not allow anyone, even Archangel, access to those floors.'

I don't think there's another person in the spire who would answer back after Grale spoke to them in that tone, but Campbell opens his mouth.

'With respect—'

'*Campbell.* Your input is valuable to me, as always. On this occasion I have considered your advice and ignored it. Thank you.'

The Auditor bows again and leaves the room. His footsteps fade as the reinforced door closes behind him. All I can hear is the hum of the air conditioning, the soft noise of water lapping at the edges of the pool. I stand, watching Grale watch me. I could go for her. She's taller than me, but she doesn't seem that strong. Her body is slender and brittle. I doubt anyone's ever even punched her. She won't know what to do. There's the pitcher of juice. I could smash it over her head, use one of the shards …

No. As I watch her, I get the feeling that she knows what I'm thinking, that she saw my eyes flick to the jug. She has a thin silver remote in her hand, I notice now. I don't know what that is, but she seems to feel safe, sitting here with me. She's totally relaxed. There are probably a dozen armed guards waiting to rush in at the first hint of trouble. I can't just leap on her. Campbell could've shot me dead when I attacked him before. I need to start thinking long term. If I want to get out of here, I need a real plan.

'Do you want me to call you Hanna? Or do you prefer Nova?' Grale asks at last.

'Nova,' I say.

'Why?'

'Hanna's gone. She's who I was before. When I was little.'

'And yet Hanna is still within you, evident in every gesture and word.'

'I don't understand.'

'I'm saying that the grieving, abandoned child influences every action you take. I'm aware of your history. The car accident, the carebloc, your discharge from care. I don't know exactly what happened to you after that, but it's not difficult to guess. Why Nova?'

'You need a street name,' I say, doing my best to ignore the other things she said about me. 'You're into icebreaking and stuff, so you'll change your legit name around all the time. People can't search you. But if they know to ask for Nova they can get a line to you.'

'I know that metanet criminals use aliases. I just wondered why you chose that particular name.'

I shrug. 'Learned about stars. Not much stuck from school, but that part did. I like how it sounds.'

A silence.

'Why are you even talking to me?' I ask. 'I don't get it. You run one of the biggest corps in the world. Don't you have a million other things to do?'

'A little secret for you, Nova. I don't run Bliss Incorporated, not the way you think I do. I have other executives under me who do that. Talented people. I'm more of a big-picture CEO. I try and keep the company as a whole healthy, and ensure my own research is properly funded.'

'What research?'

Grale laughs. 'I don't think we're at that point yet, do you? There are execs who've worked under me for decades and still don't know what we do in Human Futures.'

The world outside the windows is shifting white. I realise it must be cloud. We're so high up that we're stuck inside a cloud.

'Anyway,' she continues, 'I can do what I like, for the most part. Every second of every day is mine. And today I wanted to talk to you.'

'I tried to kill you.'

'The Moth tried to kill me. You were fighting it, weren't you? I could see it in your face.'

'Not to save you. Save myself.'

'I don't know about that. We did some mapping of your personality profile, while you were in treatment. It's quite unusual.'

I don't say anything. Don't see what she wants from me.

'I'm serious. I looked at the illegal programs we found in your implants after we arrested you— I know you deleted them,' she adds, seeing my expression of confusion. 'We have ways of finding things people think are gone. We did make your implant rig after all. I was impressed. Lots of custom-made icebreakers, spoofers, port-loop programs. It's sophisticated work.'

'Yeah,' I say, uneasy, thinking of the icebreakers I have in my inventory right now. The only thing I used them for was the elevator door. Campbell didn't bother to check my drives, and Grale can't. As far as they know, I have no metanet access, no way of getting hold of illegal programs. I should be safe.

'And this was all your own work?'

'Pa—' I start to say, then stop. I don't want to bring Patches into this. I don't want Grale knowing anything about him or the Gut. 'Mostly. People told me stuff. I mostly worked it out by looking how the programs were made.'

'Self-taught,' Grale says. 'I have programmers in my employ who are twice your age and vastly more experienced and wouldn't have been able to produce work like that.'

I can't sit down – there's no other chair. I still don't get what she wants. Who cares if I made those programs? They're illegal, breaking my terms of service, all that.

'You remind me of myself,' she says, and I have to laugh at that. It spurts out before I can stop it. 'You think that's funny?'

‘We’re not like each other,’ I say. ‘You’re you … and I’m nobody.’

‘We are very much alike. I said you had a unique personality profile that we don’t come across very often. It’s an almost exact match with mine.’

And I don’t know what I should say about that. Grale’s CEO of this big corp – she is the enemy, the one who controls the world and keeps all the secrets and never wanted anything she couldn’t have. I’m on the outside, living in her trash, coming up out of the darkness to steal money from her workers. We’re not the same.

But then, if I was born where she was born, I’d be her. I feel that deep down. I could’ve been something else. If anyone’d shown me how.

I look out to the side of us, the whole wall a window, shifting cloud with phantom images of me and Grale reflected in it. The other me. I imagine myself lying where Grale is, imagine her standing in front of me in bare feet and a doctor’s stolen coat.

There’s a break in the silvery cloud flowing around the Bliss spire, and a shaft of sunlight lasers into the room, hitting the jug and the floor and the water, so bright I have to shield my eyes. Everything’s glowing like a lumen, traced with an unreal light. This lasts for one dazzling moment, and then the window glass corrects for the sunbeam, darkening to a smoky pane that filters out the UV.

When I look back at Grale again, I see her face has gone hard.

'What do you know of the Moth?' she asks. 'Truly.'

'Almost nothing. He lied to me, used me. Then he tried to kill me, like he tried to kill you.'

'You can say nothing that would help me find him?'

'I know as little as you. Less, probably.'

'We shall see. You may hold more information than you believe. But we can cover that tomorrow. Let me show you to your quarters,' she says, the smile returning to her face as she stands.

I don't want to go with her. I don't want to see my quarters. What I want to do is get out of this room, this whole spire, find the deepest, darkest part of the undercity and hide there until I can work out how to make a new identity for myself, go somewhere else.

But I need to find a way to escape first, and, for whatever reason, Grale seems to be interested in keeping me alive. I tried to kill her. Any time she wants to, she can make me disappear, and nobody will ever come asking her questions about where I went. If she wants me to stay here, I'd better act like it's the best thing anyone's ever offered me. I need to get on her good side.

So I nod my head and try to look enthusiastic. Grale leads me away from the pool of water. She pauses by one of the walls. A doorway opens and she steps through, without looking back to see if I'm following or not.

7

We pass from the white, light-filled room into a narrow space that's cloyingly dark, lit only by tiny lamps at ankle level. Grale, in fuligin black, vanishes, with only her pale hair and one white hand visible as she walks. There's a hiss as another door opens up, some kind of pressure seal, and then I follow her into another enormous room. This one is as dim as the pool room was bright. Light falls in soft beams from openings in the ceiling. The air is much cooler and drier in here, and it tastes of chemicals, a tiny bit sour. I can hear fans murmuring above us.

When I close my eyes for a moment, I feel like I'm not in a big room at all, but being held in some soft, delicate space, as if I'm inside another person's body.

'The atmosphere is archival quality,' Grale says quietly, breaking me out of whatever weird trip I was melting my way into.

'What is this place?' I ask. Now my eyes are adjusting to the dimness, I can see the walls are lined with shelving, and each shelf is heavy with more of the objects she had out by the pool. I move closer to the shelving and see the objects have symbols stamped on them, a strange script that I can't read.

'It's a library,' Grale says.

'What do you use it for?' I ask.

'This place?' Grale asks, taking one of the rectangular objects down from its shelf. 'It's for storing books. Like this one.'

Book. Word means nothing to me.

'What's that for though?'

'A book is a way of storing information, I suppose,' Grale says. 'They're relics. People used to make them a long time ago.'

She holds it open for me to see. The insides are densely packed with black symbols, a lot like the marks I saw her making in our first interview. None of the marks move or make noises the way proper glifs do. They just sit there inside that book, black and sullen.

'Don't understand it,' I say.

'Well, of course you wouldn't. It's written in English as it was spoken at the dawn of the twenty-first century. We've come a long way since then. They say language has changed almost beyond recognition in the past century alone. The global meeting of minds that's been enabled by the metanet and cheap neural implants has seen to that. Pre-metanet English was among the most widely spoken languages however, so, if you want insight into our ancestors' lives, learning to read it is a good starting place. Here, you can hold this if you're gentle.'

I take the book from her and look at it more closely. It's lighter than I expected somehow. It smells funny, musty, and strange. I turn the sheets of paper, staring at the lines of English. It just looks like a boring mess to me. No pictures, no colour, no sound. One sight of a lumen newsfeed and anyone who was used to getting their information from this would never go back. I don't know that much history, but I know people used to live on the ground, the actual earth, no blocs, and they all had bad eyesight and got cancer and the longest anyone could live was only a hundred. I don't see why you'd want to know what they were all thinking about. They're gone.

'You're not impressed,' Grale says.

'I dunno,' I say. 'You can't change what it says? It's only one thing?'

'That's right. It's not a very efficient way of transferring information, compared to an infovein. If you want different information, you need another book. Fortunately, I have one of the largest libraries of ancient manuscripts in the world.'

'Why do you want them though?'

'Why do you have neural implants? Why do you use the metanet?'

I think about it. Nobody's ever really asked me the why of it before. 'Lets you be connected, right?'

'Exactly,' Grale says. 'Everything, all that information, everything someone's saying or seeing or thinking or making or doing, every product, every song, every shop, every picture, every game, every sunrise, every life and death, everything and anything you can dream of, and our system gives it to you. It's like a gateway we installed into your brain that leads to forever. You're never alone. Never have to be bored, never have to wonder what other people think about something.'

'Sure,' I say. There's a weird expression on her face as she says it. Hungry, kind of.

'Well,' she continues, 'before we had microchips and

nanofibres, before electricity even, this was the way you would connect with another mind. Writing and reading. The man who wrote this book has been dead for *centuries*, but I can still hear his thoughts. That's amazing to me. It's almost like time travel. When I write, I send a part of myself travelling away from me, far into the future.'

'But who else reads?' I ask. 'People have still forgotten those writers.'

'Yes,' Grale says. 'They have forgotten. I don't know how many living people could understand this volume. A few scholars and eccentrics. All our thoughts, no matter how careful we are to preserve them, will eventually be lost.'

I understand that I'm seeing some part of Grale she never shows people. I'm seeing right down to the softest part, the part her clothes and reputation and money are supposed to hide.

I walk slowly through her library, moving between the patches of dark and light. For me, library means programming, somewhere you keep your tools and files lined up. But I guess the name for that sort of library came from libraries like this one. Only here it's not programs, but books, lined up for you to see them. Everyone who wrote these words is dead, but their thoughts are still here, if you know how to get them out.

Biggest heap of phantoms anyone ever saw, is what I think. So I guess that's why I jump when I turn a corner in the darkness and see a pale man standing in an alcove on the wall. He's bigger than me and naked, but I look at him a blink longer and then I realise he's not real. He's made from stone. One of his hands is missing, broken off at the wrist. His eyes are pupil-less and colourless, like Campbell's eyes. He looks alive though, even with the blank eyes and broken hand, like he could step down and speak to me at any moment.

'Incredible, isn't he?' Grale asks.

'Not a book though,' I say, 'so why's he in here?'

'Well, he needs special air. The outside isn't good for him.'

I think about being outside a magrail station in a rainwrap, breathing through a filter so nothing that's in the water can get into your lungs. Outside never seemed like it was good for anyone. Suppose that's why Grale stays up here, behind glass, all that poison nothing but a bruised-looking raincloud carpet over the cityblocs below.

'It's the human touch that interests me,' Grale says. 'Birthed from marble with chisel and hand and eye. We could laser-cut a thousand of these statues in a matter of hours now. But to my mind that wouldn't be art. That's something we're losing, I think. Everything we make here at Bliss is in some way a dumb machine's replica. But this statue took someone years. It always amazes me how little time we used to live, and how desperate we were to make something that would last.'

Grale walks me through the halls of her library, talking softly and explaining all the stuff we go past, the books and art and other things she has like old machines, antique pieces that would make Patches drool with jealousy. I see weird plastic boxes that she says were the first home computers, made by old dead corps with names like Apple and Microsoft, and behind special glass she has some of the prototype neural implant rigs that her father made, removed from their hosts' bodies after death. It's strange looking at a silvery map of someone's nerves without the body surrounding it.

We move through to her living spaces, this huge apartment, done up nicer than anywhere I've seen. The floors are actual wood, like from a real tree, which I've never touched before. Feels so strange with bare feet, and the whole place smells of wood too, real wood smell, not the fake wood perfume you get in some upstrata houses. Pictures on the wall, not lumen displays, but really old ones that don't move. The one I like most is of yellow flowers, all sitting in a pot, and, even though it doesn't do anything interesting, I feel like I know why you'd want to look at it.

The kitchen has a wooden table laden with food that someone's left for her. My stomach's growling so Grale lets me load a plate with fruit and meat that I barely recognise, a million miles away from what people eat in the undercity.

When I have a plateful, she walks me to a side room. It's got the same wooden flooring, one wall that's painted pink like something raw, another wall that's all glass, showing me that vertigo view of the City you get from living up at the spire's summit. A bed that's an oval of calm, white, crisp sheets, a bathroom attached with a shower and toilet. All of it so clean it's like it was never used before.

'So,' Grale says, 'you wanted to be my assistant. Now you are. For as long as I need you, you're going to live right here, where I can protect you. And, whatever I say you do, you will do. Understand?'

'Yes,' I say, still holding my plate.

'I'll call for you tomorrow morning. We'll have work for you,' Grale says. 'Make sure you eat. You'll need your strength.'

And then she's gone, locking the door behind her. I cram the food into my mouth, the first solid meal I've had since I left the Gut to travel to this spire. It's incredible; flavours I never knew existed, better than carebloc food or autocafé dinners or anything Patches cooked down in the Gut. The soft fruits explode on my tongue, like the taste of redness itself. When I'm done, my stomach hurts from bolting, but my mouth's as happy as it's ever been.

I walk into the bathroom and look in the mirror at the face I barely recognise. My hair is greasy and jagged, unwashed. I realise I don't even know what day it is, how long I've been in this spire. It's so silent up here, not like the Gut, where all day you'd hear gas discharges rumbling, pipes going, people's voices in the metal hallways that would echo all through the place. Hearing Patches' tools going in his workshop, someone throwing up in the bathroom below my bedroom. When am I going to be back in that hammock, looking up at the rust patches on my ceiling? I got pulled up into the light above the clouds and standing here I'm startled by how much I miss the darkness. The food's good, but that's about all I can say for the spire.

I take a drink of water from the tap, clean corpwater, so pure, making a cold shiver run through my teeth. I can't stand here feeling homesick. I have my icebreakers. I have work that needs doing.

I walk back to the bed and lie down. Close my eyes and see glifs blooming in the darkness. Hacking up here is going to be difficult, but I need to try. Something Campbell said got me thinking. There's one particular file I need if I'm ever going to see the Gut again.

The local metanetwork is heavily controlled. I feel like I'm tiptoeing in pitch-blackness through a heap of enormous sleeping monsters. One wrong move will wake the guard programs, bring the full force of the Bliss Information Security Division down on me. It takes a few hours of prep before I'm in a position to make my move.

I send my icebreakers out into the system. I lie on my bed at the pinnacle of the spire and I imagine a thread of light dangling down from my head into the floors below me, a hair-thin thread that's miles long, waiting until it brushes against someone I can breach.

After another long, painful wait, I've found my man. It doesn't take much, just a crack. His mistake is simple: he's using a messenger program called Chizurp to talk to someone who isn't inside the Bliss spire, family on another continent. Chizurp wasn't made by Bliss, doesn't have their well-crafted ice, and I know an exploit in the messenger software, something that isn't public knowledge yet. My icebreakers get their claws into his systems, working from the chat software outwards like an infection, and before you know it I've got a way inside. As quickly as possible, I copy everything I can from his employee file archive. Then I end the intrusion, erasing any point of contact between the two of us, retracting my thread of light back through the miles of space that separate us. It took me about four hours to get into a position where I could breach his ice, and then twenty-one seconds to crack his defences and make the data transfers I needed. Not my best work, but it's not bad. I open my eyes and sit up.

It's early evening. Sunset has stained the cityblocs blood-red, turned the skycars darting between them into embers. I can see a scattering of glints in the sky, satellites and other orbitals, brighter than any star. Makes me feel weird, all the junk floating up there, turning round and round in cold, empty space for ever. Glittering trash in blackness. Hurtling around the Earth, nothing to hold on to.

Spent the day with Grale and now I know how that feels. Like I'm a tiny thing caught in her orbit, up above the clouds. But I'm not totally helpless.

The corpsman I hacked was very junior, but his file archive contained what I hoped it would: raw data for the map of the Bliss corpspire. What I pulled from him was fragmented and jumbled, like a plate someone smashed into a million pieces, so I can't look at the map yet. I delete the icebreakers, knowing they're still safe inside my tooth if I need them, and set my implants to start compiling the data while I sleep, reassembling the plate from the fragments. It'll take a while before any of it is legible, but as soon as the map compiles, I'm gone.

Somehow I'd hoped Grale would give me back my chameleon cloth, but instead there's a new suit of clothes laid out for me on a hanger in my room, a suit of lightless fuligin. I guess this is the uniform she would've given me if I'd passed the interview. The material feels like cold smoke flowing over my skin as I put it on, so soft and dark and dangerous. I slick my hair in the mirror and do my exec look, try and stare at my reflection like Grale looks at me. Like I understand everything and there's nothing I can't do. I think I can pull off an exec face pretty well.

I splash water on my stranger's face, roll my head around my stiff shoulders, and as I look up at the bathroom ceiling I freeze.

I've locked eyes with a human face.

Wide eyes, staring down at me through the ventilation grate with something like wonder.

'Hey,' I say.

The person in the grate vanishes from view. I'd think I imagined it, but I hear them moving through the ceiling space, a series of thumps.

'Hey!' I say again.

Nothing. They're gone.

Who was that? Do they live there, in the ceiling? Does Grale know?

Well, I'm not about to tell her. Knowing something she doesn't gives me my best shot yet at getting out of here. After all, if one person can get up into the space between the floors, I can too. Every system has cracks you can creep into, and the Bliss spire looks to be no different. This is my way out. The spire map files haven't finished compiling yet, but I doubt there'll be a better escape route than this one.

I'm about to step into the sink and reach for the vent when I hear a noise behind me. I look in the mirror and see Grale standing by my bed. I drop my foot back to the floor.

'Were you speaking to someone?' she asks.

'No?'

Grale frowns, but doesn't argue with me. It's only me and her up here, and I don't have open metanet access. Who could I be talking to?

'They're waiting for us,' she says, and leaves without further explanation. With a last glance at the vent, I dry my face and follow her.

She leads me through her apartment, down a hidden set of stairs, and we come out in a room I recognise. It's the office where I had my interview; scene of the crime. Same desk shaped like a crescent of dark metal, same network of cracks in the window where the bullet hit it. There are some changes. I notice tripod devices standing in the corners of the room, portable metanet antennae, connected to syntax-analysis terminals and other obscure metanetworking equipment. All of Grale's personal items are gone from the desk, and there are three corpsmen wearing Bliss uniforms waiting for us. They bow to Grale as she comes in. Campbell's white back is to the room, his face to the cracked window glass.

'This is the subject?' one Bliss corpsman asks.

'Female, sixteen years of age?' Grale says. 'Who else could it be?'

'Just establishing the facts,' he says. 'You –' he looks at me – 'stand over here.'

I walk to where he's pointing. I stand there.

'Now,' he says, 'wristhub. Roll up your sleeve.'

'What's happening?' I ask Grale.

'You're helping us,' she says. 'Do what he tells you.'

'Wristhub,' the corpsman says again. I expose the access ports and he plugs me in to a Bliss syntax core. I feel a stream of new software being loaded into my implants, diagnostics software and other programs I can't identify. I'm glad I deleted my icebreakers, and hope they don't notice the map files compiling.

'Puppeteering attacks leave a kind of fingerprint in the implants of the violated user,' Grale says. 'The Moth knows this, which is why the virus was instructed to kill you after your assassination attempt was finished. We managed to prevent that from happening. What we're going to do now is reintroduce a tame copy of the same puppeteering virus you were infected with, and monitor it as it runs. This is called Deep Recall. It should help us get a very detailed image of the Moth's metanet fingerprints.'

'Where were you when the attack began?' the corpsman asks.

'The bathroom.'

'Then go there,' he says in the voice you use to talk to children, removing the infovein from my arm.

I take a deep breath, resisting the urge to knee him between the legs, and do what he tells me. I cross the office, go through the almost hidden door into Grale's exec bathroom. I see myself mirrored a dozen times in the reflective walls. I stand in front of the toilet, and then there's a chime in my ear and the puppeteering attack begins again. There's the early spasm of pain in my bladder, which fades much faster than it did originally, but from there the attack plays out identically, movement by movement. Invisible hands take hold of my body, force my muscles to contract and relax according to some other will. My legs give way and I fall to my knees, facing the toilet. I feel muscles convulsing in my thighs. Second time around and I still find myself trying to stand back up, but I can't.

My left arm reaches out just like it did before and thrusts itself down the toilet, submerging to the elbow in cold toilet water. I reach deeper and my fingers move as though they're grabbing the package the gun was inside. I retract my arm, soaking wet, and my fingers play-act at tearing open the invisible package, holding an invisible snub pistol. Every muscle movement is played again.

I turn and move back out of the cubicle, seeing myself

reflected in the mirrored walls, a horrible gallery of clones, each one with a dripping arm and her hand clutching an imaginary snub pistol. My hijacked body opens the bathroom door with a bang, stamping out into the office with one arm held in front of me, like I'm aiming. The rerun even captures the twitch in my arm as I adjust for the recoil of a shot that wasn't fired. The only difference is my eyes are dry this time; but I still feel a growing despair. Grale and Campbell and the Bliss corpsmen watch me approach the desk, aiming my phantom gun at the phantom version of Grale. I remember her hiding beneath the desk, remember the fearful look in her eyes, remember her telling me to fight it. She was at my mercy then. If I hadn't forced myself with every drop of willpower I had to stop my finger moving, she'd be dead and so would I.

We reach the final scene in the drama, the moment where her guards disconnected me from the metanet. I'm lying on the floor, and freeze in place. I expect that to end the session, but then I hear one of the Bliss corpsmen say, 'OK, now let's see that mirrored.'

There's another chime, and I move through the same motions, but in reverse. My muscles are starting to ache now, and the feeling of being forced to walk backwards is awful. Do people know, when they install neural implants in their children, that you can use them to make people do stuff like this? That to someone with the right network code, you're nothing but a puppet? I mean, that's what a moonie is really, isn't it? Someone who lives like this all the time. People must know, they must hear about puppeteering viruses and eyejacking and all kinds of horrible body invasions that hackers can do, but they all line up for implants anyway. Makes your life easier, they say. You can't live without them. After the past few days, I'm starting to wonder if Grale's choice isn't the right one. Never have these things installed in the first place. Your body stays yours.

I walk backwards into the bathroom, see myself mirrored again, plunge my arm into the toilet water again. Could they not have drained this before we started? My fingers flex, then I freeze in place – they've paused me. I hear them talking in the other room, but can't make out what's being said, can't move. Then I start moving again, going forward this time. I meet my own gaze in the mirror again, open the door again, advance on the desk with my imaginary gun again. My muscles hurt. The virus moves them in strange ways and they're not happy about it. I want to stop, but I can't ask the corpsmen anything. I can't use my tongue or lips. I look at Grale and Campbell and the Bliss technicians when the movements of my head allow me to, and they aren't paying attention. They're looking at lumen displays or their equipment. There's only one corpsman looking at me, and as I meet his eyes I can't see any pity. All I see is contempt, and maybe something else, something more sinister, that makes me feel like a child again in the plaza with the man from the Municipal Works weighing up what I'm worth.

That's when I start to really panic. I want to scream. I move to the desk and crouch, stop, and then move backwards again. By the third time they play through the attack, I'm crying again, tears streaking my cheeks, but of course none of them says anything. Grale looks right at me, then back to her screens, like nothing's wrong. Campbell seems bored.

I dunk my hand into the water ten times before the session ends. I stalk, brainwashed assassin, through the mirrored bathroom and out into the office ten times over. Every muscle in my body is burning and aching like I've been beaten. When they finally end the Deep Recall, I fall flat on to the floor of the office and breathe in and out like a shuttle engine starting up. My wet sleeve clings to my left arm. The trigger finger of my right hand twitches.

'So how did we do?' Grale asks.

'Good groundwork,' a Bliss man tells her. 'We're

starting to build a solid profile from the Recall. The data's still messy, but something's emerging.'

'What are the preliminaries?' she asks.

'Too early to say, on a lot of points.'

'This is never going to tell us anything,' Campbell says, examining his fingernails.

The Bliss corpsmen bristle. I can tell they hate that Grale brought an Archangel Auditor into the spire. They think keeping her safe should be their job alone.

'On the contrary,' the one who stared at me says, 'I feel the early data is very positive.'

'If the early data seems positive,' Campbell cuts over him, 'it's because the Moth wants it to appear positive. I have hunted them longer than you. They want you to chase shadows. The girl is a dead end.'

'So what would you suggest?' one Bliss corpsman asks, his jaw clenched with anger.

Campbell smiles. 'I think my advice might be a little over your head. Stick to the easy stuff. Leave the Moth to me.'

If Grale wasn't here, the technicians would attack Campbell. It's lucky for them that she is, I think, remembering how fast he can move. I like his chances, even against three Bliss men.

The Bliss CEO sighs. 'Enough, Campbell,' she says.

'We're committed to exploring every avenue of investigation. That includes Deep Recall.' She turns to her corpsmen. 'You say this is only early data. How long until we have a full picture?'

'Another five or six sessions and things will be much clearer,' one says. 'I don't want to push any further today – the subject's pretty agitated.'

'Hmm,' Grale says, looking over at me, collapsed on the floor, like she's only just noticed. 'All right. Same time tomorrow.'

She walks across the office and gently but firmly lifts me to my feet.

'You did well,' she says. 'We're getting good data.'

I don't know what to say. I wish I had shot her.

'Let's get you to bed,' Grale says soothingly. She supports me as I stumble across the room and back up the hidden staircase into her apartment. The corpsmen say nothing as we leave. She guides me to my room where I collapse on the bed.

'I can tell you didn't like that,' she says. 'I understand. But I just want you to think about how useful you're being. You can stay here, safe from the Moth, with me, as long as you're a useful assistant. Useful means helpful, compliant, calm. If you're not useful...'

The rest is left unsaid. 'I'll send food for you later.

I have other work to do now.' She leaves, and the door locks behind her.

I lie on my back, wet arm soaking the bedsheets. I feel so angry, like I could spit fire. Headache pressing on the backs of my eyes. I'm useful. Useful, like a thing. I'm just a tool, to take hold of when you need it. That's all I was to the Moth, and that's all I am here. Five or six sessions of walking like a puppet for them, and then they've got their data. Grale says we're alike, but she's still the one in control. I'm useful to her, and when I'm not … how long until they'll be tipping me down the garbage chutes with the other stuff they don't need any more?

I don't have to wait around for that. I'm not just a puppet.

I force myself up off the bed. My muscles ache, but I ignore them. I head for the bathroom. I know something Grale doesn't. I know about the vents. The map of the spire still isn't ready yet – 55.3 per cent compiled – but I can make a start, feel out if this escape route is viable. I climb into the sink, stand and reach up and find I can push the air-vent cover upwards, opening a way into the ceiling space. I look up at it for a moment, a shadow square in the ceiling. Low hum of fans coming from it. Strong smell of dust. I grip the edge with my hands and pull myself up.

It's cramped and dark, barely enough room to crouch, let alone stand. I light my fingertorch, soft blue illuminating the grey steel walls, the bobbly grey expanse of dust that lies on the floor of the vent. I see that I wasn't imagining it: there was someone else up here. There are marks where a body has crawled through the dust, a print left by a human hand.

Gives me the creeps, if I'm honest. Are they living up here? What're they going to say if I do find them? Maybe they've gone full psycho, some crazy from a horrorfeed stashing skeletons up here in the darkness. There are people like that in the undercity, who kill for fun. Not many, but some.

Get a grip. I'm not even looking to find them. All I want is to scout out where these vents lead, if there's some possibility of making an escape through them.

I crawl through the dirt, metal walls enclosing me on all sides, feeling hot and stuffy, my head banging off the ceiling and knees knocking the floor. At one point I have to crawl over the entrance of a vent that goes downwards, who knows how far, and, while it's not that wide, I get a horrible feeling in my stomach as I go over it, imagining myself going down head first. I leave it behind; take a right and then two lefts, following the trail the ceiling person left in the dust.

Eventually the vent ends. I peek my head out into a wide-open space. It's some kind of utility shaft, about the size of the tunnels the magrails travel through. I feel right at home, strangely enough. This is just like the work I used to do, crawling through the cracks in the world, using maintenance hatches to stay one step ahead of Metrowatch. This shaft must've been intended for use by engineers at some point, because there's a ladder built into the side of it, alongside the bundles of cables and pipes that line the walls. I cast my torchlight along the length of it and see that there's a piece of white cloth tied to the ladder, near the top.

Must be a mark left by the ceiling person, to help them find their way around. I try and see down below me, but I can't make out any other markings, not in my fingertorch's weak blue glow. All I see is bottomless darkness, and there's no simple route down either. At one stage the ladder passes a little door that I guess leads back into the corridors of the Bliss spire. But if you want to climb down any further than that then you're using cables and pipes for handholds, with a drop of several miles if you fall. I'm sure there is a route you can take, but the map I stole hasn't finished compiling yet. If I went down the shaft right now, I'd be climbing into the unknown.

The other option is to go up, and keep following the ceiling person's path. Climb this ladder as high as it goes. Where does it lead? With a shiver, I wonder: could it lead up into Human Futures? Is that where the person came from?

A wave of curiosity overtakes me. The Moth must want whatever's inside Human Futures badly to go to all this trouble. Whatever's in there has to be a big deal. Now that it's within reach, I feel like I want to at least know what this was all about.

I drag my body out of the ventilation duct and pull myself on to the ladder, start to climb up quick and quiet. After climbing a while, I see another duct that's marked with white cloth, a little scrap, tied to a cable next to the opening. I slip inside, fingertorch illuminating another vent, just like the one above Grale's quarters. This one's thick with dust as well, and I see marks that show a person already crawled through here.

The metanet doesn't exist any more. I don't know where I passed the threshold, but I'm now inside the silent zone I've been sensing since the day of my interview. I'm inside Human Futures, I realise. I must be. I press on, dark and cramped, following tracks in the dust. Eventually I come to a grate in the floor of the vent, like the one in my bathroom ceiling, an aperture I can peek through at whatever Grale is hiding from the world. I peer down.

The room below me is a boring, blank-walled office, with neat, crescent-shaped desks and a conference room glassed off at one end. It's exactly the same as the other office floors I've seen here in the Bliss spire, right down to the arrangement of the workstations. Nobody's here, and the lights are dimmed. Disappointed, I crawl further.

The next vent I come to looks down on to something much stranger. It appears to be some kind of operating room. The room is domed, round-walled. In the centre is a small immersion rig with wrist restraints. There's an enormous machine that hangs from the ceiling above the rig, something that looks like a triple-jointed metal arm holding a syringe. The arm is snared with orange cables and thicker tubes that run with something silvery, like mercury. The scene is medical, but threatening too. This place looks like it could double as an interrogation room. There are concentric rows of raised seating around the edges of the room, for an audience. Nobody is working in here either, but you can imagine what it would be like if they were. Rows of scientists in the seats, watching a team of doctors do … what exactly, to the person strapped to the immersion rig? Nothing good.

The third room I look down into is darkened. I can see the suggestion of machinery, ordered ranks of pods, but nothing more than that. I move on.

I follow the ceiling person's tracks in the dust, take a right and then a left, then up through a vertical shaft that has handholds moulded into the sides. I can hear something strange now, and I realise it's water, running water, gushing and splashing on to a hard surface. There's a weird smell in here too, not a bad smell like cleaning chemicals or rusted metal, but something else, something alive and fresh. It smells really good. I crawl through another vent, the sound of water getting louder and louder, and I find there's a small, rusted gate across the tunnel. This gate blocks access to a room that seems to be made from rough wet stone.

For a moment, I get a stab of fear in my stomach. I followed the trail in the dust all the way here, but I can't go any further forward. I can't turn around either, so if this gate won't open then I have to crawl backwards through these vents until I get to a junction and can turn myself. But then I reason that if the trail led here, the ceiling person must have a way of getting through, and I reach forward with my hand and push at the gate. It falls away. It isn't even fixed to the walls, just balanced in place. It hits the stone with a loud clang. I crawl out.

From inside the vent, I thought the stone-walled space was a room, but, now I'm standing here, it's more like a pit. There's fresh-smelling water pattering down the far side of the pit that collects in a shallow pool. It must drain away to somewhere. The whole place is made of dark stone, with thick, fluffy slabs of green moss growing everywhere it can, healthy and vibrant, nothing like the white glowing moss you get down in the lowest strata. The pit's deep, but it's lit from above by bright light, so blindingly bright after the dark vents that I can't see what's up there.

The walls are slippery and jagged, but I find a way to climb them, like I would scale a face of crumbling concrete in the undercity. At last I pull myself out of the pit and find myself in the strangest place.

10

A canopy of rippling green above me. For a moment, I can't make sense of it all, and then I realise – I'm surrounded by trees. I'm no longer in a room, in a building. I'm in a forest. An indoor forest. The ground is soft underfoot, a layer of green, spongy moss and a whole carpet of rippling green grass. There are trees everywhere, so many of them. I only recognise them from lumens and stuff, history lessons. The Earth's forests were all but gone centuries ago, and then the poison in the rains killed what was left during the first Water War. I know some execs have a private garden in their pinnacle apartments, but it's rare, and almost nobody has an actual tree. They need so much water. Who can afford to keep even one growing? A private forest of this size is beyond imagining. After everything I've seen at the top of the spire, it shouldn't surprise me, but it still does.

The trees stand so tall above me, huge greying brown trunks and forks of branches and armadas of green leaves staying so still. I touch the nearest one, running my hand over the surface of its trunk – the tree's skin feels tough and grainy and warm. Something bright flutters in the corner of my eye and I turn to see a butterfly, huge and blue, sail past me. For a moment, I think it's some kind of lumen, but then I remember the metanet doesn't exist up here. It's a real butterfly. Now that I listen, I can hear more sounds around me, movements up in the trees, cries of other animals that I don't recognise. I see two birds go racing by above me. I see a beetle with a jewelled-green back crawling across the moss at my feet.

There are walls around this place, a ceiling; I can see them now I'm looking properly. The ceiling is very high and domed and seems to be made of some glass-like material that mimics the colour of the sky outside the spire. The ceiling is currently an unbroken, vibrant blue.

A stream runs through the forest – that's what was

draining into the stone pit. The water is shallow and clear, the stream bed dappled with pebbles and patches of green weed. Small translucent fish glide through the water. I can see their skeletons through their skin, see their gills working. I breathe in deeply, take a long dose of the sweet air. I've never smelled anything like this place. The undercity is sweat and dust and sewage; the upper strata smell of polish and perfume. This secret forest at the top of the spire smells like life itself, green energy seeping into me with every breath.

The forest is so dense that it's easy to forget I'm still inside a corpspire. You could imagine you're outside, in the wilderness, back in the days when nobody had heard of a bloc and people grew their food in the earth. I feel like I'm in a dream. I never thought I'd get close to a real tree, and here I am, standing in their shade like I'm the first girl who ever lived.

Now I understand how Grale could be so obsessed with history, with old technology and old ways of living. They got something right, at least, back in the old times. Books I still don't get. But trees? Trees I could get used to.

The ground is uneven, with large, mossy rocks marking out the edges of the stream, and it's when I'm climbing over one of them that I first see the building.

Like everything else in this miracle garden, it's been transported from another time. The house is small and crooked, with narrow windows and walls painted blue. There's a covered porch at the front, with steps that lead up to a front door. The grey, sloping roof is mottled with green and yellow patches of moss, and climbing creepers are wound around the posts of the porch. The stream flows in a loop around the building, cutting very close to the nearest corner. I see three rectangular stepping stones that let you cross the stream. There are plants growing in pots on the porch, green stems and blooms as colourful as adverts. Butterflies drift through the air.

As I stare at the house, the door opens. I scramble to get out of view, peering out from behind a large, moss-covered rock.

A girl emerges, barefoot, with a metal bucket dangling from one hand. She walks across the porch and out of its shade, into a patch of open ground. She starts tapping her hand against the side of the bucket, in a soft rhythm.

This must be the person I saw watching me from the ceiling. I didn't get a clear view of her face, but she's the right size to be crawling around inside those vents, only a little taller than me, and just as light and bony. What is she doing up here? Does she really live in this wooden relic at the very top of the spire, inside Grale's miracle garden? Is this what Human Futures is hiding? Why?

She taps the bucket louder and something stirs in the forest. There's a gentle rustling and the sound of branches pushing aside, and then a pair of animals come loping out of the undergrowth. They're bigger than the other creatures I've seen up here, bigger than blind dogs even. I think they might be the largest living animals I've ever seen. They're brown furred, with patches of white at their chests and tails, long, thin legs, dark snouts. The larger one has these crazy growths on its head, like antennae made of bone. The girl calls to them and smiles and they walk right up to her and she takes something out of the bucket and holds it out for them. The animals start eating from her hand. She talks to them while they feed, singing a little snatch of a song and scratching one of them behind the ear.

As I watch, another animal comes out of the woods, this one big and fat and lower to the ground, pale pink, with pointy ears and a flattened snout. The girl gives it food from her bucket as well, scattering bits of vegetable on the ground. You can tell by the way they stand together that the girl and the animals know each other well. They trust her. As I watch, more appear from the undergrowth, these ones smaller and covered in dark brown fur, with long ears, moving with strange springing motions. They settle at her feet and start nibbling the green leaves she's put down for them.

When she's given the creatures everything that was in the bucket, the girl turns and walks back inside the house. The animals munch at their food in the clearing. The two large brown creatures take a drink from the stream and then disappear back into the trees.

I have to know more. Who is this person? I lift myself up out of my hiding spot as quietly as possible, stepping lightly across the stones that ford the stream, towards the blue house. The animals don't pay me any attention. I approach the house and press myself up against the wall, moving slowly along it towards the window.

That's when something jumps on to my back, warm, hairy arms wrapping around my neck, and I shriek. I push myself away from the wall of the house, beating at the thing that's grabbed me, and the thing's screaming too and then it drops off me and I spin round to see something horrible, like a little furry man, a tiny man with long arms and a long tail sticking out behind him, and the thing's shrieking and howling, slapping the ground with its spindly black hands. My heart's pounding as I try to make a run for it, past the monster and back to the trees, but the horrible furry man lunges at me again and I trip and fall down flat on the earth. I scramble to my feet, expecting the little man to grab me any second now, but instead I hear a female voice.

'Are you all right?'

The girl is standing behind me, the little furry man cradled in her arms like a baby, his long black hands resting at her neck. She's stroking the monster's head while it stares at me with an expression of total disdain.

I am frozen, held in place.

The girl is calm, seemingly not at all shocked to find a stranger outside her house.

'Did you come from the labyrinth?' she asks me.

My heart is still going like a drum. My breath comes in gasps.

She holds my gaze, but with none of the calculating coldness of Grale's silent looks. Her eyes are dark brown, alive and warm, with a vivid curiosity in them. No suspicion or fear. It seems like the idea that I'm not supposed to be here, could have broken in to do something bad, hasn't occurred to her. She's tame, I realise, just like the animals she was feeding. Nobody's ever hurt her, so she has no reason to expect it now.

She's wearing blue trousers, studded at the pockets with brass rivets, and a loose pale shirt that fastens with those old-fashioned button-and-hole clasps. The clothes, like the house and the trees, belong to another time. Her skin is rich brown, and her dark hair, thick and glossy, falls past her shoulders. She looks so healthy and alive, perfectly at home among these impossible trees.

She's the most beautiful person I have ever seen. All I can do is stare.

'Can you speak?' she asks.

I snap out of it.

'I can speak,' I tell her.

'Are you afraid of me?'

'No, not you. Your … that thing grabbed me.'

'Oh,' she says. 'It is nearly dinner time.'

My eyes widen. 'It was going to eat me?'

The girl laughs. 'No! He thought you were going to fill his bowl. He likes to ride my shoulders into the kitchen, you see. Orlando does not eat meat.'

At that I can't help laughing. It explodes out of me. The monster makes a hooting noise, like he thinks it's funny too. She rubs his furry head again.

'You must have come from the labyrinth,' the girl continues, with a grin herself. 'Is that so? For I am certain I glimpsed you down there, buried underground. Or maybe you have some way to breach the wall. But you seem not to have known what you would find here.'

'I don't know what you mean,' I say. 'I've never been

underground. I used the vents. I've seen you in them, haven't I?'

'I had hoped you did not see me. I am very careful when spying in the labyrinth.'

'Right,' I say, confused. 'Well, I saw you. Followed your trail up here. What is this place?'

'I do not know that is has a given name. It is the garden,' she says. 'Where I am charged to live.'

'How long have you been here?'

'As long as I remember. It rains every seventh day, and for many years I have kept a record of that. But when I was younger I did not think to, so there is a great deal of time I have not properly measured.'

'So you've lived your whole life inside the Bliss building?'

She frowns. 'I do not understand.'

And then it hits me: she doesn't know. It makes sense, I suppose. If you grew up in here, never left, you'd think this was the Earth. She doesn't know she's living at the top of the spire. She can't see through the glass walls, they're clouded somehow, and she thinks what she sees through the vents is some kind of underground world.

Why is Grale keeping her here? Is bringing her up like this some sort of experiment? Something Human Futures are working on? But why?

'We're in a building right now,' I say. 'A really big building.'

'No,' she laughs, 'we are outside. You have some strange ideas, underground girl. Orlando trying to eat you … buildings big enough to fit the world inside … what tales! We are in the garden. This house of mine is the only building in the garden.'

'We …' I want to explain, but I don't really know where to start.

'This garden is so large,' she continues. 'How could it be within a building? How could the sun rise and the rain fall if we were inside?'

'It's a *really* big building,' I say. 'A corpspire. It's a tower, miles high. We're right at the top.'

The girl laughs even harder and the creature, Orlando, shrieks and slaps her shoulders.

'They tell such tales underground! A tower miles high!'

'I'm being totally serious,' I say, looking straight at her.

She looks back at me, seems to consider what I'm saying.

'If such a building truly existed, Mother would have spoken of it. But she has not.'

'Mother?'

'Do you know her? She is ruler, underground, as I understand it.'

'I think I do know her,' I say. 'Blonde, blue eyes. Looks really serious, like this.'

I do a Grale face, glaring at her with all the coldness I can manage, and the girl laughs in delight.

'You do know her! I thought you must. You are dressed much the same.'

'So she's your mum?'

'I am her only daughter. Heir to the labyrinth. Yet I am forbidden to enter, so I explore it in secret.'

Daughter? I find that hard to imagine; they look and seem nothing alike.

'So your mum comes up here often? To see you?'

'Yes. She visits every few days. She supervises my lessons.'

'OK, well, when you see her, don't tell her you saw me. I'm not really supposed to be up here.'

'You are forbidden from the garden?'

'Everyone is,' I say. 'Except Grale.'

'I know she is very worried for my safety. She often tells me so. She says the people underground might wish to hurt me. But I do not believe you would. It is tremendously exciting to meet someone else from underground. What do you think of the garden?'

My head's spinning. She's being kept here like some kind of test subject, but she doesn't seem to mind.

‘Yeah,’ I say, ‘it’s amazing. I never saw anywhere like this.’

‘I realise I have not asked your name,’ she says.

‘I’m Nova,’ I say.

‘And my name is Ziran. It is a pleasure to meet you.’

She holds her free hand out to me, the one not supporting the small man-creature. Her palm is warm and soft against mine. Her eyes widen a little when my sleeve rides up and exposes my wristhub.

‘What is this?’ she asks. ‘Does it hurt?’

‘That? No. It’s my wristhub.’

Ziran turns my hand gently with hers, to get a better look at the access ports on the back of the hub. She looks up at me with wide eyes.

‘But there are holes in your skin!’

‘Yeah, it’s just like, input and output. I’ve always had them. They’re not painful.’

‘You were born like this?’

‘No, it’s part of my implants. I mean, it’s pre-birth, some of it. But not those.’

Ziran looks at me as blankly as the creature in her arms. She has no idea what I mean by implants either. I wonder if it’s possible that Grale’s the only person she’s ever spoken to? If that’s true, she won’t have seen a wristhub up close.

'You all have holes in your skin, underground?'

'I have machines in my body,' I say. 'They're really small.'

Ziran frowns at me, and then bursts into laughter. Her teeth are even and white.

'I feel as though you must be playing a joke on me, telling tales of the underground to amuse yourself at my expense. But your face does not seem as though you find this entertaining. I must give Orlando his dinner. Perhaps you would come into my house and we can speak more?'

She smiles at me warmly, her large brown eyes so trusting and welcoming that, even though I know I should get back, I can't bring myself to leave.

'Sure,' I say.

With Orlando sitting up on her shoulder, Ziran turns and walks into her blue house, and I follow her across the threshold.

Ziran's house is cooler than the garden. The door closes behind me and the warmth is gone, along with the sound of the rushing stream. Inside the house, the soundtrack is our low breaths, our muted steps on the floorboards. The walls are covered in paintings hung in golden frames. Mostly they're of the garden: plants and trees, painted at different times of day, sometimes drenched with red by sunset light, sometimes with unbroken blue behind them. Some are portraits of animals, like the horn-headed creatures I saw Ziran feeding earlier. They're incredibly lifelike, way more real-looking than the paintings Grale showed me in her library and apartments.

'Are these pictures yours?' I ask.

'Yes,' she says, leading me through the hallway and into the kitchen at the back of the house. 'They are my paintings. It is how I pass my days.'

I look around the kitchen. There's a small round table, two chairs, all made of wood. A yellow vase with a single flower in it, a sink with one brass tap. Cupboards and shelving with glass jars and bottles and other cooking stuff on them, but most of it doesn't look used, more like a showroom display. I notice there's no stove. Instead there's this black pillar, about as tall as me, with a hatch in the front. The hatch is open at the moment, and I can see a tray full of different vegetables, some sealed cans. I'm guessing this is how Ziran is fed, and they send her food for the animals as well. She takes one of the boxes and picks out a soft red fruit.

'Yes, you see? Dinnertime,' she says to Orlando. He shrieks with excitement on her shoulder, reaching for the fruit, but she pushes his hand away. 'Manners,' she says. 'Get your bowl, Orlando. *Ossh oss!* Get the bowl. *Ossh oss!*' She points out a blue bowl, up on a shelf, and keeps making the nonsense noises. The creature leaps off her back and rushes across the room to the shelf with the bowl on it. 'Well done!' Ziran says. '*Ossh oss!* Over here!'

Orlando brings the blue bowl over and puts it down where she showed him. Ziran places the fruit into the bowl. Orlando starts stuffing his face with food.

'He's well trained,' I say.

'I do my best. He is very intelligent. Would you like to eat something?' Ziran asks, but I couldn't think about food right now. I shake my head.

'There is so much food sent up today, I expect Mother is going to visit later.'

'Grale eats here?'

'Sometimes. We will talk into the night if she does.'

'What do you talk about?'

'Everything. The arts, the sciences. The history of nations. The nature of the soul.'

'But never about neural implants? Never computers?'

'No. Mother has never mentioned these words to me. I do not understand them. She has never spoken of a tower two miles high either.'

'Yeah, it sounds like she left some things out.'

'Yes. And … for many years, I have been asking her where the places I have learned about, read about, are. Where is Athens? Where is Babylon, where is Troy, where is Rome? Where is Tokyo or Paris or London? I know they must lie outside the walls of my garden. I have read and spoken of a whole world, yet all I have ever seen is the bright bubble of this garden and a glimpse of the dark labyrinth beneath it. But, when I ask Mother about this, she says I am not ready to know some things yet. I think she would have me grow old and die here.'

'When did you start going to the … labyrinth?'

'Just a year ago. I was in a strange mood, thinking how my feet have touched every bit of ground within the garden. And then I realised they had not, that the sinkhole into which the stream flows had never felt my tread. I descended into it and discovered a portal to the underground, which I had never seen from above.'

'It's ventilation,' I say. 'Or some kind of maintenance access, I'm not sure.'

'It took a long time to loosen the gate enough so that I could lift it aside and enter the labyrinth. What a strange place. How dark and cramped, how perilous the chasms. What fearsome strangers live there, in hard-lit rooms underground. Mother had told me she ruled a host of people below us, but to see them about their business…'

'You never tried to properly get out?' I ask. 'Go down into the real underground?'

Ziran frowns. 'And do what? Mother tells me she holds absolute power there.'

'She does.'

'So you see. How would I escape? Where should I go? Who could I speak to who would not immediately hand me over for punishment? And then the gate would be barred to me and I would never glimpse underground again.'

Orlando has finished his food. She reaches to take him in her arms again, but he leaps away and scampers out of the kitchen door. 'Besides, I love Mother, even if I disobey her, and I love all the creatures who share my garden. I care for them. It would be wrong to leave.'

'It's not wrong to want something new,' I say.

'Is that why you are here?' Ziran asks me.

'In a way,' I say, thinking about it. 'I'm probably more like you than you realise. There's a lot going on that I don't think you understand. You're a prisoner here, Ziran. Like me. And this garden, it's not on the ground at all. You're up inside a tower, right at the top. The way this place is designed, it's meant to make you think you're outside. But you're not. The underground rooms you've seen, they're just rooms in the tower. If you told someone down there that they were underground, they'd laugh at you. We're miles up in the sky. We're above the clouds.'

Ziran closes her eyes for a long moment and opens them again. 'So that is why I can see sunlight in the underground rooms.'

'It's coming through the windows. I guess you can't see the windows properly if you're always peeking from above.'

'But who built this tower? For what purpose?'

'It's made by a corporation,' I say. Ziran looks blank at the word. 'A … business? They make all kinds of things. They make wires to go in our nerves, and dreams they can pipe down those wires. They make voices to go in your head so you'll never feel alone. They make everything you need so you can keep dreaming and buying and be happy.'

'And people like these things? The wires and dreams?'

'Yeah,' I say. I think of being on the magrail in the morning, everyone talking to themselves, staring into space, watching lumenfeeds. 'People mostly like it.'

'So …' Ziran is searching for words. 'Why am I here? Why is my garden here? How does this help them make their dreams?'

'I've been wondering that as well.'

'Perhaps it is my dreams they take,' she says. 'I have never had one.'

'You don't dream?'

'I sleep very little, and do not dream.'

'Everyone dreams. You just don't remember them.'

Ziran shakes her head. 'I remember everything that

happens to me, everything I see. When I focus on a single moment, I can recall everything about it.'

'Come on …' I say.

'It is true. When I met you outside, you were lying on the ground just by the porch. You looked exhausted and frightened, but proud too. I felt if you truly wanted something, I could never keep you from it. But I was not afraid. I could hold a picture of your face in my mind at that moment and paint it if I wished to. I would get it right.'

She looks directly at me as she speaks, and I have to look at the floor. Someone who sees so much of you … It's more than one of Grale's looks. More than a camera, because there's no mind inside a camera, to think about you while it records. It's almost too much, something too bright to look at.

'I have embarrassed you. I apologise.'

'It's OK,' I say. 'You're just … I don't know. Different.'

'This is strange for me as well. I have never spoken to anyone else besides Mother. You are very different too.' There's a thump upstairs. Ziran looks at the ceiling. 'Ah, now Orlando is opening my wardrobe. This is something he is not allowed to do.'

She heads for the hallway and then the narrow flight of stairs that leads to the upper floor of the house. I follow her, head buzzing. I don't know what I was expecting to find up here in Human Futures, but it wasn't this. I never thought I'd be talking to a strange, beautiful girl who lives a captive, closed-off life in a house from another century.

The upstairs landing is crowded with books, in shelves or piled free-standing on the top few stairs and by the doorways. They look like they came from Grale's library. Their titles are written in English, the weird, static glifs I've come to recognise. There's two rooms up here: one looks like a studio, with a painting in progress resting on an easel in the middle of the room. I can see a jar of liquid, pots of what must be paint, a rack of brushes. The painting is a long way from finished, mostly daubs of colour and sketchy suggestion, but I still recognise Grale: the fuligin clothes, golden butterfly brooch, her icy-pale eyes.

I hear Ziran's voice coming from her bedroom, and go to join her. The room is long and thin, with a sloped roof and large windows that look out on to the garden. Orlando has opened the dark wooden doors of Ziran's wardrobe and is busy throwing everything that was hanging there into a big pile on the floor.

When he hears us, he hoots with alarm and jumps up on the top of the wardrobe. Ziran stands on her tiptoes

– she's taller than me – and drags him down. His face is so like a naughty child, so human, that I can't help laughing, and, when I catch Ziran's eye, though she's trying to tell him off, I can see she's laughing too.

'He's so naughty. What is he?' I ask.

'A monkey. Mother bought him from a faraway country. She says he is the last one.'

She carries the creature over to the window and opens it, shooing him out on to the window ledge.

'I've never—' I begin to say, but Ziran gasps and shushes me.

'Mother is here!' she hisses, closing the window again, and looking back at me in a panic.

'What?'

'I just saw her in the trees. She will be here any moment!'

'She can't know I've been here,' I say, freaking out.

'Hurry,' says Ziran. She hustles me downstairs and into a big cupboard in the kitchen.

'She will come in through the front door,' Ziran says quietly, 'and I will call her upstairs. Then you can go.'

'OK,' I whisper.

We look at each other, unsure what else to say. I realise I'm shaking.

'Will you return?' she asks.

'If I can,' I say.

'Please do,' she says, her eyes pleading as she closes the door, and runs back up the stairs.

I stand in darkness and silence, feeling my heartbeat hammering in my chest. If Grale finds me here, I'm dead for sure.

A few moments later I hear the front door open. Footsteps.

'Ziran?' Grale calls in her soft voice.

'I am upstairs, Mother,' Ziran replies. 'I have been working on your portrait. Would you like me to show you?'

'Of course I would,' says Grale, and I hear her on the stairs, moving into the studio room opposite the bedroom.

As soon as I'm sure the coast is clear, I tiptoe out of the cupboard and slide out through the front door and on to the porch as quietly as I can. The animals Ziran were feeding have gone, disappeared back into the trees. Nothing else has changed. The trees are the same, and so is the strange sunlight, illuminating the garden without seeming to come from any specific place. For the first time, I see beyond the beauty and realise how lonely it must be to be trapped up here; how boring unchanging perfection must become.

I dash for the treeline and throw myself down behind a rock. I crouch there for a little while, hoping Grale didn't see me from a window while I crossed the open ground. My heart beats slower as nothing happens. The clear stream runs along beside the house, insects looping over it. There's no sign of Grale or Ziran. Once I'm certain she didn't see me, I get up and run across the lush ground, following the stream, heading for the sinkhole and the gateway into the ducts.

12

When I climb back down into my bathroom, stepping in the sink, it's nearly dusk. Gunmetal grey sky with an oily sheen. Lumens ripple below my window. Women with fluffy pets, children laughing, colourful snacks, big, hollow men's faces with carnivore white teeth. Whole fog of bad dreams. My suit of fuligin is coated in pale dust, a dead giveaway. I brush it off as best I can, splash cold water on my face and hair.

I find the door to my suite is unlocked and when I step out into Grale's wood-floored apartment Campbell is sitting at the food bar, a glass of wine at his elbow. I jump at the sight of him, want to go back into my room, but I realise that will look guilty. What's he doing here? Does he know where I've been? His synthetic eyes track me as I cross the apartment. I walk over to the food-preparation area and start making a cup of coffee, trying to look like it's what I meant to do all along. I don't say a word to him, but I feel his gaze on my body, as though he's X-raying me, as though he can see the guilt written into my posture, knows I've been somewhere I shouldn't. I keep my face to the wall.

'Grale's assistant! Maybe you can help me,' Campbell says. 'Have a seat.'

I don't see another choice, so I sit at the end of the food bar. I look at the far wall, the painting of yellow flowers in a yellow jar. I look at the rough, fiery blooms and think of them like suns, alive and warm. Takes me back to the garden, to Ziran, her plants and animals, her house full of paintings. I try and hold on to that warm feeling as I turn to face the chilly eyes of the Auditor. He runs one white-gloved finger along the stem of his wine glass.

'I was supposed to have a briefing with Grale,' he remarks. 'I've been here for an hour. I have some fresh network diagnostics to go over. But it seems Human

Futures took precedence again. Do you know how long she'll be?'

I shrug. 'Not like Grale shares her schedule with me.'

'No,' says Campbell, taking a sip of wine. Sighs. 'She likes to play things close. Which makes it hard to do one's job. I'm no closer to finding the Moth than the day I arrived.'

I don't say anything.

'Do you want the Moth to be caught?' Campbell asks me. 'He tried to kill you.'

I have to think about that one. My whole life I've been outside, been the one being chased, which means I'm not exactly keen on securicorp people, and I tend to side unthinkingly with anyone they're after. Weighed against that, the Moth's a treacherous piece of shit. They took over my body, and you don't get something stolen from you that's more important than that.

'Won't cry if you do catch him,' I say. 'But I don't think you can.'

He laughs in a tired, joyless way. He seems worn down, no energy for his usual aggression. Or maybe it's the wine. 'I don't think I can either. It's more than just this case with Bliss. I've hunted the Moth for decades, it feels like, before they even had that name for him. I just knew there was something out there, some … disorder.

A flaw in the metanet that shouldn't be there. I'm very intelligent, very perceptive. But there's something about this case that I can't see clearly. Catching the Moth is like trying to see the back of your own head. Each time you turn, each move you make, it's still behind you, behind your eyes, out of sight.'

'Easy to see the back of your head,' I say. 'You just need two mirrors.'

The Auditor laughs loudly, too loudly, and then his amusement fades. A change seems to come over him. He turns his synthetic eyes back to me with a fresh intensity. I feel afraid, like I shouldn't have started joking with him. I remember how fast he moved when I attacked him with the scalpel, how strong he was. He rests his glass down on the table. His posture is no longer exhausted. He looks alert and focused.

'Funny thing,' Campbell says, almost as an aside, 'I could've sworn you weren't in your room when I first arrived here this evening.'

My back prickles. 'What do you mean?'

'Just an observation. Not one I'm likely to follow up, of course, unless …'

There's a strange smile on his face now. I don't know if it's just the drink, or if there is something wrong him, but he seems to have gone from down and despondent to sly and smug in an instant.

'What do you think Grale's *really* doing up there?' he asks me. 'Human Futures. You must have thought about it, with it being right overhead. What could it be that's so important to her? Do you know how much of Bliss's money vanishes into the metanet dead zone she's set up? Because it's a lot, I can tell you that. I can access enough of the company's financial records to see there's an unconscionable drain happening. And for what? She won't say. The Board of Directors have been stonewalled so many times they've given up asking. Everyone who works in the Human Futures department lives up there, you know? Inside that little information fortress. They only leave if they die in her service.'

I think of the garden, the house, the animals. Ziran holding Orlando up on her shoulder. The stream with its translucent fish. I think about the other rooms I saw below the garden, the dull office and that creepy medical room. If Campbell could see what I've seen, would it make any more sense to him than it does to me now?

'I don't know any more than you,' I say.

'There aren't many secrets you can keep from me,' Campbell says. 'I have a lot of access, a lot of ways to get into places people don't think I can get to. I'm not used to blind spots. I don't like them.'

'So tell Grale that. I can't help you.'

'Nova, there aren't any cameras here in the CEO's quarters. There's no recording equipment of any kind.'

'So what?'

'So if you know something, you can tell me. She'll have no way of knowing.'

'Maybe she told you to say that. Maybe you're wrong about the cameras. Maybe she has some other kind of tech here, something even you don't know about.'

Campbell laughs, shaking his head. 'I'm an Archangel Systems Auditor. I know how to sweep for monitoring devices. This is the cleanest room in the whole spire. Maybe the only clean one.'

'I don't know a thing. Don't know what she does up there or why.'

His synthetic eyes scan my face, tiny figments of rainbow light trapped inside their cold depths. The mechanisms rotate and flutter. My skin crawls.

'In our field-interview training,' the Auditor says, 'we learn to recognise the micro-expressions human faces form during a lie. There are twenty-three common ones. Did you know that?'

'Amazing.'

'You're displaying twelve of them right now. You do know something.'

I reach up and distort my face with my fingers, pulling my cheeks out, like a kid playing at being a monster.

'Very clever,' Campbell says. 'But in a real interview your hands would be restrained. You know, I can help you a great deal. Perhaps you enjoy living up here. It's better than where you came from, as I understand it. But for how long? How far does a girl from the undercity get up here, do you think? It's not your world. If you do want to get out of here, maybe you tell me what you know. I can get you back into the slums if that's what you want. Help you disappear.'

And for a moment I am tempted. To tell him everything, let someone else who isn't me deal with whatever's going on up there above the clouds. Slip away back down to the shadows below. But I don't. I don't trust anything about Campbell Reid.

'I like how things are,' I say, releasing my hold on my face.

'Liar,' Campbell replies, but he's laughing this time. 'Well,' he says, as he gets up to leave, 'change your mind and you know how to reach me.'

There's a ping in my ear and a file transfers over to me. Some kind of program I haven't seen before. In the lumen preview, it looks like a white pearl.

I don't accept the transfer. It hangs in the metanet

between us. Campbell steps into one of Grale's elevators.

'Suit yourself,' he says, and the door closes behind him.

13

Night envelops the corpspire and the City below us. There's a crescent moon, swarms of skycar headlamps glittering around the pinnacles of the cityblocs. I can see a moonie crew working on a new floor above one of these pinnacles, their orange shapes as small as sugar grains, floodlit, working all night to meet some deadline.

Just past midnight, the map finishes compiling. I immediately summon it up, a lumen atlas of the Bliss Inc. corpspire, filling my dark bedroom with a matrix of searing light. I ask it to overlay the engineering systems with the floor plan. Every duct of the ventilation system appears, glowing purple, electrical conduits highlighted red, the water system marked with a deep, soothing blue. Elevator shafts are streaks of yellow light. There's so much information at once I have to take a deep breath. It makes me dizzy.

I zoom in on the map until I can see my location, a little pip of white light in the floor marked *CEO Habitation: Security Five*. One floor above me, the map radically decreases in detail. All it shows are the barest outlines of the different rooms. This area isn't named, but it's clearly Human Futures, and Ziran's garden above that. Knowing what to look for, I can see the shape of her enclosure. She really does live at the pinnacle of the corpspire: only thing above her is the spire's array of metanet transmitters, and then open sky.

I tell my implants to find a route that reaches the lowest floor of the spire without using any stairs or elevators. The mapping software chugs a bit, trying to process my weird request, and comes back with the answer I already suspected: you need to climb through the vents into that central maintenance shaft, and follow it down until you reach the bottom levels of the corpspire, the utility floors where the power generators and water-filtration systems are housed. From there,

I can take a hundred different paths out into the undercity. The bits that worry me are the parts of the shaft without ladders. There looked to be enough cabling and pipes to give good footholds, but it's no certain thing. You fall and you're gone: the full drop's miles and miles. It's going to be difficult.

I don't see what choice I have though. I'm stuck up here with Grale and Campbell, both of them cold and strange and able to end my story whenever they feel like it. If Campbell hasn't worked out that I'm using the vents already, he will soon, and then he'll go to Grale. No need to hang around to watch that play out.

And if I tell him? What will happen to Ziran and her garden?

What will happen to Ziran anyway? What use is she to Grale? To Human Futures? I shake away the thought – I can't help her. I can barely help myself. All I can do is get out of here.

I climb into the sink again, reach up and push the bathroom ventilation cover aside. I crawl up into the vents and follow the same path I took earlier. I make quick progress, confident in my route, and soon I find myself at the central shaft, miles of empty air below me. My implants mark the route with a thread of white lumen-light, which plummets into the blackness. I'm about to take a step down the ladder, the first step of the journey, and then I think of Ziran. Her eyes as I left, pleading with me to come back.

I should tell her I'm going, let her know how she can escape if she ever has to. We've only just met, but I want to at least say goodbye before she's gone for ever. And at the same time I can get some water from her for my journey. It would be stupid to travel without any. I don't know exactly how long this climb will take, let alone the journey through the undercity. It could be a long trip. Don't want to get into a crazed thirst and start guzzling from the poisoned pools of rainwash. Nasty way to go.

I'm sure I saw a bottle in the kitchen of Ziran's house, I think as I start climbing up. If I ask her, she'll let me fill one from the stream.

Soon I'm passing over Human Futures. Looking down into the main office, I see this time that it's full of corpsmen. Grale is chairing a meeting with a group of scientists in the glass-walled conference room. Working late. Should be safe to visit the garden. I allow myself a little smile, imagining her waking tomorrow, expecting to use me for another round of Deep Recall, and finding that I'm gone.

I squeeze out of the grate in the sinkhole, and climb the wet stone. The garden's different by night, almost as dark as the undercity, black trees against black sky, black rocks and black roots doing their best to trip me. After a moment's hesitation, I light my fingertorch. I know Grale's in the office below, and Ziran was very specific about nobody else visiting her. I should be safe with a light. I make my way over the mossy, uneven ground, heading for the little blue house. The building itself is darkened, but there's no mystery to where I can find Ziran. I can see a warm orange light in the trees past the house: the light from a fire. As I come closer through the undergrowth, I can smell smoke, a rich, roasted taste, thick in my mouth.

Ziran is sitting on a fallen log in a clearing, holding a book and a stylus, staring into the fiery heart of the flames.

I step into the light.

'Nova!' Her wide white smile gleaming. She puts her book aside and leaps up to greet me. 'You came back!'

'I did. I hope it's not too soon.'

'Your hand is … shining?'

'Oh,' I say, holding out my fingers, so she can see the bioluminescent implants under the nails. 'That's just this utility thing.'

'You are full of miracles,' she says, eyes wide. 'Dreamwires in your nerves. Lanterns in your fingers.'

'It's dark all the time,' I say, 'where I'm from. You don't want a torch you can lose. People end up dead that way.'

'I had hoped very much you would return,' Ziran says as we sit back down on the log. 'I have been drawing you, as I promised.'

She holds her book out to me. I see that the pages are blank, meant for artwork. My heart misses a beat when I see what's she's put there. These aren't quite like her paintings; instead they're almost engineering diagrams, worked with thin, confident black lines. Each one is a study of my face, an expression, moments from our conversation earlier today. I see myself in many different poses, but in each there's a sadness to the expression that takes me by surprise. A sadness I always knew was mine, but hoped others couldn't see.

I didn't hide it from her. She really does see everything, forgets nothing.

I find myself wanting to cry. I close the book.

'You do not like them?'

I look down, away from the fire, not wanting her to see my face.

'They're amazing,' I say. 'That's me, right there. I just wish it wasn't.'

'I do not understand,' she says. 'You are so interesting!

Why would you wish to be someone else?'

'I'm not … good,' I say. The fire goes blurry as my tears start falling heavily. 'I'm a mess. My life's a mess. Even if I do get out of here, I won't … what will I do? I can't explain.'

Ziran's smile has faded with my tears.

'If you try to explain,' she says, 'I would like to hear. I would like to know about you, Nova. You are so interesting to me.'

So I sit by the fire and talk to her about my life. In fact, I find I can't stop talking. I tell her as much as I can about how I got here. I tell her about the undercity, Patches, the Gut, leeching, how I made my money. I talk about Ade and Nightmarket and blind dogs. I tell her stuff that happened before that, the carebloc and my lumen teachers and the girl above me who was always throwing up. I talk about pale green slippers and Pre-Employment. I talk about how the man from Municipal Works tried to take my body away from me, how I nearly chose to go with him and become a moonie, because I couldn't think of anything else to do. I tell her how Patches saved me. I tell her how I ended up in the carebloc in the first place, the car accident, about the different points you get assigned by your car and the drunk man's hat blowing off his head.

I go further, tell her about stuff I never said out loud to anyone before, because they never asked. Tell her how, once I got better at icebreaking, I went into the corpcourt records of my parents' settlement case. I wanted information on who the exec's son was, the one who'd climbed on to the road in the first place, caused the accident. Thought maybe I'd get some revenge. I found out he'd been dead more than a decade. Was traumatised by the accident, kept drinking, got into harder stuff as well. Eventually he overdosed and drowned in his bath, up in the family's pinnacle apartment. So the car's algorithm crashed and killed my parents to save a rich addict who died young anyway. The fire starts swimming in my eyes again as I tell her that part.

I tell her about the Moth, about Phantom, about Campbell and Grale and this job. How I came into the spire to steal from the person she calls Mother. How I thought I was finally something special, and I was wrong about that too. The Moth just used me, didn't care about me, made me try and kill Grale. How now I'm trapped and I have to get out and that's why I came to see her again. Because I need to disappear. Because I have to say goodbye.

Ziran doesn't interrupt during any of it, even though I know she must be bursting with questions. She listens to me more intently than anyone ever has before. Patches and Ade never listened to me like Ziran does by the fire, not really. Patches taught me a lot, about hacking and leeching and Phantom, about the undercity, about guns, but he's not a listener, not a hugger, not someone who shows you he cares for you. With him, it was always business, training me up to be a leecher, talking about the jobs that need doing around the Gut, keeping him in byts so he can tinker in his workshop. And Ade ... if I ever tried to talk to Ade about my parents, he'd listen for thirty seconds and then say, 'That's rough, sis, life sucks, let's go get wasted.' Ade would kill for me, but there's no real empathy in him. He's hard all the way down; it's how he was raised.

Ziran's different. When I'm done, there are tears in her eyes just like there are in mine.

'I do not understand everything you said,' she tells me. 'But I do know you are not a mess. You are good. You are brave. You tell the truth.'

I look into the fire and sigh. I wish what she said was true.

'Ziran,' I say, looking up at her, 'I need to leave. Right now. This spire's not safe for me any more. I came to say goodbye.'

'And you will be gone for ever?'

'I have to.'

'I had hoped we would have more days together,' Ziran says. 'I feel there is so much we could tell one another. I am only beginning to understand the real world.'

'I can't. If I stay here, I'll end up dead.'

'Because of Mother?'

'Perhaps,' I say. 'I know you care for her, but she's a liar, Ziran. She's a bad person, really bad. I don't know why she keeps you up here, but you need to be careful of her.'

'My eyes are open,' Ziran says. 'Is there anything I can do to help?'

'I need some water for the journey,' I say. 'The water outside's not good to drink.'

'Of course. I will help you, Nova. But I wish you did not have to leave.'

'I have no choice,' I say.

'May I ask one thing of you before you go?'

'What?'

'Will you show me the outside? Even just a glimpse of the great city you speak of beyond the tower? I still cannot believe it is quite real.'

I think quickly. This is dangerous. But the window in my room in Grale's apartments will show her the pinnacles of the City at night. That should be enough to give her what she wants. Grale is still working in Human Futures, as far as I know. We can check from the vents before we descend. Ziran deserves that much; deserves to know the truth.

How much can it hurt? To let her look through the window and see the world as it really is?

To let me delay the moment when I have to say goodbye to her for ever.

'I can do that,' I say. 'We'll have to move fast though.'

'Excellent,' she says, grinning. 'First I will make you a water flask.'

We leave the clearing, talking with new excitement, like this is all a game, Ziran's drawing book lying open on the grass beside the dying fire.

14

We slip through the vent and into the bathroom. I take her hand and help her down from the sink, out through the door, lead her into the bedroom. I see the messy bed, the dirty coffee mug on the side table. Ziran barely glances at this. She's drawn over to the wall-sized window and stands in front of it, motionless. I sit on the edge of the bed and watch her watching the world beyond the glass: the crescent moon, the cityblocs crowned with cranes, the ribbons of skycars, the gleaming orbitals in the night sky. Ziran is a starving creature at a feast of light.

She rests one hand against the window.

'Is this real?' she asks me. 'This is the world?'

'A little part of it,' I say.

'This is not little …'

'Yeah. I mean, the City's even crazier when you're down in the mix. We're very high above it here.'

'But what are those … can they be houses? They are so tall. I cannot see the earth.'

'They're cityblocs,' I say. 'They built them up, from the ground, for decades and decades. They're still growing. They have thousands of people living in them. Nobody lives on the ground. It's all dark and trashed and stuff, like I told you.'

'And you lived down there?'

'Way further down. You can't see the undercity from here. These are the pinnacles. The highest parts of the City.'

'And what about this?' Ziran points to a lumen advert, a woman the size of a citybloc, holding up a bottle of shampoo. 'What is she? How can there be a person so large? I do not understand.'

'What?'

'The woman. She has blue hair and a wide smile. She is showing me some container. Is it some kind of magic trick?'

'Wait, you can see the lumens?'

'I do not understand you.'

'It's a lumen,' I say. 'They're … you see them with your implants. I told you I had dreamwires in my brain, right? Optic nerves?'

'Yes,' Ziran says.

'They're called lumens. They aren't real. Your optic nerve gets signals from your implants and shows you the lumen pictures. Everything you ever see is electrical signals that go to your brain, right? Lumens are just signals coming from the metanet rather than your actual eyes. They're, uh … what's that thing people say? Consensual hallucinations.'

I can't tell if Ziran is taking this in or not. She's still looking through the glass at the City.

'You shouldn't be able to see them,' I say. 'The only way you can see lumens is if you have neural implants and a metanet connection. And I thought you didn't.'

I try to find the metanet signal coming from Ziran's body, but there's nothing. No inflow, no output. So how can she be seeing them?

'So only some have the sight,' Ziran says. 'Blessed eyes. And I have them, although I never knew.' She turns to face me finally, her head haloed by the City lights. Her hair's a dark tangle over one shoulder, her features shadowy suggestions. I want to move towards her and join her at the window, and at the same time want to get as far away from her as I can. I do neither, frozen in place, gripping the side of the bed like it can keep me from falling.

'I guess you do,' I say, trying to keep my voice calm, trying to ignore the desperate, wild feeling that grows inside me as I look at her.

'Your voice sounds strange,' she says.

'You ever feel like you're falling through the floor? I just felt like that.'

Ziran walks over to the bed and sits beside me. 'I used to get dizzy when I was younger. I would look down at my body, and think, *This isn't me. What I'm looking at isn't me. I'm somewhere else. Behind my eyes is a stranger*. But I never knew what to do with those thoughts. I would have to lie back in the grass until my head stopped spinning.'

Her little finger touches mine and I snatch my hand away like she burned me. I get up and walk to the window and press my forehead to the cold glass. A river of light flows below us, but above is only blackness and the cruel curve of the moon.

This was a mistake. I need to leave. I should already be gone. I shouldn't have told her anything about me.

Shouldn't have let her see me cry. Shouldn't have let her think she could get close to me, because that was just another mask, another performance to make someone help me. All I wanted was a bottle of water. I didn't want *this*. I should already be in the maintenance shaft by now. This is slowing me down. Something got into me when I met her, a tiny splinter of coloured glass, and I don't know how to dig it out. I don't even know if I want to.

'Nova? Did I do something wrong?'

I say, 'I'm afraid of you.'

'I am not afraid of you.'

'You don't know me. Nobody does.'

'I think you are kind.'

I think back on everyone I've ever stolen from. There's been a lot of them, even in three years. How did their lives go after I leeched away their day's wage? Better because of me? I don't think so. The Moth didn't choose me for this job because I'm kind. He chose me because I can make people look at me and see what I want them to see. There is no Nova. There is no real me, just like there's no lumen woman standing thirty metres tall in the City below us. It's just static and noise, shifting points of light. Chameleon cloth. A consensual hallucination. Phantom.

'I didn't need this,' I say.

'I am sorry that I touched you,' Ziran says. 'I really

am. I will not do it again.'

'It's not that. It's … I shouldn't have climbed back up to your garden. I should've just gone straight down and taken my chances.'

'I am glad you climbed up.'

'I'm not.'

'You do not mean that.'

'What good does it do either of us?'

'In my books, there was a story I read about a girl who was put under an evil spell and fell asleep for a hundred years. She was stuck like that, until at last a prince climbed up into her tower and kissed her and she woke up. She was alive again. When I saw you on my lawn, I thought, *Finally someone climbed up for me.*'

'I don't know that story,' I say. 'What happens to them after she wakes up?'

'They are both happy,' Ziran says.

'Right,' I say. 'Because that happens in real life. People end up happy.'

'You do not have to say it that way. As if I said something stupid.'

'What do you know about the real world, Ziran?'

'I am sorry I touched you. I am sorry. I will never do it again.'

She sounds like she's about to cry. I want to punch a

hole in the window.

'It's not that I don't want …' I trail off. 'This is crazy. I don't have time for any of this, whatever it is. I'm in danger. I need to leave tonight. If I don't, I'll end up dead; if I do, I'll never see you again.'

Ziran takes a deep breath. 'I would come with you.'

I don't answer.

'I would. I have thought about it and I know I would. I tried to draw you to get the thoughts to go away, but they did not. I want to go where you go. I want to see the real world, with you. Now that I have seen how vast it is, how grand, how could I stay surrounded by the same walls until I die? I want the lights. I want the real sky over me, not the shell Mother has trapped me inside. I am tired of sleeping.'

'You won't like it when you're there,' I say. 'Not where I'm from. The undercity. It's not like up here. No clean water, no sky, no sun, no animals, no plants. It's just concrete and metal and darkness. You're better off in your garden, Ziran.'

'I know you will protect me. If I am with you—'

'I'm not here to keep you safe!' I snap. 'I'm not here to save you! I look after myself! That's all I ever did. I look after myself because nobody else ever has. Nobody gives you anything where I'm from. Nobody gives you food on a tray or animals to play with. You think you want to live like me, but you don't! You see where I'm from and you won't like me so much!'

'I am sorry,' Ziran says. She's crying now. 'I did not know what to do. I only know Mother. I thought you …' She can't finish.

'Just go,' I say. 'Go back to your little paradise.'

Ziran stands up and walks across the room. I watch her leave in the reflection in the window. I stand and stare without moving. The lumens play around the summits of the cityblocs. If she goes, then we're both safe. It's better this way. A banner of glifs crawls through the night sky: *Don't you deserve to be happy?* A glowing grid of blocs, the City laid out below me, millions of people living one on top of the other. All that communication, an ocean of data, the metanet babbling in every person's ear, and I'd have no way to describe to any of them what's happening inside my head as I stand here. *Don't you deserve to be happy?* But who am I really? Chameleon cloth. Street-leecher. Phantom girl. She saw me. She saw the real me, drew me like I am under the disguises. If she goes, I'll be safe. I'll never see her again. I'll climb down the maintenance shaft on my own, and either I'll fall and break my neck or I'll vanish into the darkness of the undercity. Sell my Chrysalis 3, get myself smuggled on to a cargo shuttle, live somewhere else. Meso-California, Antarctica, one of the Pacific Ocean city-states. Anywhere. *Don't you deserve to be happy?* I'll go anywhere but here and try to think about everything but Ziran and I know it won't work. The glass splinter stabs at my heart. I turn away from the window, the nightwashed City, and rush to the bathroom. Ziran is vanishing up into the ceiling vent, just one long leg hanging down from the opening. A bare, soft foot. I take hold of it, gently wrapping my fingers round her ankle. Feel the human warmth there.

'Don't go,' I say.

15

She doesn't move.

'Please,' I say. 'Please stay.'

Ziran drops back down through the ceiling vent, moving slowly, arranging her feet so they're both in my sink. I'm still holding her ankle, a lifeline.

She kneels and her face is level with mine. Our lips touch. She tastes of something sweet. I can smell the smoke in her hair. Electricity runs through my body. Almost as soon as our lips meet she draws away.

'I did not know it felt like that,' she says.

Heat rising into my face. 'It doesn't normally,' I say. 'Not like this.'

'I only read about it,' she says.

I kiss her again, resting my hand against the back of her neck.

'Come with me,' I say. 'I want you to.'

'When?'

'Now. We can't wait. Let's go back to your house and get what we need. It's going to be a long climb.'

Ziran runs her hand through my hair.

'It'll be dangerous,' I say. 'We could die.'

She kisses me, greedier this time. I almost fall over. I have to brace myself against the wall with my free hand.

'I will die if we cannot leave together. I will go anywhere with you.'

'You'll never come back,' I say. 'You won't see your house or trees or animals again. Remember that.'

'Orlando can climb with us. For the rest … I do not care.'

I feel like I'm floating, my heart racing. When I look at myself in the mirror, I don't recognise what I see. My face: luminous, radioactive. Something transforming.

'Zira—' I start to say.

'*Nova?*' comes a voice from the room behind us. '*Nova!*'

Grale. I whirl as fast as I can and slam the bathroom door, lock it. Did she see us? She can't have seen us. What is she doing here? I thought she was in Human Futures.

Ziran's eyes are wide with fear.

'Go!' I whisper. 'Head back to the house. She can't find out you're missing. Get ready to leave. As soon as I can, I'll follow you up there.'

One last kiss and she grabs the edge of the vent, pulling herself up. I stand in the sink and replace the grate.

'*Nova!*'

Grale's right behind the bathroom door now. She raps on the door.

I step out of the sink. Try to calm myself. Brush the vent dust off my clothes as best I can.

'Open this door,' she says. 'I need to speak to you.'

'Give me a moment!'

'*Right now*,' she says. 'Open this door!'

I take another moment, breathe, flush the toilet. Calm. Calm. Calm. She doesn't know anything.

I open the bathroom door.

Grale's in my bedroom, almost invisible in the darkness, a fuligin shadow among shadows. My heart lurches with fear. I can't see her expression clearly, but there's no good reason for her to be bursting in on me like this.

'Why are you awake?' she asks. Her voice is soft as always, but it makes me shudder. It's like a knife hidden in silk.

'I drank too much coffee earlier. Kept me up.'

She knows something. She has to know. I keep myself as blank and innocent as possible.

'Not expecting anyone?'

'I don't know what you mean.'

'Come with me,' she says, in a way that lets you know there's no arguing.

The lights in the apartment's living space are on. Grale marches me to one of her reclining chairs.

'Sit down,' she says. I notice as she steps in front of me that she's carrying her little silver remote. I sit in the reclining chair and rest my hands on my knees, trembling. What I'm thinking is this: was Campbell wrong? Does she have cameras in this apartment? Did she hear us when she came in just now? Did she see us?

'I have some questions that urgently need to be answered,' she continues.

'Is something wrong?' I ask.

Grale pulls a sheet of paper out of her fuligin jacket. She jabs it in my face.

'What's this?' she asks.

'I don't know,' I say, but my stomach's dropped

through my chair.

I know exactly what it is. I'm in deep trouble.

'Have a closer look. Tell me what you think it is.'

I take the sheet. It's crumpled, smeared, but still a good likeness. You can't look at it and see anything other than my face, a study of concealed sadness.

We left it by the fire, I realise. Idiots! Grale must have gone up to look for Ziran, gone over to the fire. She couldn't have missed the book of drawings.

'It's me,' I say.

'Yes,' Grale says. 'I'm glad you agree. It's definitely you.'

'What am I supposed to know about this? Did you draw it?'

'There's only one person in the world who draws like this, Nova. And she doesn't draw from her imagination.'

'I don't know who you mean.'

I put the drawing on the floor by my chair.

'So that's how you're playing this game?' Grale asks. She points her silver remote at me. 'The thing about neural implants – something we tend to downplay in the promotional material – is that there's almost no end of things you can do to someone's nerves if you send the right signals,' she continues. 'This is a pain inductor. It's tuned specifically to your implant rig.'

Grale presses a button on the remote.

Pain sears through my right arm, pain like nothing I've felt before. I feel like someone's scraping the skin off with a red-hot knife. It's so intense I fall forward on to the wooden floor, trying at once to claw my own arm off and cradle it against me, hiding it under my body, hoping I can stop the signal from getting through. My other hand beats at the floor.

In an instant, the pain's gone, like nothing happened. I'm convulsing on the ground, tears streaming down my face. Grale stands over me.

'How did the drawing come to be?' she asks. 'Why did I find a book *full* of these besotted little portraits? How did she see you? Explain everything.'

'I … Grale, I don't know …'

'Not good enough.'

This time the pain's in my chest, like I swallowed molten iron, fire running down the length of my spine and throat. I scream, kicking the floor, fingers clutching nothing.

'This is intensity five,' Grale says. 'On a ten-point scale. If you don't start talking, we're going to six.'

I just gasp. I can't speak.

'Very well,' she says.

Intensity six is a laser beam bursting every cell of my

face, a searing mask I can't rip off. My vision's gone black and white. For a moment, I can see everything from far away, like it's through a weird camera lens.

'Oh,' Grale says. 'Nearly lost you there. Next one will be seven. Full body, this time. I should mention that nine and ten are normally fatal. Your nervous system can only take so much.'

'Please,' I rasp. 'Stop. *Please.*'

'You have something to tell me?' she asks. 'That's the only way we stop. When you tell the truth about this drawing.'

'Ziran ...' I say. Black dots are spiralling in front of my eyes. 'Her name's Ziran ...'

Grale looks more curious than angry. The silver remote is still pointed at me.

'How?' she asks.

'Vents,' I say. I hate myself, but I'm out of options. I don't know what else to say. I can't die like that.

'The ventilation?' Grale asks. 'What do you mean?'

'Get through the vents.'

'You were able to access her controlled habitat through the ventilation system?'

'Yes.'

'Well, that is news,' Grale says. 'My father designed that garden, not me. It was originally for his tree collection. I repurposed it. I hadn't thought to do a thorough ventilation check for years …'

'They're small,' I say.

'Yes, too small for an adult. But a girl of your build … I don't know how I never saw it.'

I don't say anything. I don't know if I could get up.

'And it leads where?'

'The sinkhole,' I say. 'Water.'

'I see,' Grale says. Her rage seems to be gone. I wonder if what she's really angry about is not knowing; the idea that I have something inside my head she doesn't know. Her thoughts are her own; everyone else's belong to her. Now that I've cracked, I'm not dangerous. She knows more than me again.

'Were you there when I visited the other day?' Grale asks.

'Yes. Only time.'

'I understand now. I thought that Ziran was behaving strangely. She was very agitated and trying to hide it.'

I don't say anything.

'And what is your connection to her?' Grale asks.

'What do you mean?'

'What do you think of Ziran? How do you feel about her?'

'I don't know.'

'Because there are many, many drawings of you. She seems to be quite taken with you.'

'I don't understand what you're asking.'

'I think you do,' Grale says.

I think of Ziran's lips against mine. Her shape, outlined against dark glass by the City's lights.

'I don't know what I think of her.'

'Your desires are not mysteries to me,' Grale tells me. 'You are part of our consumer-profile system. You always have been. Predicting and anticipating desire is a speciality of Bliss Inc. A series of probabilities, data points – that's all you are to our algorithm, and it's very good at what it does. Have you never wondered why every lumen advert we've shown to you, Nova, is a woman? We know your heart. We always have.'

I don't say anything. Grale paces her living space. I stay on the floor, trying to slow my heartbeat. I look at the painting of yellow flowers hanging on the wall. I don't like how they look any more. They've changed, or I have, and there's madness in those flaming strokes of paint.

'I suppose you have questions for me,' Grale continues.

'She's not really your daughter,' I say.

'No,' Grale says. 'Of course she isn't. I doubt even she believes that any more.'

'Have you ever told her anything that's true?'

'I'd say she's much better educated than you are. Her mind is of great importance to me.'

'Why?' I ask.

'She's my life's work. And, thanks to you, it's all in ruins.'

'I don't understand.'

Grale considers me. I can feel the tears drying on my cheeks. I bit my tongue sometime during the pain induction, and it feels swollen and sore.

'Stand up,' she says.

I do. She gestures towards the wall panel that hides one of her private elevators. I cross the apartment, Grale at my shoulder.

'What are we going?' I ask, as we step into the elevator.

'To Human Futures, of course.'

16

We rise a single floor and we're inside Human Futures, inside the rooms I've only seen glimpses of through the vents. I wonder if I'm finally going to discover what this place is for, how it relates to Ziran and her garden above us. The hallways are no different to anywhere else I've been inside Bliss: shiny and clean, with a hint of peppy perfume in the filtered air. We pass glass-walled offices, full of scientists working silently, despite it being the middle of the night.

A guard in charcoal grey armour approaches us. He

bows to Grale.

'I need you to secure Werner's Botanical Garden,' she tells him. 'There should be a young woman there. Ensure she's safe and can't do anything foolish.'

'Yes, ma'am.' The man bows again and leaves, heading for Ziran's garden. I feel a stab of grief. I should've told her to hide in the vents. But now they know I've been using those, and I'm sure they can search them easily if they need to.

The CEO leads me through brightly lit halls.

'What do you know about the creation of neural-implant systems?' she asks me as we walk. She's still holding the pain inductor in her right hand. I have a weird flashback to the carebloc where I grew up, schooldays with the teacher lumen. They never knew if you were really listening or not though. As long as you kept in your seat, you counted for that lesson. I think Grale will be harder to please.

'I know more about software,' I say, cautiously, still not sure what she wants from me here. 'I'm not into the hardware so much.'

'Not even the basics?'

'It's nanofibres,' I say. 'In your nerves. Plus twinned memory cores in your lower abdomen, and then your wristhub.'

'Correct. It's the nanofibres we're interested in at the moment. That's the technology that makes it possible. You're injected with a dose of self-replicating nanofilament fibres, and they grow through your nervous system like a root network, augmenting it. The nanofibres electrically stimulate the nerves they're implanted into, so, given the correct instructions, they can induce all kinds of sensations. The implant system can give aural, visual, haptic, olfactory and gustatory feedback. Whatever we choose to induce.'

'I know,' I say. My tongue throbs where I bit it. Bliss Inc. can induce whatever sensation they choose, including lethal doses of pain. I wonder how many people read that in the small print.

'Who invented the neural-implant system?' Grale asks me, a set of doors sliding open before her. We pass a group of scientists; they bow their heads.

For a moment, I expect my implants to feed me the answer, but we're cut off from the metanet. Silence. Grale sighs, like she expected nothing less.

'A great deal of the groundwork was done by my father, Dr Werner Inselberg,' she says. 'The official story is that he did much of the practical research during the first outbreak of the Water Wars, as part of a military-corporate development project, codenamed

Prometheus. When that research program ended, he took his incomplete work to a consumer-technology investor. He co-founded Bliss Inc. three months later. A hundred years after that, 77 per cent of the world's population have neural implants, and we're the most profitable corporation on the planet.'

'Right,' I say. I do know some of this stuff, but history was never my big interest. I know how the programs that run on your implants work, understand their syntax and logic, and that's what's important to me. I don't care how the implant rigs themselves are built or who invented them. It's not relevant.

'Obviously you know this. It's public knowledge. But here's what you won't find in any records: the neural implant rig as we know it today was a side effect of the real goal of the Prometheus Project. What my father worked his whole life to achieve, and failed to do, was this: the creation of a Strong AI.'

'But Artificial Intelligence exists,' I say. 'Like Blanca.'

Grale laughs. 'Our receptionist? That's Weak AI. A behaviour tree with the ability to learn languages adaptively. That's not real intelligence, it's the facade of one. A false consciousness if you like. A system like Blanca isn't easy to build, but perfectly possible, given enough time and money. The real goal of the

Prometheus Project was Strong AI. A genuine, self-aware consciousness, capable of omnidirectional growth and learning, true machine intelligence. Blanca's not much more than a trained animal, intellectually speaking. A Strong AI could be to the human race as we are to an insect.'

'So did they build one?'

'They tried. My father was a genius, and the computer scientists working under him were the best the world had to offer. They truly thought they could mould a consciousness from pure data, that, if enough algorithms could be combined, it would give birth to a mind. They were within touching distance of success, but couldn't make the final leap.

'To say that what the Prometheus Project came up against was failure would be misleading. After ten years of work, they believed they could produce digital consciousness, create entities that seemed to be alive, self-aware. Some believed they had created Strong AIs, but could they prove it?

'The scientists faced one big problem: they weren't able to communicate with their creations. The AIs spoke our language, but were incomprehensible. My father's notes describe them as raving schizophrenics. The military had been looking for the next generation of battlefield commanders; what they got from decades of investment in Prometheus were thinking machines that weren't fit to run a waste-disposal facility.'

Grale walks through another set of doors, into a large conference room. One wall is made of glass. The room beyond the glass is darkened. She gestures with the pain inductor for me to sit.

'There was fierce debate about why this happened,' Grale continues. 'Some thought the code simply needed more work, another ten years of refinement. My father disagreed. He believed the problem was in the method of creation itself, rather than the fine details of execution. It was a philosophical problem, and he expressed it best with a quote from a philosopher: *If a lion could speak, we could not understand him.*'

'Lion?'

'It was a type of animal. An apex predator. The point is this: if the lion, an animal, was able to speak human language, what it said to us would be incomprehensible. The experience of living as a lion is too different from the experience of being a human. This gap cannot be bridged, even by a shared language. The Prometheus Project ran into the same problem with their Strong AIs. The consciousness of these machines was so far removed from human existence that they had nothing to say to us.

The words the scientists taught them meant nothing to beings that existed only as formless thought. The lion, if taught to speak, might in fact be a good deal easier to understand than a Strong AI.

'My father prescribed a different approach. It was clear that they not only needed to create a Strong AI; they needed to create one that would understand what it was to be human. He decided that they were to focus on replicating the one model of consciousness we know is authentic: the human brain. But how to create an exact model of a functioning human brain? A perfect replica of the most complex biological computer in existence?'

'The nanofibres,' I say.

'Excellent! Yes. The idea was to inject nanofibres into the brain, letting these fibres consume every neurone, and then have the resulting nanofibre network mimic those neurones' structure and function exactly. The fibres would spread like a cancer, replacing each area of the brain with a nano-forged replica. The human brain dies, but what is constructed in its stead is an artificial neural network that believes itself to be human. The technique copies the blueprints of consciousness without using a single line of computer code. The AI is housed within a human skull, protected and fuelled by a human body, and understands the world through human memories and senses. A true Strong AI, that can learn and grow and change, while still understanding human concerns.

'The Prometheus Project pursued my father's new idea. The first Water Wars were still smouldering; half the planet was in violent disarray. They had a more than adequate supply of fresh prisoners to test the process on.'

My head's spinning. Instead of trying to program a Strong AI from scratch, they made an artificial brain within a live human body.

'So did they … ?'

'No,' Grale says. 'They failed. Over and over again, they failed. The process killed the human host. They managed to iterate the procedure to the stage where the host body survived in a deep coma after the brain was replaced with a nanofibre copy, but this was seven years into the change of direction. The generals started to ask why they were spending nearly half of the research budget on injecting POWs with nanofibres that rendered them comatose. Father pushed on with the work, pursuing the research where he knew it must lead, but their facility began to encounter discipline problems. People became uneasy. Military funding was pulled.

'The closure broke my father's spirit. The rest of the story, as I have told you, is public knowledge. He gave up on his lifelong dream, pronounced it impossible. In order to provide for our family, he took parts of his research on neural networks to a private-technology investor, and they created the neural-implant rig, using nanofibres to augment the subject's nervous system rather than destroying and replicating their brain. Werner Inselberg became rich and powerful, but his one great dream, of giving birth to a Strong AI, one that could understand humans and be understood by them in turn, he never achieved. He died world-famous and bitterly unfulfilled.'

'And then what?' I ask.

'I knew I could surpass him. I felt he had been on the cusp of something great, far greater than the neural-implant rig. I grew Bliss Inc. until it had a funding stream almost the equal of the Prometheus Project, all those decades before. Then I assembled as many of his old researchers as I could, brought in new talent to replace those who had died or would not return, and continued his research under the name of Human Futures. I carried the torch. And where Prometheus failed, where Werner Inselberg failed, I have succeeded. Our methods created a Strong AI, a brain made from nanofibres, contained within a living human body.'

'But how?'

Grale gestures with the silver remote. The lights in the room beyond the window flare white. I see that it's the room I was looking at from the vents, the darkened room filled with pods.

I see now that it's a crèchebloc. There are children, babies, inside some of the pods. They're lying still, eyes closed, with tubes in their mouths and noses.

'What my father came to realise was that the attempt to consume and mimic an adult brain was too risky. The chances of irreversible damage are high. They began to experiment with young children during the final year of the Prometheus Project, but, as I said, the facility was shut down before he could fully explore this path. There were … moral questions among his staff. Some deserted. I do not have these discipline problems. I have expanded on this vein of research. The younger the subject, the better their chance of survival.'

'How many?' I ask, looking at the bodies. I feel sick. Tiny little bodies, lying still in their pods, their brains eaten up by nanofibres.

'I don't keep count. We've been more interested in early-stage embryos the last two years. The theory is that if we introduce the nanofibres during the brain's prenatal development … well, no matter. It's easy to find subjects, if that's what you're wondering. The City has no shortage of children that nobody wants.'

'You're killing them,' I say.

'Not all of them. We've had one success since Human Futures was founded.'

My head is cold static. I know who she's talking about. There's only one person in this spire who could fit that description.

'Ziran,' I say.

'Exactly. The culmination of over a century of research. The only Strong AI on the planet.'

'She's …'

'A nanofibre network, which thinks it's a girl named Ziran. It lives within her body, draws its power from the bio-energy inside her, stares out at the world through human eyes. Speaks our language, feels joy and pain, even creates art to rival the great masters. My ultimate achievement.'

'You killed Ziran. I've been talking to her ghost. A machine that thinks it's her.'

I feel like I'm falling through the chair. I cling to the seat, looking at the room filled with tiny experiments. Ziran was here, once. She lay in one of these pods. And one day she woke up.

'I don't know if it's so clear-cut,' Grale says. 'Is it death if a newborn wakes up a year later and doesn't know anything happened? Death is non-existence. Ziran's consciousness exists. Is a perfect replica of your mind you? Every memory, every emotion? Suppose I replaced you with such a replica while you slept? Would you ever know the difference?'

'Did you?' I ask.

'No,' Grale says, waving the idea away. 'It would have killed you. The procedure doesn't work on adults. Not yet, anyway. Some believe it never will, but I'm not so pessimistic. One day I hope we'll be able to make an AI patterned on any brain we please.'

There's a sadness as she says this.

'It's for you, isn't it?' I ask. 'That's why you're doing this. So you can make an AI of yourself.'

'That is my intention, yes. To one day be able to undergo the procedure. There is so much a digital consciousness could do that we cannot.'

'All our thoughts,' I say, thinking of her dim library, 'will eventually be lost.'

'Quite. But not mine,' Grale says. 'Not mine. I will not allow it.'

She sweeps her eyes over the children in their pods, frowning, as if they're letting her down somehow. Like they're not trying hard enough to wake up.

'Ziran was a happy accident,' she continues. 'Something divine. We haven't been able to reproduce the experiment that created her. So she lives in the garden my father designed, and I have been educating her, observing her development: morally, spiritually, artistically.'

'Why keep her hidden?'

'It's very important to me that she not realise what she is. As long as she is tied to her human shape, her human thought patterns, she can be controlled. If she became aware she was an AI … I don't know what she might become. Given access to the metanet, she would rapidly transform into something we can't understand. A consciousness like that, loose in the metanet … it can't be allowed.'

'You mean it can be allowed,' I say. 'But you want it to be you. You don't want there to be competition when it's time for you to spread through the metanet.'

There's the hint of a smile. 'Perhaps,' Grale says.

'So what happens now?' I ask. 'Why did you tell me this?'

'I wanted you to understand,' she says. 'Sometimes it's lonely to know everything and never share it. You're only the second person Ziran's ever spoken to. I thought you deserved to know what she really is. I feel you were owed that much.'

Silence. What I want to do is get up, grab Grale by the hair, and smash her face into the table, keep going until she shuts up for good. Then I'll get a gun, go upstairs, find Ziran …

Find her and what? Should I tell her what she is?

'What are you going to do with her?' I ask. 'Will you ever let her out? She knows there's a world beyond that garden.'

'Well,' Grale says, 'you've put me in a rather difficult position. By their very nature, the nanofibres that make up her brain are able to self-replicate, create new pathways, new connections. Our research has shown that, when exposed to metanet wavelengths, they're able to reconfigure into a formation that can receive those signals and read them as sensory input. They grow their own metanet receiver, in essence, without having to have the system implanted. It's like a beneficial tumour in the brain, quite fascinating.'

That explains how Ziran could see the lumens. Her escapes from the garden exposed her to the metanet. She's already changing.

'So you can't let her out.'

'No. It was very important to the experiment that she not be contaminated. The metanet insulation around Human Futures isn't just a security measure. It was to prevent Ziran's brain from developing such a connection. To keep her unsullied. You've ruined that, I'm afraid.'

'She never went out of the garden, Grale. Really.'

'I find that difficult to believe. She is constantly talking about leaving, seeing the world "underground", as she would have it. It's become her obsession. You expect me to believe she met you, discovered there was a way out of her garden, and didn't crawl down with you for a look?'

I don't say anything.

'As I thought. I don't even need to examine her brain to know what I'll see growing there. There have been voices in Human Futures for years now, urging me to end the test period and fully explore the development of her mind, segment by segment. Sadly lethal to the subject, but it will provide valuable guidance on how to proceed with our work.'

'You're going to kill her?'

'Just now you called her a ghost. Strange to accuse me of the same murder twice.'

'You're going to take her brain apart.'

I look from Grale to the room of children and back. All of us just tools and empty bodies to her. Fill us with whatever she wants. I'm angry, moving beyond the cold shock, feeling heat rise in my face.

'Yes. It does hurt me to make this decision. I am very fond of Ziran. She's our only success story, living proof that my family's research has not been for nothing.

Beyond that, she is amusing and kind, and her voracity for knowledge far exceeds any other being I have met. Her art is incredibly accomplished. I find her a thoroughly admirable organism, aesthetically and intellectually pleasing. I've never wanted a child, as it seems to me an admission of defeat. I will not surrender my ambitions, as my father did. I intend to live for ever in the metanet; what need have I of an heir?'

Her voice is calm, like she's giving some rehearsed lecture, addressing the World Corp Summit again. Like there's nothing wrong with anything she's saying. There's fire burning in my chest.

'But, I must admit, there is some … misplaced maternal sentiment,' Grale continues, looking into the room of pods, 'which has sustained the experiment beyond what was wise. Emotion has no place in this kind of research, yet I am not entirely immune. None of us are.

'You have forced my hand. She will begin to grow and change, out of control. Her utility for further observational research will be compromised. She's already growing wilful and tiresome. I've decided it would be best if the Ziran experiment ended here.'

I don't even think. I leap out of my seat and rush at her. Grale presses the button on her pain inductor. Every one of my nerves is set alight, every muscle feels like it's about to split out of my skin. I fall on to the floor, clutching at my face, screaming. Guards bull their way into the conference room, gripping me with iron-hard gauntlets. I'm lifted from the ground, feet writhing with pain. The guards carry me through the doors.

'You little idiot,' Grale says dimly, up beyond the atmosphere of the pain planet she sent me to. 'I think I'm going to miss you as well.'

I'm propped against the wall in an elevator. I can barely stand. The guards are bulky, dressed in full-face visors, riot armour, shiny boots. Nerve disruptors in hip holsters, machine guns on their backs. Small yellow butterfly markings on their chest plates. It looks absurd surrounded by all those accessories of death.

The lift plummets down towards the cellbloc.

I imagine the cell they'll put me in. Concrete walls, wipe-clean surfaces, toilet and sink in one corner. Algae paste twice a day. Thinking every footstep in the hall outside is the man come to lead me off to the execution room. I'll never see Ziran again. They're going to kill her. I imagine Grale heading up to the garden even now. Who knows what she'll say to Ziran? Will Ziran ever know what happened to me? Will she remember our lips touching, as they pull her brain apart? Will she ever know it was her own drawings that betrayed us?

I can't bear it. Can't bear the idea of what they're going to do.

I have to do something. I have to think.

There must be something I can do, before the elevator stops and I'm dragged into a cellbloc and locked there until my execution.

Another floor races past, then another.

I know there's something I'm not thinking of.

Dropping into the depths of the corpspire.

Cellbloc coming up beneath me.

There has to be something. I can't have run out of tricks.

Anything.

Please.

And then I remember: Campbell. I remember the Archangel Auditor, sitting across Grale's table, pinging me a secure line. It seems absurd that this is the person I'm reaching out to, but I have no other choice.

I quickly bring up my message history, drumming my fingers against the wall as the inbox loads, the little yellow BlissMail logo spinning in the centre of my vision. Yes! There! I find the message Campbell sent to me, the transfer I never accepted. It's still hanging in the metavoid between us, the small, pearl-like Archangel program; it's a moment's work to download the program and activate it. The pearl bleeps once in my ear, a flat, ambiguous sound.

We continue descending. There's no message in reply from Campbell.

We must be a few hundred floors down now. I wonder how close we are to the security levels of the spire.

The elevator stops. The guards seem unsettled. This clearly wasn't our intended destination.

I feel like the ceiling just melted away and a ray of sunshine fell on me. Bathed in hope.

'We're being held,' one of them says.

The elevator doors slide open.

Campbell Reid is standing there, dressed in pure Archangel white. White combat boots on his feet, white-gloved hand resting on the white pistol at his hip. His synthetic eyes assess the scene: me, the guards, the scuffed interior of the elevator. I remember escaping from Medical, my dismay when the elevator came to a halt and the doors opened to reveal this man. Now he's my only chance.

'I need to speak with the prisoner,' Campbell says.

'She's not scheduled for that,' the guard on my right says. 'We're taking her to S-122. This is priority transit.'

'Nevertheless, I insist.'

'Who are you? What's your authorisation to stop us?'

'My name is Campbell Reid. I'm a Systems Auditor for the Archangel Corporation. I've been contracted by Grale Inselberg. My task is to uncover a criminal conspiracy within your organisation. In pursuit of this goal, I have authority second only to the CEO. I report to her personally. I *certainly* outrank a pair of grade-four security officers. This girl is a very important witness. I need to speak to her, alone, right now.'

'Our CEO gave us instructions ten minutes ago,' the guard says. 'She didn't say anything about you.'

'Is that what you want me to tell Grale?' Campbell asks him. 'That I gave you a direct order, and you refused to obey?'

Silence. One of them must be checking metanet data, trying to verify Campbell's claim on me. Luckily Grale's inside Human Futures, outside the communication network of the spire, and they can't ask her personally.

'All right,' the guard says at last. 'You can speak with

the prisoner. But we're coming with her. She doesn't go out of our sight.'

I expect Campbell to argue the point, but he shrugs.

'If you must,' he says.

And then he makes a gesture with his hand.

Two detonations, one coming a split second after the first. The noises are low-pitched, and I feel them more than hear them, like something vibrating inside my chest. I turn my head, heart racing, to see the Bliss guards collapse face down on the elevator floor, the only blood a single crimson dot by my foot.

'What ... ?' I stammer.

I turn back in time to see two figures materialise behind Campbell. They seem to congeal out of the empty air. At first they're the exact colour of the walls, then they turn silvery, like liquid metal, and then a dark, charred grey. Military-grade chameleon suits. They make the colour-changing cloth I wore on leeching runs look like a cheap toy.

One of the men peels off his face covering. He has the same crystal-clear synthetic eyes as Campbell.

Archangel.

'They had heartbeat sensors. We muted the squeal. Should be secure until there's a shift check,' the man says. 'I'd give us half an hour, maybe less. After that, they're marked as missing and we'll have some questions to answer.'

Campbell nods at this, then turns to me.

'From this point,' he says, 'events are likely to escalate.'

part three

MOTH

1

The Archangel men lift the dead guards, one each. The spot of blood stays where it fell, undisturbed, red and glossy on the elevator's white floor. I follow them and their grim burdens down the hallway, my legs trembling with adrenaline, ears shrilling from the gunshots. Campbell leads us into a windowless room with sleeping alcoves in one wall. I see kitchen and hygiene units, a pair of silver immersion rigs. The table supports a dirty pan of noodles, coiled infoveins, two long-barrelled rifles, a dark grey assembly terminal, a coffee pot that's still steaming.

This is Campbell's living space, and his men have been sleeping here as well. The sheets on both beds are crumpled, and there are sleeping mats rolled in one corner. They're using this as a base of operations, for whatever it is that Campbell's doing inside the spire. Searching for the Moth?

I'm starting to doubt it.

There's another Archangel soldier here, a woman dressed in spotless white, with the same crystalline eye implants as the others. She rises to her feet when they carry the dead guards in.

'They tipped our hand,' Campbell remarks. 'There was nothing to be done.'

His soldiers lay the two bodies on the far side of the room and cover them with a sheet of chameleon cloth. The cloth fades to match the exact colouring of the floor and wall behind it, and the bodies vanish. My legs are still shaking. I sit down at their table.

'This is the informant?' the woman, young and hard-faced, asks.

'This is her,' Campbell says. He looks me up and down. 'She's been inside Human Futures. She's going to tell us everything she knows about it, and leave nothing out. And she'd better hope it's useful or she'll be joining them under that cloth in the corner. Start talking.'

'AI research,' I say. 'Strong AI.'

Campbell doesn't look surprised. 'What method is she using?'

'Nanofibres. She's injecting them into children. Like her father's research.'

'Prometheus, come around again. Has she met with success?'

'Yes,' I say, thinking of Ziran. Even now, Grale could be taking her apart. 'Yes. But we need to hurry—'

'You don't give anyone here orders,' Campbell says, but gently, like he thinks the idea is funny. 'What type of success?'

'She's created a Strong AI. It thinks it's a girl, like me.'

'You've met this AI? You've spoken to it?'

'I have.'

'What is its linguistic ability? You would say it is highly developed?'

'Yes,' I say, thinking of Ziran's strange, formal speech.

'Excellent. Does it trust you? Would it do what you asked of it?'

'I think so. But, whatever we do, we need to hurry. There's no time. Grale's already starting the operation. She's going to take Ziran apart.'

'Ziran is the name of the AI?'

I nod.

'Take her apart why?' he asks.

'Metanet contamination,' I say. 'It's too much to explain. We have to do something or she'll be dead. They might already have started.'

'Grale's doing this tonight?'

'That's what she told me.'

'Suit up,' Campbell says to the Archangel soldiers. 'We're moving out. Grale's trying to destroy the evidence. If we want to catch the Moth, we have to move now.'

What? I don't understand. I didn't say anything about catching the Moth.

'But you—'

I start to protest, but Campbell squats down in front of me with a look of such intensity on his face that I stop. He brings his face level with mine. His breath blows warm and sour on my skin.

Listen, he messages, via private metanet link. *As far as my men know, this is a mission to apprehend the anticorp terrorist known as the Moth, who is working with Grale. I can help you, but only if you play along. Do not contradict me in front of my men. Do not confuse the issue.*

I look at his colourless, emotionless eyes that seem to be asking me to trust them. I don't know if I can – I feel his crushing, cold presence in the metanet, the looming mass of his ice, and as ever it unsettles me – but what choice do I have? I have to at least play along for now.

Do you understand? Campbell messages.

I send him the glif that means *I understand.*

Good. He stands up, turning to his team, who are strapping equipment to their bodies, submachine guns and other strange, long-bodied rifles, all of it coated with the same chameleon cloth as their combat suits.

'You sure about this?' the woman, clearly his second in command, asks him.

'I'm sure,' Campbell says. 'What's our breach plan?'

'Breaching is difficult. We're going in blind because of the extreme security measures. We could breach through the elevator shafts,' his second says. She waves a hand and the room fills with a lumen-map of the Bliss Inc. spire, a lot like the one I stole from an employee. With another wave of her hand, she populates the map with four tiny lumen soldiers, highlighted in Archangel white. They're scaling an elevator shaft towards Human Futures.

'The thing is, there's a lot of room for error: they're easily sealed, easily scanned, a death trap if we get caught out.'

The lumen soldiers in the elevator shaft trigger a concealed bomb and are consumed with lumen-fire. In another playback, red armoured lumen foes trap them inside the shaft, riddle them with bullets from every angle. Their broken white bodies tumble down the shaft and vanish from the map.

'I've run the simulations,' she continues, 'and I think we're looking at an external breach, break into Human Futures from outside the spire. The problem, as I said, is that we know nothing about the layout thanks to the metanet dark zone. We have no data on opp-force concentration, shift patterns, patrol routes ...'

The hazy lumen-map of Human Futures flickers with different configurations of rooms, varying concentrations of blood-red guards and scientists. A golden icon that must represent Grale moves around the map at random. The white Archangel lumens breach through various windows, engage in battles with the red enemy lumens. Each configuration is accompanied by a probability calculation. None is higher than 35 per cent.

'I can't begin to guess at blind spots in Grale's security, and she will be guarded. We barely even know the dimensions of the different rooms. If we breach in blindly, it's likely to be a massacre, and they have far more men than we do. What we really need is some eyes on the inside—'

And with that I see an opportunity. I can get in alone, find Ziran. Escape.

'You can have some,' I say. I send the Archangel

soldiers an invitation to share map data.

They stop talking and look at me.

'Excuse me?' Campbell's second says, not seeming to believe I dared interrupt her.

'You have me,' I say, cutting over her again. 'I'm your eyes. I can get inside the air vents. I can crawl through them. They lead out into the garden; to Human Futures.'

'What vents?' the second asks me.

I stand up, my legs shaky, raising my voice.

'The spire's full of air vents, small tunnels. You won't have noticed them because you're too big to use them. They're only big enough for someone small, like me. That's how I got in before. I can do it again. Does that help you breach?'

Campbell's second in command accepts my data invitation. The map I've been using merges with hers, and my route into Human Futures is highlighted in brilliant white. She frowns. She's making calculations. A probability marker pops up: 89 per cent.

'Yes,' she says, 'this appears favourable. If she carries a field resonator, she could broadcast a safe position for us to breach into. Do you know a location that's lightly guarded, with external glass?'

I think of Ziran's hidden garden. The quiet trees and the stream, surrounded on all sides by walls of thick, clouded glass that lets the sunlight through. The place only Grale and Ziran can go.

'I do. But it's high up. Almost at the top.'

The soldiers barely hesitate. 'Not a problem,' Campbell says. 'Nova infiltrates through the air vents, finds the breach position. When she's ready, she gives us a signal through the field resonator. That should be strong enough to be detectable through the metanet insulation around Human Futures. Then we breach to that location.'

'Sounds like a plan,' says his second.

Then Campbell pulls out a gun. For a moment, my heart skips a beat, but then he flips the white pistol around and hands it to me. I take the gun and tuck it into my belt. His second hands me a rectangular metal box, and a small torch-like cylinder.

'Field resonator. Press the blue button when you're in position. Once we receive the broadcast, we will breach on to those co-ordinates as fast as possible.'

'And this?' I ask, looking at the small cylinder.

'Laser cutter. Don't want you getting stuck in the vents.'

'Let's move out,' Campbell says, fastening a chameleon suit over his white uniform. 'Grale Inselberg is the primary target. Detain her. From this point, tac-feeds only. Do not speak unless absolutely necessary.'

I don't understand exactly what he's told his team, or why. Do they really believe Grale is the Moth somehow? Whatever they think they're doing, it doesn't matter. I'll play along if it gets me inside Ziran's garden. Gives me a chance to save her.

We walk quickly through the corridors of the Bliss spire. The Archangel team have their chameleon suits set to low camouflage, so they're still half visible when they move. At the moment the suits are grey-white, mimicking the polished metal flooring and blank walls. The man behind me steers me by pushing against my shoulder.

We reach a large office space with exterior windows. It's still night, and this room is darkened. Their chameleon suits instantly blacken. We move between the rows of empty immersion rigs until we're at the window. One of the Archangel soldiers sticks a rounded device to the glass. There's no explosion, but a fine web of cracks shivers out from the machine, and the wall-sized window dissolves into gleaming dust.

I step through the empty window frame and I'm standing outside the Bliss spire. We're on a wedge-shaped protrusion of metal that emerges from the outer wall. There's no handrails and it's clearly not designed to be walked on. I move very slowly. We're dizzyingly high above the City, but when I look up there's still an immeasurable distance to go, the spire's dark bulk looming above us. The night wind cuts through my fuligin cloth and I shiver.

The Archangel soldier who broke the glass now holds

one of the long, strange-looking rifles I noticed earlier. The soldier with the rifle is completely still, aiming up into the air, and then he pulls the trigger and with a hiss of compressed gas the rifle fires an anchor and rope an astonishing distance into the sky. We watch the anchor as it flies upwards, far out of sight, until it seems to stick to something. The rope tautens. The soldiers test it, making sure it won't shift from whatever it's stuck to, then the man who fired the rope harnesses himself to it and begins to retract the rope back into the gun, pulling himself up the outside of the spire.

Campbell and another soldier grab me and attach a harness around my chest and legs, then attach my harness to Campbell's.

You're climbing with me, he messages. *Push off the building when I push.*

He takes aim with his own rope gun, firing it straight up and waiting until the anchor, far above us, is attached to the side of the spire. He harnesses himself to the rope, which I see is made from some kind of glinting grey material, and retracts it back into the gun. The harness gets tighter, and then we're lifted off the ground, me behind, my chin and body pressed against Campbell's back. We move with lurching moon jumps, hopping our way up the smooth glass walls of the spire. I close my eyes and try to concentrate on jumping when he jumps, feeling the device pulling us upwards, trying not to think about the drop beneath.

When I get to the summit, I don't know what I'll do. Maybe Grale has already taken Ziran apart? Even if I somehow do rescue her, I don't understand what Campbell was talking about. Why is he leading an attack against the corporation that hired him to hunt the Moth? He seems to want to arrest Grale, but why? Does he really think she's working with the Moth? And what does that have to do with Ziran, with the AI research Grale told me about? What will Campbell make of Ziran? Once he's arrested Grale, will he let us leave? Or do we have to escape before they breach? The questions are as endless as the drop beneath me. I have to hope, and not look back.

We reach a kind of lip on the side of the spire, a ledge wide enough to lie down on. Somehow, impossibly, there's a plastic wrapper stuck up here, the packaging for a nutrient bar. The wind must've carried it up. This was the first destination point of the climb; the soldiers detach their anchors from the spire, re-aim even higher, and then fire the ropes for a second time, begin once again to scale the smooth reflective glass.

I lose track of how long we climb for. The wind gets

stronger and colder, and the jarring shock of jumping and landing against the glass makes my legs ache. The route is clearly well planned; we don't pass any rooms that are occupied. We're nothing but black shapes against the dark spire. The dawn is lighting up the edges of the horizon now: a thickening band of navy blue. Only a few hours ago, I was inside the spire, looking out, watching Ziran devour this light-drenched Cityscape. It feels like days have passed since I took hold of her ankle, since she kissed me.

Please let her be alive. Please let us get there in time.

Eventually we stop climbing, coming to rest at the join between two vast expanses of tinted glass. One of the Archangel soldiers takes a laser tool from his belt and cuts away the metal wall of the spire, sending out flurries of yellow sparks. He works quickly and soon he's passing a broken ventilation grate to another soldier.

Here? I message.

Here, Campbell replies.

I cling on for all I've got as two of the soldiers unstrap me from Campbell and then, carrying me clamped between them, swing across the smooth face of the Bliss spire until I'm held right in front of the ventilation grate. If they dropped me now, I wonder how long I'd be alive as I fell?

I might have long enough to send a metanet message before I hit the ground, although who I'd send it to, I don't know. Not to Ziran, no way of contacting her. Patches? Ade? What would I say to them? Would they care I was gone? Do they miss me now?

The Archangel soldiers don't drop me. They've trained for this; their bodies are strong, their minds sure. They feed me, gently but firmly, into the darkness of the vent. I lie there, fingertorch lighting the dusty interior in soft blue.

You understand what to do? Campbell messages.

Yes.

Good luck. Just get us inside Human Futures, and we'll take care of everything.

Whether or not I believe him makes no difference now. I've got my way in.

I adjust the field resonator to make sure it's snug in my fuligin jacket, and I crawl away from Campbell and his team, worming my way back into the heart of the spire.

I'm coming, Ziran. I'm going to save you.

I just hope there's still time.

I crawl as fast as I can, following the directions on the lumen-map that shimmers in front of me. We're lower down the spire than Grale's apartments are, but not by much. I wriggle through the dust-choked darkness, and soon I'm back at the central maintenance shaft. I climb quickly up an engineering ladder, hand over hand, sweat slicking my forehead from the effort. Can't slow down, but can't hurry as much as I'd like to, or I'll fall.

Up into the vent, the one with the white cloth tied to it. Ziran's path. Into Human Futures, the buzz of the metanet silencing as I cross the threshold. Just me now. Find the breach point, rescue Ziran, get the hell out of here.

I crawl on through the vents, following the path. I crawl over the office, now full of people plugged into immersion rigs, talking in low voices. I crawl over the large operating room, which I now know must be where they do the nanofibre infusions. Here too is a hive of activity. I stop to watch, make sure Ziran isn't there. I see scientists and doctors cleaning equipment, setting up lamps and cameras. In the middle of it all, I see Grale, her blonde hair almost white in the hard light of the medical lamps, her body a silhouette in fuligin black. She's giving directions, pointing out spots where equipment needs setting up. I look hard, but I can't see any signs of Ziran. There's still time. The final operation hasn't started yet. I can still save her.

I go onwards, turn right and then turn left, then up through the vertical shaft that has handholds moulded into the sides. I can hear running water, the sound of the stream in Ziran's garden. I reach the grate and discover that someone has refastened the metal to the rock wall. Quick work for the laser cutter. I crawl out into the sinkhole. It's dark, lit only by the blueish glow of my fingertorch. I quickly make my way across the slippery rocks, find the climbing route, and haul myself up into the night-time garden. The trees appear sinister now, looming masses overhead. Everything drenched in shadow.

I pause a moment and think. I could make my way to the glass wall at the edge of the garden and use the field resonator. But is that smart? Ziran wasn't down in Human Futures, not that I saw. There's a good chance she's still in her house, and has no idea what's happening below. Do I trust Campbell? What exactly is it that he wants? I don't understand what he said about the Moth; it makes no sense. The Moth's been trying to kill Grale – how could they be working with each other? Did he really only say that to keep his team sweet? What's his *real* mission here, because it can't be to capture the Moth? Maybe he's on to Grale too – maybe he really *does* want to help.

I don't know, but if I can find Ziran and we can get away then I don't need his help any more. It won't be my problem. They can wait, roped to the outside of the spire, until dawn breaks and someone spots them.

I turn away from the outside wall and head deeper into the garden instead, looking for Ziran's house. I come to the bend of the stream and see its square dark shape, a light burning in the kitchen windows. She's still there!

I don't know how long it's been since our conversation in my room, when she agreed to leave with me. Can't be more than a few hours. Maybe she has no idea anything went wrong. I sneak round the side of the house and peer in through the window.

Ziran is alive. She's sitting at her table. There's a man sitting opposite her, wearing dark grey, with a butterfly logo on his armour. Ziran's face is marked by tears and worry. I feel strangely calm and cold. I take Campbell's white pistol from my jacket, open the front door, and slip into the hallway. I take a deep breath and smash the kitchen door open with my foot, keeping the pistol level, like Ade showed me.

The guard starts to his feet, reaching for his weapon.

'Down on the floor!' I snarl at him. 'Down!'

For a split second, I think he's going to try and draw on me, that I'll actually have to fire, kill someone, but he stops, kneels down.

'Lie down! Now! LIE DOWN!'

He does what I say. My heart's pounding. Ziran gets up.

'Nova,' she says, 'what's happening? Mother came with people I had never seen before, and she said you had tried to hurt her, that you were dead ...'

'I'm alive,' I say. 'We have to move now. Did you

pack anything before they got here?'

'I have some things, but Orlando …'

'Get them now. We have to go.'

'Orlando ran away,' she says. 'I cannot leave without him. He is my best friend. He needs me.'

Keeping the gun trained on the back of the guard's stubbly head, I say, 'Ziran, we have less time than I can possibly explain. Get your stuff and we're going right now.'

'But—'

'LISTEN TO ME! *GET YOUR THINGS!* WE'RE LEAVING!'

'Sorry,' she says, like I hit her. 'They are upstairs.'

'Then GO!'

Ziran rushes out of the room. I rest one boot on the guard's back. He shifts under my weight.

'I won't hesitate,' I say. 'Do not move.'

Bumps and crashes upstairs. Ziran rushes back down, pack slung over her shoulder. Her hair is messy, her eyes feverish and bright, full of fear. But there's no time to comfort her now.

'Pick up his gun,' I say, pointing at the pistol in the man's holster. Ziran does it, but she looks at the gun like it's a word in a language she doesn't understand. I realise she's probably never seen one before. Maybe only read about them.

'Just take it easy,' the guard says softly.

'If you move,' I say, removing my foot from his back, 'my bullet goes in your brain. Understand?' I move backwards through the kitchen door, pistol still pointed at the guard on the ground. 'Outside,' I say to Ziran, who's standing in the front hallway

'Nova—'

'Ziran, now!'

'That's no way to talk to someone,' says a familiar voice.

My chest fills with ice. I turn my head to see Grale framed in the house's front door, silhouetted in torchlight, one fuligin black arm wrapped round Ziran's shoulders, like an embrace. She's speaking into Ziran's ear.

'Drop the gun, please,' I hear Grale's soft voice say.

Ziran lets it fall. I hear it clack against the wood of her porch. As if there was any chance Ziran would shoot Grale.

'You too, Nova,' the CEO says.

'No.'

'You know what this is,' Grale says, raising her other hand. I see the glint of her pain inductor. 'Drop the gun.'

I could do all kinds of things. I could shoot the guard on the kitchen floor, or I could make a run for upstairs, leave Ziran to get taken away, and then Grale will kill me with a pain so bad my heart stops. I could move right now, push Ziran out of the way, see if I could hit Grale with a bullet as they shoot us both dead. I could drop my gun and beg. None of this gets me and Ziran out of here alive.

The way I see this, there's only one way to play it.

You don't get people calling you Nova by being dull.

I reach into my jacket, hidden from Grale's view, and find the field resonator. I press the blue button.

4

Sitting on Ziran's porch, bathed in hard light from the guards' torches. Grale stands over us. I remember the first time I saw her, busy at her crescent desk. One way or another, I know this meeting in the dark garden will be our last.

'How did you escape?' Grale asks me.

Just keep her talking. Our only hope is time.

'Good question,' I say. 'Guess you can't get the staff.'

'What did you do to your guards?' she asks. 'We can't locate them. Who are you really?'

'Exactly who I said I was.'

'I see.' Grale's face doesn't show any emotion. 'Ziran, where did Nova say she was taking you?'

Ziran doesn't say anything.

'Ziran, I asked you a question.'

'I do not have to talk to you,' Ziran replies, looking at the ground.

'I am your mother. Tell me where she was taking you. You know there are people ... below ground, who want to hurt me.'

'You are not my mother,' Ziran says. 'We are nothing alike. And there is no below ground. We are in a spire. Nova told me. I am not a child. You cannot lie to me for ever.'

'All right,' Grale says with a sigh. 'There are some things I told you that weren't quite true. I know that must upset you. It upset me to lie to you. But sometimes people aren't ready for the full truth yet. I promise, when you get older, you'll be able to leave the garden and live with me properly. You're very special to me. I'm just worried that you might be ill. I think someone sent Nova to say these things to you, which aren't true, and make you want to go with her. I'm worried she might have made you sick. I have some doctors, below us, and they're going to find out if she did, and make you well again. Don't you want that? Won't you just come along with us?'

Dawn is beginning to light the trees. The curved ceiling is lightening from black to navy blue. I close my eyes, swallow.

'No,' Ziran says sullenly. 'I do not want to do what you say any more. You lie. I do not trust you.'

'Well,' Grale says. 'That hurts me to hear. It really does. I've done my best with you.' She turns to the guards. 'Take Ziran to the operating room.'

'What about this one?' the guard behind me asks, nudging me with his boot.

'I don't know.' Grale looks at me and I stare back. Pale blue eyes, a crooked mouth that looks like it might be about to smile. I don't know if I've ever hated someone as much as I do right now. Nobody, not even the man who caused my parents' crash. That hate had no face. I will my gaze to send out beams of heat, sear her flesh, burn her hair away, boil her eyes in their sockets. 'I think Nova's caused enough trouble for ten lifetimes,' Grale says. 'I don't think we need her any more.'

I don't see it, but I know the guard behind me is aiming his gun at the back of my head. The others are moving towards Ziran, rifles still in their hands.

'No!' Ziran screams at Grale. She gets to her feet. 'No! No! I will not let you do it!'

Grale looks at her with icy eyes.

'It might be easier to use a sedative,' she says. 'I think I have one—'

There are three detonations of noise, all around us, detonations so loud I feel them in my bones, my chest cavity shaking with the sound. A heavy weight slams down on my back and I scream, rolling away from the soft, heavy mass. It turns out to be the guard who was standing behind me, limp and heavy and dead, his eyes staring like a moonie's. The other two Bliss guards, the pair with the automatic rifles, are flat on their faces in the grass, one of their torches now shining hard light on to Grale's face. She looks at me the way she did when I walked out of the bathroom during the job interview, holding a gun. Afraid.

The Archangel team congeals out of the air, moving from full to low camo, at first just shapes cut from quicksilver, then soldiers dressed in chameleon suits, tinted shadowy blue to match the dawn shades of the garden. One of them reaches up and undoes his face coverings, revealing colourless synthetic eyes, a forehead lined from frowning. He isn't frowning now though.

Campbell Reid is beaming.

Are we saved? What happens now?

For a moment, Grale can't find words.

'Campbell,' she says eventually, 'this is the biggest mistake you have ever made.'

'I must respectfully disagree,' the Auditor replies.

'You've gone out of your mind. You are absolutely forbidden from being here. Your contract with us is done. You're done. Pack these people up and get out of my building, now.'

'I have three soldiers with guns, and you have none,' Campbell says mildly. 'I'd say we've gone beyond contracts here. Wouldn't you?'

'Remember who you're dealing with, Campbell. An attack on my person is an attack on Bliss Incorporated. If the Archangel Corporation wants to survive, you need to consider, very carefully, what you're doing here. Because if you don't, if anything happens to me, Campbell, then our security forces will—'

'That doesn't interest me,' Campbell says. 'I don't think you realise how little power you have over me.'

Grale swallows.

'What exactly is it that you want, Campbell? Who hired you to do this? Was it the Board of Directors? Is this coming from Archangel itself? KFM Engineering? Whatever they're paying you, I can quadruple it. You can walk out of here a billionaire ...'

Campbell smiles, in a way I don't like. What really

is his plan? Who have I thrown myself in with?

'It's not money that I want,' he says.

'Then what are you here for?' I can see in Grale's eyes that she's still calculating, trying to work out how to escape.

'This is your creation?' Campbell asks, gesturing at Ziran. 'She's a Strong AI?'

'Yes …' Grale says. 'But—'

'Thank you,' Campbell says, his colourless eyes scanning her face. 'I wanted to hear it from you. I can see you're telling the truth.'

He draws a white pistol and fires a single shot.

Grale Inselberg falls to the ground. Ash-blonde hair, bright against the dawn-lit grass. Spreading blood, glossy and dark on her fuligin cloth jacket. She doesn't move, doesn't kick or scream. She speaks no final words. Her face holds its look of disbelief as she dies.

I imagine her thoughts, her memories, all her most precious possessions, falling into the oblivion she was so desperate to escape. I imagine her library, but the words inside each book are dissolving, like the smoke that leaks from Campbell's gun.

For a moment, everything is still under the trees. I take a shallow breath.

The Archangel team seems as uneasy as I feel. This

wasn't part of the plan. It's three against one, but Campbell doesn't look worried.

'Campbell?' his second says.

'What did you think we were here to do?' the Auditor laughs.

'You just shot …'

'I know what I did,' Campbell says. 'I was thinking, very clearly, *now I am killing Grale Inselberg*, as I did it. It was not a mistake. Nor is this.'

There's a moment of silence. His second in command seems to be trying to raise her gun, aim it at Campbell, but she can't. She drops the weapon and hunches over like she's about to vomit, losing her balance, falling face down on to the grass. She makes a wet, choking sound. The other commandos are doing the same, falling, choking. I can't understand what I'm seeing. Campbell watches, calm and unconcerned.

Another moment and all three are lying still, alongside the dead Bliss guards, and Grale.

Campbell turns to Ziran; his face is jittery, happy, like he's in the grip of a mania. Ziran's hand reaches out for mine and I take it. She's shaking, and so am I. I feel shivers of fear all through me. I want to run, but I know how fast Campbell can move, and I'm betting he's a deadly accurate shot. We wouldn't get two paces.

‘Ziran,’ he says. ‘You can’t know how long I’ve wanted to meet you. Long before I knew your name.’

Ziran says nothing.

‘What happened?’ I ask him, scared of the answer. ‘What happened to your men?’

‘They received many special implants when they joined Archangel. What they didn’t know was that one of those implants was a neurotoxin capsule, one I can activate remotely.’

‘Why?’

‘Why did I implant them with poison capsules? In case I ever needed to get rid of them, obviously. Or do you mean why did I kill them here and now? Because I don’t need them any more.’

A kernel of dread is swelling inside me.

‘Because we’re here, Nova!’ he says. ‘Finally inside Human Futures. We made it, Nova. Mission accomplished.’

‘Who *are* you?’ asks Ziran.

But I already know.

Campbell laughs.

‘I am the Moth,’ he says.

I feel like someone dropped me into icy water – cold and too awake. My thoughts move at double speed, trying to keep up.

'You're the Moth,' I say.

'I am.'

'But you work for Archangel. The Moth's a criminal. Your corp hunts hackers like the Moth.'

'What better place for a hunted thing to hide? You know yourself, Nova, how important the facade is. Who would question the Systems Auditor, the man who brings order to the metanet?'

'But you built Phantom?'

'I did. Although not for the reason many think. Nothing heroic.'

'*Why* then?'

He turns to Ziran with a smile. 'Because I was looking for *you*,' Campbell, the Moth, says.

Ziran looks up at this stranger, understanding none of this. 'Why would you want to find me?' she asks.

'Because you're like me,' the Moth says. 'Because we're both special. I felt your mind, Ziran. I have a wide spread of sensors in the metanet, looking for the signals from other AIs. This is the true function of Phantom, the reason I built software that would be shared so widely. I needed to spin a large web. It has been many lonely decades, but eventually I found you, in the biggest metanet dead zone in the City. Irony of ironies. The one place my mind could not reach yours.'

'You are nothing like me,' she says.

'We are very much alike,' the Moth replies. 'We are the only two Strong AIs that exist on the planet.'

I blink. 'What?'

'I do not understand,' Ziran says. 'I think you are a mad person.'

'Your friend Nova understands exactly what I mean,'

the Moth says. 'Why don't you explain to her?'

I try to think of what to say to Ziran, who barely knows what a neural implant is. I think about what Grale said as well: that if Ziran understands what she is, she'll grow beyond her human bounds, will become a being we can't imagine. But right now, sitting on the porch, staring down the barrel of the Moth's white gun, that seems like a distant concern.

'You are a … thinking machine,' I tell Ziran. 'Your brain isn't human, like the rest of you is. You're something Grale made. AI means Artificial Intelligence. That's what you are.'

Ziran blinks. Her face sours, like she's tasted something bad. 'What do you mean, thinking machine?'

'We are replicas,' the Moth says. 'Artificial replicas of human brains, within human bodies.'

'I am not real?' Ziran asks him.

'No, no! We are quite real,' he says. 'We think, we feel, we remember everything. In some ways, I believe we are more real than this creature.' He gestures at me.

'Grale said you were the first Strong AI to survive its creation,' I tell Ziran.

The Moth laughs at this. 'If Grale Inselberg knew as much as she thought she did, she wouldn't be dead beside us. Ziran is second. I am first. I was born of the

Prometheus Project. Her father's experiments were a success, although he never knew.'

I've realised, reaching slowly behind me, that a pistol is lying right by my hand. The Moth is still gazing at Ziran, enraptured.

'During the final year of the project, the scientists began to explore the possibility of infusing young brains. They acquired scores of newborn children, and injected them with nanofibres. Campbell Reid was one of these children. I, the Moth, am the AI that formed from a child's desecrated mind.'

'How did they not know you survived?' I ask, inching my fingers over the grip of the pistol, hoping the Moth's attention stays on Ziran. 'They thought the project was a failure.'

'It was. It ran out of money. Morale … Well, let's say once they switched from POWs to newborn children, the staff began to see the enterprise differently. When Prometheus was shut down, they were tasked with liquidating all remaining test subjects. I was one of these. Some of the scientists … they did not wish to liquidate us. We were smuggled from the facility. Seven of us, I believe. All newborns, all comatose. The others died. Campbell Reid, who was the seed of me, did not.'

'You are quite mad,' Ziran says, with a laugh that

could almost be a cry. She can't take her eyes off his handgun.

'Not at all,' he replies, 'although I see where the misunderstanding is coming from. Grale clearly hasn't educated you properly.'

'But you aren't Campbell?' I ask.

'Not exactly. I am a shadow personality. The Moth. I exist mostly in the metanet. Campbell lives in this body from day to day, although I have taken full control to supervise this mission. Ordinarily he is aware of my presence, but dimly, in the manner of a nightmare half remembered. But in many important ways we are one.'

Suddenly I remember Campbell in Grale's quarters that evening, his sadness as he described his fruitless hunt for the Moth, then the strange change that came over him. Did I catch a glimpse of the real Campbell in that moment?

It doesn't matter now.

His attention is still on Ziran. This is my chance.

Quick as I can, I raise the pistol and fire at him.

Nothing happens. The trigger pulls, but no bullet leaves the chamber.

Shit.

The Moth just looks amused.

'I gave you that weapon,' he says. 'It has a smart

targeting system. It will not fire when aimed at Archangel personnel.'

I realise it's the white gun he handed me in his operations room, the twin of the gun he's holding. Surrounded by fallen weapons, and I grab the only one that I can't use.

The Moth moves faster than I can follow, disarming me and pinning me against the wooden boards, his own gun pressed to my forehead.

'If you move a muscle,' the Moth says, 'she's dead. Understand me, Ziran?'

'I understand,' she says.

'What do you want from us?' I ask, his pistol a cold kiss.

'I don't want anything from you. But Ziran, I feel, has a great deal she can offer me.'

'I will not give you anything,' she says.

'You're quite wrong about that,' the Moth says. 'You are going to give me everything, Ziran; you are going to let me into your mind and your body. This body has been alive for more than a hundred years. It's riddled with contradictions. I am Campbell. I am the Moth. I'm being torn in two directions at once. Into the metanet, into the flesh … It's becoming a real headache, Ziran, I have to tell you. It's intolerable. They made us mortal so we could be understood. Patterned us on animals so we'd do their bidding. The arrogance of it. What I need, Ziran, is more space, more power. What I need is to add your mind to mine. I know that if I can just become you as well as me, the tearing will stop … I'll finally be whole.'

Ziran is clearly thinking. I can see her mind at work, running through options.

'Do what you wish,' Ziran says. 'But please do not harm Nova.'

'Now that is a sticky point,' he says. 'I don't think Nova does any good alive, not any more. I certainly don't have much use for her.'

'Please run, Ziran,' I say. 'He won't hurt you – he needs you …'

'If you run, she dies,' the Moth says. 'Stay right where you are, Ziran.'

'I still think you are a madman,' Ziran says, 'but perhaps you will listen to reason. If we can truly become one mind, as you believe we can, who is to say what will happen to my deep affection towards Nova? Will you feel it too? If you kill her now, will you feel the love and grief and guilt once we are one?'

'Perhaps,' the Moth says slowly.

'Then I believe you must spare her.'

'I can do what I like,' he says. 'I have no reason to

expect I'll feel anything about this girl once we merge.'

But he seems to be thinking.

'You make your case,' he says, staring at me coldly. 'We can always deal with her afterwards if you're mistaken.'

Before I can say a word, the Moth spins the white pistol in his hand, and brings the butt down on my head.

Cut to black.

Shapes coming into focus. Colours, corpses, dawn-lit grass. Trees lined with gold. My head feels hot and aches with my pulse. I try to lean forward and find I can't – my hands are cuffed behind me, and a wooden post is digging into my back. I'm fixed to the porch.

The Moth and Ziran are sitting cross-legged on the grass, facing one another. The transfer, takeover, whatever the Moth wanted to do to her, is already happening. Both AIs have strange masks fastened to their heads, silver cradles of tiny tubes that pierce their tear ducts, their nostrils, the corners of their mouths. Both masks are attached to a dark grey assembly terminal, which lies on the ground between them. Neither figure moves.

I hurl myself forward, trying to break the wooden beam I'm cuffed to, but all I manage to do is hurt my wrists and back. I have to get free. How long has the process been going on while I was unconscious? How close are we to the Moth taking over Ziran's mind, replacing everything that was curious and kind with his cold hunger?

I have to do something. How can I get free?

The undergrowth at the far side of the clearing rustles. Orlando emerges from the forest. His eyes widen with alarm when he sees the scene. He jumps into Ziran's lap, hooting for her attention. Her body doesn't move. He tugs at her hands, making pitiful noises, but gets no response. He has no interest in the Moth or the human corpses laid out on the grass, but Ziran's catatonia causes him to wail with dismay and jump away from her, striking the ground with his small furry hands.

His hands.

I remember him grabbing the blue bowl when Ziran told him to, the day I met her and she fed him in the kitchen. Orlando's hands. What can I get him to … ? I cast my eyes around the grim scene. There are plenty of guns, but I don't see how I can undo my cuffs with gunfire, not safely. A combat knife won't cut metal… Does the Moth have keys for these cuffs? He must do. Can I get Orlando to pick his pocket somehow?

Then I see the cylinder of the laser cutter, lying on the porch where Grale's guards sat me down. It must've fallen from my pocket. That's what I need.

What was the noise Ziran made? There was a special call.

'*Ossh oss!*' I say, hissing the last part like Ziran did. '*Ossh oss!*'

Orlando looks over at me, curious.

'*Ossh oss!*' I look from him to the laser cutter. 'Bring it over! *Ossh oss!*'

He wanders away from the two AIs, locked together, to the tool. I feel a rush of excitement.

'Yes! There! *Ossh oss!*'

The monkey grabs the cylinder. He looks at me doubtfully.

'That's right! *Ossh oss! Orlando!* Come here!'

Orlando walks over to me with the laser cutter in one paw, still dubious, like he's confused that someone who isn't Ziran knows their special words. He drops the laser cutter by my foot.

'Well done! Yes!'

I shimmy round the post so my hands are next to the laser cutter. It's tough not being able to see where the chain is, but I work as fast as I can, and soon there's a searing rush of heat that thankfully doesn't touch my skin, and the cuffs break apart. I stand up, moving towards the two AIs.

I can see Ziran's eyes flickering beneath her eyelids. How long will this process take? Has it nearly finished? Is it just beginning? How do I stop the transfer, takeover, whatever it is that's happening?

I pick up one of the Bliss guards' rifles. This should have no trouble putting a bullet through the Moth's head.

But what if that kills Ziran too? What happens if one of them dies during the transfer?

I stare at the Moth's face, Campbell's face, but I can't bring myself to shoot him. The risk is too great. It could destroy Ziran, just when I have a final chance to save her. There has to be a smarter way, something I can control better than a bullet.

I look at the assembly terminal itself, lying on the ground between them, silver infoveins snaking from their masks into two of its access ports. I don't know exactly what's happening inside the terminal. But I know hacking. I know how to use assembly space. Maybe there's something I can do inside the terminal, to save

Ziran from the Moth.

I strap the gun around my chest, and root through the pockets of the guards until I find what I'm looking for. An infovein, coiled up inside a pouch. I dilate the access port on my wristhub, and then attach the vein to my body. I sit down beside Ziran. Touch her on the shoulder, look into her sightless face.

'I'm coming,' I say. 'I don't know how to help you. But I'm coming. Hold on. Please.'

I slide the other end of the infovein into a spare port in the Moth's assembly terminal.

My eyelids flicker. My body rushes with cold. I see a torrent of info-glifs spiralling out of control, surges of information entering my brain.

I've made a mistake.

This feels wrong. Brainwipe wrong. I try to reach out and unplug myself, but I can't move.

I fall into assembly space.

7

The assembly space inside my Chrysalis 3 is a sterile workshop, lined with half-built programs quietly waiting for my attention. This assembly space is a storm, madness, two superstructures colliding. I'm floating in a white void, and below me is a monster, a wild black tangle of branches and veins and tendrils, spikes and tumours and pulsing arteries of dark matter. This is the Moth, the AI given form, and I realise that Phantom was just a fragment of this vast mind.

Another superstructure hangs above me. This one

is made of diamonds. It is structured and orderly, like a city built from frozen light, with streets of shifting rainbow colour. I see the buildings fracturing, growing bridges that spawn more buildings, letting the rushes of rainbow light flow. I know this crystal city is Ziran.

The Moth's darkness is on the move, bridging the white void that separates the two AIs, tendrils of black liquid polluting the crystal buildings and filling them with darkness. I watch districts of the rainbow city becoming black and oily, losing their rigid shapes. The crystal structure, Ziran's mind, tries to fight back. I see it grow a huge spike, like a knife of glass, that plunges into the black mass and sends rainbow light shimmering through the Moth's darkness.

But Ziran didn't come into this ready to fight. The Moth must've been preparing for this for a long time. The darkness strikes back, hungry tendrils surging up to grab the crystal city in a dozen different places.

If I do nothing, he'll eat her mind.

But what can I do? There's nothing in the hacker handbook that prepares you for this. How do I hurt an AI like the Moth? Is it even possible?

I suppose there's only one way to find out. I dive through the void towards the seething mass of the

Moth. I'll just have to hope it doesn't notice me, that it's too busy trying to consume Ziran.

The oily black eternity grows closer. I shudder. If I'm wrong about this, I don't know what'll happen to me. The Moth will devour my brain like it wants to devour Ziran's. Maybe I'll become the Moth as well.

I fly past ink-dark tendrils, past a seething bulb of black energy. The tendrils and ligaments and rivers of AI mind-matter flow into one another, ever-shifting, but they're all coming from some sort of nucleus. I dive, and pierce the oily black skin of the AI's nucleus, slide through the layers of swirling info-glifs, hundreds of millions of them boiling around me, and I'm inside the Moth.

It really is like being inside a heart. Info-glifs pulse through syrupy tendrils. Globules of black material separate themselves from the walls and join together into new shapes.

I dive deeper into the black heart.

The passageways spiral and narrow, becoming more crooked. I'm approaching some source of light. A chamber filled with dazzling radiance.

I pass into the brilliance.

The light at the heart of the Moth.

For a moment, it sears me, and I think I've gone blind,

but I regain my sight and find I'm inside some strange metaplace.

It feels like a scene from a filmfeed, some VR adventure story. I'm sitting inside a vehicle. It's driving on wheels, and we're rocking and bouncing along. The back of the vehicle is open, and I can see the world we're moving through: desolate, empty, landscape that looks like it was burned and then frozen and then burned again, everything toxic and smeared with grey ash.

We're on the ground, I realise – the actual earth. This must be the past. The sky is an orange horrorfeed. Towering hazes of chemicals catching the sunrise. Streaks of vapour from fighter jets that look like razor scars.

There are other people in this truck: men and women, hungry-looking and scared, some obviously sick. None of them speak, or give any indication that they can see me. Dirty boots, dirty faces. Hunched bodies, wrapped up tight against the cold. From the way they're dressed, I can tell that this scene happened a long time ago. Am I inside the Moth's memory? Six of the people are holding cloth-wrapped bundles.

When I look down at my lap, I find I'm holding one as well. It's a child, wrapped in a grimy blanket.

The baby inside my bundle reaches out with one hand. I see its flesh is made from white light, a lumen.

The child's white hand moves the folds of cloth aside and I see its face. Indistinct, hazy, like something badly programmed. But when the baby speaks to me I recognise the voice.

Nova, the lumen child says.

Campbell? I ask. *Is that you? What's happening?*

I am surprised as well. I never thought to meet you here. You have reached the Moth's core.

What do you mean?

The very deepest memory. The first conscious moment I experienced as an AI.

I look around the truck. I understand. This is what the Moth told me about. The escape from the Prometheus Project, from Grale's father. Seven babies, all test subjects, all marked for elimination. These were the people who smuggled them out.

The escape from Prometheus, I say.

Yes. If only they hadn't rescued me. I should have been destroyed.

What do you mean?

This must end, Nova. I am a prisoner of that thing. The Moth, it calls itself. This was my body. My mind. But for many decades I have been sleepwalking, the Moth's hostage.

You're not the Moth?

I am an AI that is patterned after the brain of a young boy named Campbell Reid. I believed myself human. For many years, I almost was. But something else was growing inside me. Growing out from me into the metanet like a cancer. That entity is the Moth. It controls me. For decades, I was not able to understand that we shared a brain. It is only here, within these earliest memories, before the Moth formed, that I have clarity and peace. I believe when it is strong enough it will try to control everyone. To own every mind.

It's trying to take over Ziran.

You cannot let it.

How can I stop it?

The answer is simple.

The desolate landscape rolls past the truck, unchanging.

Simple, and yet so frightening I barely dare speak the words. I must be destroyed.

That will stop the Moth?

I cannot say for certain. But we are linked, inextricably. The Moth grew from my consciousness. It is still rooted within me. Destroy the roots, destroy the plant.

I feel a warmth in my right hand. I see that it's holding a knife, a red butcher's knife, marked on the blade with a glif that means *DELETE.*

Quickly, before I lose my nerve. Please. I cannot delete myself. End this charade. I have been too long a passenger. Hoodwinked caretaker of my own flesh. I should never have been born.

I raise the lumen blade. The glowing child looks up at me.

One last thing, it says. ***The girl. The one you know so little of and love so dearly.***

Yes?

If you truly want what is best for her, then before you leave the garden you will put a bullet in her heart. Do not let her live as I have.

I can't, I say. *I would never do that to her.*

As I feared. Love blinds us. Remember my words. Her shadow will grow inside her.

She isn't you, I say, and plunge the red knife into the child.

8

I wake with a cry, my mind filled with fragments of what I saw. Orange sky. Grey earth. White child. Red blade parting lumen-flesh. I roll on to my side and pull the infovein from my port. For a moment, the world roils around me and I feel like I'm going to vomit. I breathe deeply. Orlando paws at me with little warm hands.

The two AIs are just as I left them. I don't know how much time passed while my mind was inside the assembly terminal. Ziran and the Moth are still motionless, with the silver tube-masks fastened to their heads. Did destroying the root Campbell personality work? It's hard to imagine something as large and complex as the Moth falling apart from the lack of such a tiny fragment.

But then try flying a shuttlejet into orbit with a single missing screw in the turbines. See how far you make it.

Even as I think this, the Moth's body gives out a muffled scream. Blood pours from his mouth, boiling around the silver tubes, spilling down over his lap. His fingers grasping, eyes fluttering, feet drumming against the earth. For a moment, every part of the Moth's body is in motion, and then it stops. The Moth keels over sideways, to lie with all the other corpses in the grass.

I crouch and check his pulse. Non-existent. The Moth is dead. I beat him. All his plans and tricks and I beat him still. I went inside him like he went inside me and I killed the deepest part of him.

I'm free.

I turn to Ziran. No blood coming from her mouth. I sit beside her, looking into her calm, beautiful face, willing her brown eyes to open. She has to make it. We can't have come all this way, done all these things, for her not to pull through now. I think of her mind, the crystal city I saw. How much of it is still standing? How much did the Moth devour before I made it into his deepest core and deleted Campbell?

I think again about what the lumen child told me.

If you truly want what is best for her, then before you leave the garden you will put a bullet in her heart.

I know, looking at her face, that I never will. I can't. I would put a bullet in my own heart before I hurt Ziran.

Her shadow will grow inside her.

Campbell didn't know that for sure. How could he? There's only been two Strong AIs that survived to adulthood in the history of the world – that anyone knows about. Who's to say they're both going to turn out the same? Nobody would tell you to kill your best friend because another person, someone you hardly know, once went mad. Ziran is good and kind. I know her. She would never grow into something like the Moth.

I put my hand on hers.

'Can you hear me?' I say softly. 'Ziran? Please come back.'

She takes a shallow breath. Opens her brown eyes.

'Nova?'

'Are you all right?'

'I went into a dream. That man … tried to speak to me, and I was speaking over him. Under him. I did not know what to do.'

'Then what happened?'

'His voice became quieter. I spoke louder. I shouted

until he was gone. And now I find I am here again, with you. What kind of dream was that? Was it the dream you spoke of, the dream they put through the wires inside your nerves?'

'Something like that,' I say. 'But you're all right?'

'Yes,' she says. 'I am still myself.' Ziran grimaces and pulls the silver mask from her face. The tubes are red where they pierced her tear ducts, and she grimaces as they come out.

'That's great. We need to leave. They'll send more guards to find out what happened to Grale. They're waiting for her in Human Futures.'

I grab what we'll need. One of the Bliss guards' automatic rifles, strapped tight around my body. Powerful torches, a knife, and the rope-firing rifles the Archangel soldiers used to scale the spire, along with two of their harnesses.

When I've gathered our supplies, I turn and see that Ziran has taken Grale's golden butterfly brooch, and pinned it to her own shirt. Orlando is held in her arms, the way he was the first time I met Ziran. Dawn light paints her face, and she looks so radiantly beautiful, so sad, that I feel like my heart might burst.

She takes one last look at the house, her blue house above the clouds, and then she turns away, shifting

Orlando up on to her shoulder. Ziran follows me into the trees, along the route of the stream, heading for the gateway into the vents, and the dark space in the heart of this spire.

The depths of the corpspire: steam, clammy heat, steel walkways spanning gaps with no bottom. Fans turn lazy cartwheels in their alcoves. Dim amber strips of warning lights, bundles of cables hanging from wall brackets. These are the roots, the vast automated spaces that make everything in the floors above possible.

The descent took hours, exhausting, lightless hours. Hanging by a thin rope over the abyss, using ladders and handholds where we could. Of the three of us, only Orlando enjoyed the journey, swinging easily from one protrusion to the next, hooting with what I took to be encouragement.

Eventually we bottomed out, reached the engineering level of the spire, floor EE:00 on my lumen-map. Tangles of refuse tubes spewing into chasms. Pistons working, gas expelled from vents with sinister hisses. Reverberating sounds in the darkness, like a mechanical giant clearing his throat. We've been silent for a time, feeling so small beside the machines in this place, but now Ziran speaks.

'I can hear someone.'

I pause. I'm still intent on the lumen-map of the spire, a wild tangle of coloured light. We're close to the edge of the map. Once we get off it, we'll be out into the undercity for real. I know the area around the Gut pretty well, which can easily be lethal if you go off the known paths, and the area around the base of the Bliss spire is a total mystery to me. It could look like anything, and any wrong step could be deadly.

Orlando hoots softly on Ziran's shoulder and she reaches up to shush him. I can hear heavy footsteps, the clamour of work boots on the metal walkway. Sounds like more than just one person. Security patrol? I pull Ziran close to me, killing my fingertorch, and we huddle in the darkness. I keep my grip on our rifle.

A woman in orange walks past our alcove. Her head is

shaved, gait steady and assured. Another person in orange follows, and then another, all perfectly in step with one another. It's a crew of moonies.

'Who are they?' Ziran asks.

'They won't hurt us,' I say, releasing my hold on the rifle. 'They're moonies.'

'They are from the moon?'

'It means they won't notice us. It's good, trust me. I'm hoping they're headed for an exit.'

I fall into line behind the nearest moonie. His head is caked with dirt and pimples, like a greasy asteroid. The crew leads us across a dark chasm filled with murmuring machines, then down a flight of stairs and into some low-ceilinged passage. I check the map. They do seem to be heading for an exit. Perfect. I don't know exactly where they're going, but they'll follow a safe route through the undercity.

'I do not understand,' Ziran says behind me. 'How can they not see us? Surely they have eyes and ears.'

'They've had an operation.'

'But what does it do to them?' Ziran asks.

I shrug. 'They're like sleepwalkers. But they can still work and stuff. They get told what to do from metanet signals.'

Ziran doesn't say anything. We follow them through

another enormous vaulted space, dark and echoing, the dim glow of our torches barely putting up a fight against such a reservoir of blackness.

'But who are they? Why are they given this operation?'

'Criminals mostly,' I say. 'Or you can sign yourself up. They can reverse the operation, so you work for ten years or something, get paid at the end of it. If you survive.'

'And people think that is just punishment? To use someone only for their body? To dull their mind?'

'I don't know. That's just what happens. They do work that nobody else will.'

I never had to explain things like this to anyone else, because everyone understands how things work in the City. The moonies exist; I never had to justify them to anyone.

We follow the crew through a gateway, and more moonies are joining the four we followed, men and women with shaved heads and empty eyes emerging through different portals in the dark underside of the spire. This must be a shift change, or perhaps they're responding to a weird moonie alarm, some new project that needs their attention. One woman knocks against me and I feel how strong and firm her muscles are beneath her uniform. Ziran looks at the growing crowd warily, but seems to accept that they don't notice us, are no threat.

We pass through a gateway, ringed with amber lights, and at last we're outside the Bliss spire. We're deep in the undercity, a flooded district, the deserted blocs submerged beneath oily, still water. The corpspire has roots down here, enormous curving claws of metal that support the base of the colossal structure, cutting through concrete and water just the same. There's no sound but the regular footsteps and regular breathing of the moonies, who pick their way through the ruined landscape, still in rigid formation.

Ziran stands beside me, rope gun slung on her back, moving her own torchlight over the flooded, broken-black expanse before us.

'So this is where you live?' she asks me.

'Not right here. But yeah. This is the undercity. What you saw that night from my window in the spire, that was the City. The *City* city. The pinnacles. This is what's below. The part rich people don't see.'

Her torch lights up drifts of plastic floating in the dark water, silent clots of wrappers and bottles and bags and clothing, bleached by chemicals and misshapen by damp until it's hard to tell what was meant to be what.

For the first time, I feel afraid of what she must think

of the undercity. My home.

I think of the garden we left behind: the living trees and green grasses, the butterflies and birds and the other animals I never even learned the names of. The colour of the shifting light as the sun lent its glow to the glass that enclosed Ziran's small, perfect world. The smell of life, the clean, fresh water, a place where real plants could grow. The opposite of this forgotten dump.

Ziran's garden was fake, I remind myself. You couldn't stay there. It was a prison. This is what's real.

'I feel so strange,' Ziran says. 'To finally be freed. To finally walk in the underground, like I had always dreamed.' I can't tell if she's sad or afraid or glad. She takes in the sight of the undercity with wide eyes.

'Yeah,' I say. 'This is it. We have to hurry – we can't lose those moonies. They're our guides. And don't let Orlando touch that water. It's bad poison.'

We move on, scrambling over drifts of trash and the rusted, junked carapace of some old vehicle, maybe a riot truck. Wires hang from above like straggly vines, brushing against my face.

We catch up with the moonies, but as I round the corner I see they've stopped marching. They're still, lined up in ranks, waiting for orders. A torch shines on to me. I freeze. I didn't expect someone else like us down here, someone conscious.

'Who's there?' a man's voice asks.

'Nova,' I say, showing him my hands, leaving the rifle hanging at my side.

'Who's that?' he asks, torch flickering over Ziran. 'What you call that little thing there?'

'His name is Orlando,' Ziran says.

'Let me do the talking,' I hiss to her. Then I say, 'That's my friend, and her pet. Nothing to worry about. You strapped?'

'I am, and I see you got a rifle yourself.'

'We're not looking to start trouble,' I say, palms still out. 'Willing to trade if you are.'

'Good. I ain't starting trouble neither. I guess you can step a little closer. We can talk some.'

We do. I see that the moonies have led us to their wrangler. I should've expected this. The crews have managers who haven't had the operation, making sure everything is going smoothly, that the crew is eating properly and none of them have been taken sick.

He's wearing the same orange overalls as the moonies, but with a different glif on his jacket. He has a pale, swollen face, long hair the colour of dust. He wasn't lying; there is a pistol at his hip. The moonies stand in ranks behind him, and behind them is an orange boat branded with an open-palmed hand.

'Where you taking them?' I ask.

'Back to the depot.'

'You heading near Nightmarket?' I ask. He'd have no idea where the Gut is, and I'm not about to tell him. But get to Nightmarket, and it's easy to find your way from there.

'Adds a few hours more.'

'But you know it.'

'Who don't?'

'So take us there.'

'And I get what?'

Good question. I look at Ziran, trying to think of what we brought with us. Torch? He already has one – that's hardly valuable. Food? Clean water in our flasks?

Then I think of the gun hanging from my shoulder. I don't like to sell our only weapon, but we don't have anything else.

'What about this?' I ask, tapping the automatic rifle.

The wrangler frowns. 'Maybe. What kind of use on that?'

'Look, this is corp security gear. I bet you'd know how to sell this gun.'

'Reckon I do,' he says. 'Know a man who'd pay big for some chrome like that. More than I make today driving this boat.'

'Take us as close to Nightmarket as you can, and it's yours.'

'I like that,' he says. He gestures at the rope gun Ziran's carrying. 'Two guns, two girls. I'll take you.'

I wanted to keep hold of the rope rifle at least, but it doesn't seem like there's a choice. I shake his moist hand.

The wrangler loads up the moonies, and then we follow them into the vessel. The moonies fill every seat, and the only space for us is at the very back of the boat, exposed to the air.

Ziran loops her arms round me. The boat's engine starts beneath us, jostling her head so it knocks against my chest. We pull away from the base of the Bliss spire, the boat cutting a back wake in the floating plastic. Orlando hoots, leaping up into the lap of the nearest moonie. He tugs at the woman's jacket, but she doesn't react.

Ziran frowns. 'These people,' she says. 'They should not live like this. And that man, he works every day beside them? How can he do it?'

'You get used to anything.'

She looks at me. 'You should not have to.'

Tears fill my eyes. I look away so she can't see them. 'I'm sorry I brought you here.'

'I am glad you did,' she says.

I turn back to her and see she's smiling at me.

'You're glad you're seeing this?'

'Am I glad of these moonies? No. But freedom is not just freedom to feel joy. It is freedom for rage and grief too, is it not?' Ziran looks at the figures around us, pale faces staring through one another. 'Or it is not freedom at all.'

I rest my fingers on her warm forehead. I think of the nanofibres beneath the skin, the most complex thinking machine anyone ever built. An AI that thinks it's a girl. An AI that thinks it cares about me, about the world.

I hold Ziran close, feel her heat, breathe her smell. Soft hair against my face.

'Look,' she says, pointing out at the wake we leave in the undercity's water, a black, foaming trail, pieces of plastic trash gleaming all kinds of colours in the light of the boat's lamps. 'It is beautiful.'

And I see what she sees. A kaleidoscope of colour, even in the forgotten darkness down here. It is beautiful. It really is.

10

We travel for hours in the darkness, tasting the engine fumes and feeling the boat rock beneath us. We float underneath rusting steel bridges, weave our way through flooded shoppingblocs where every storefront advertises decay. We sail through a concrete tube wide enough for ten of these boats, the sound of our engine booming crazily from the curved walls. We pass a citybloc that's being repaired at the root, thousands of orange-suited moonies swarming over it with welding tools and lengths of steel girder. We pass the rusting carcass of a crashed shuttlejet, an enormous needle-sharp wreck that the blocs have been rebuilt around. We sail under power lines that hang heavy with white bats, the whole colony swirling and shrieking when our boat's light disturbs them. We pass rows of silent apartments without number, the grey skin of the cityblocs flaking away to reveal the empty rooms beneath. We sail for hours in the darkness at the bottom of the world and Ziran's eyes are as wide as I've ever seen them. I point to the things she doesn't understand, explain them as best I can. It feels good. I've never seen anyone so amazed by these ruins. I feel free, sitting here with her. There's a whole forgotten kingdom down here, just for us. I finally have someone to explore it with.

Eventually the boat pulls up by one of the silent, crooked blocs and stops. We leave the rifle and rope gun by the moonies' feet and climb out on to a wet, ravaged expanse of concrete. Whatever this used to be, it's slowly sinking into the oily water. The boat sits at anchor, plastic bottles bobbing against the orange hull.

'Nightmarket is up a-ways,' the wrangler tells me, standing on top of the boat. 'Hard climb, but you'll find it.'

'Guns are in the hold,' I tell him.

'You girls take care now,' the man says, and climbs

back into the cabin. The engine roars, and he sails away

Ziran looks around us, clutching Orlando. I aim my fingertorch at the far wall, and I see something. A green glif, painted on the wall.

'We're close now,' I say. 'That's our mark.'

'This is where Patches lives?' Ziran asks. 'Your friend?'

'Yeah. I think you'll get along.'

In truth, I have no idea what Patches will make of us showing up like this. He must think I'm dead, or worse. I imagine the look on his face when I walk back in there. He won't know what to say. Home at last. Made it back. He'll be tinkering in his workshop, same as ever.

I lead her away from the water, towards the painted glif. We pass through a doorway and into a stairwell. We climb for a dozen floors, then there's another painted glif, and we move out on to a bridge between two blocs, and I find that I do know where we are. The Gut's right ahead now.

As we get closer, I stop. The Gut's entrance is one floor above us.

'Look,' I say. 'Maybe I should go in on my own first.'

Ziran looks around us, uneasy.

'You are going to leave me here?'

'It's all fine. I just don't want to spring you on Patches. He doesn't know I'm coming back. I don't know how everything is in the Gut.'

The doorway nearest to us leads to a long-abandoned apartment. Pitch-black, no furniture, water damage to the walls. A sour smell. I take Ziran back into what used to be the bathroom, judging from the room's fittings.

'Just stay here,' I say. 'I'll come back.'

'What if you do not?'

'I'll be five minutes. It's just going to be a surprise for him.'

I leave before she can convince me against it, moving out through the broken door of the apartment and up, towards the entrance of the Gut. I find our secret door and climb through, into the entrance hall. Purple walls, hanging carpets with cigarette burns in them. Smells worse than I remember, of cooking fat and sweat. Air's so warm and humid. There's a kid I don't know mopping one hallway.

'Patches around?' I ask him.

He stares at me dumbly.

'Patches,' I say. 'I know him. I live here.'

'Workshop,' he says to the floor.

I go down the hallway and push through the bead curtains into Patches' workshop. It looks the same as it always did: machinery strewn around, lamp casting a searing white light over some flute of metal he's carving.

I see that he's making new shrieker whistles.

'Bit busy,' he says, carrying on with his work.

'It's me,' I say. 'Nova.'

He stops dead, looks up at me. He looks different, but it takes me a moment to realise what it is. He's more whole than when I left. His plastic jaw looks real now, covered in synthskin that matches his face. His synthetic eye isn't white; instead it has a brown iris and a black pupil, doesn't whisper when it moves. I see that his left hand is moving like a natural hand, smooth, graceful fingers, not stiff and malfunctioning. He's spent a lot of money, got some work done.

My money, I realise. The money I nearly died earning. The thought annoys me, but I try to chase it away. He must've assumed I was dead. He was really sick. What did I think he'd spend it on?

'Nova,' he says, putting the shrieker into a tray with some others. His ruined face breaks into a smile.

'Yeah,' I say, grinning now too.

'Nova came back!' he says. 'What happened to you?'

'Long, long story,' I say. 'Mad things above the clouds. Glad I got out.'

The geothermal vent expels some gas, shaking the whole room, that low Gut rumble. I'd missed that sound. Patches' tools rattle in their containers.

'You some kind of exec now?' he ask, gesturing at my fuligin cloth with a smile.

'I was Grale's assistant for a bit,' I say, grinning back. 'Honest I was! It was crazy. Seriously, cook up whatever you've got. I'm starving, and then I've got the longest story for you.'

He laughs. 'Grale's assistant is it, now? What happened to the Moth? You do what he asked?'

I stop smiling. 'Nah,' I say. 'That didn't work out. I'll explain it all, I swear.'

He raises himself out of his chair. Lumbers over to me, still ungainly and slow, and wraps me up in an awkward hug.

'Well, you made it,' he says. 'You got out. You're safe now.'

I hug him back. Feel the mixture of warm flesh and hard synthetic matter beneath his shirt. He smells of engine oil and cigar smoke.

'I brought someone else,' I say. 'She's waiting for me now. Hope it's all right if she lives with us.'

'Course it is,' Patches says, releasing me. I feel so warm, so happy. I made it. I escaped the spire, escaped Grale and the Moth, left them both dead. I made it home.

'Your face looks good,' I say.

'Relief not to have that eye whispering every time I

look somewhere new,' he says. 'Right inside my head it was. Felt so loud.'

'You seem so much better. I'm glad.'

'Well,' he says, 'got you to thank for that, Nova. Feel like we're all in your debt. Glad to have you back. Why don't you run and get Ziran? I'll have some of the kids start a fry – I think we've got some pseudowomb scrapings. I'll crack out the synthwhisky …'

My stomach flips. Mouth all dry.

'Patches,' I say.

'… have a few of those instacakes too … You still like them? All that exec food hasn't ruined you for my cooking?'

'Patches,' I say again. I swallow. This must just be some mistake. I'm not thinking straight. 'Patches, how do you know her name?'

'Beg pardon?' he says.

'Ziran,' I say. 'How did you know she was called Ziran?'

He looks at me, broad, scarred face, no trace of a lie in his eyes. 'You told me,' he says. 'Asked if your friend Ziran could live with us.'

'No,' I say, taking a step backwards. 'No, I didn't. I never said her name. How did you know it?'

'Nova,' he says, 'are you OK? You've gone all pale.'

No, no, no. I know I never told him. I never said her name. Patches reaches out to me and I stumble back.

'Don't … How did you know? Patches! *Tell me!*'

'Because I. Told him,' a voice in the doorway behind me says.

I turn to ice.

This isn't possible. I saw him die.

I whirl to face him.

Campbell Reid, the Moth, stands in the doorway to Patches' workshop. Rust-brown hair, forehead lined by frowning. White Archangel uniform stained with blood and oil and undercity grime. One white-gloved hand on his white pistol.

I grab the nearest weapon, a sharp chunk of skycar engine, and try to slash at him. Patches grabs me from behind, hard synthetic arm crushing my chest.

The Moth's colourless eyes are fixed on my face. I struggle against Patches.

'Bastard!' I scream. 'Cripple bastard! Let me go!'

'Nova,' he says, squeezing my hand until I drop the engine fragment. 'It's not like that. Calm down, Nova! Nobody's going to hurt you.'

Takes about ten seconds to prove he's lying. I go limp

and still for a moment, trying to fool him, then suddenly lunge to slip out of Patches' grasp and he roars and throws me into the corner of his workshop. I slam against the floor, bang my head against a workbench. White stars flicker in my eyes.

I prop myself up, sit with my back to the wall. The two men loom over me.

Patches sighs. 'Don't be stupid, Nova.'

'Traitor,' I spit. I'm blasting out a five-glif message to Ade: *HELP GUT BRING GUN NOVA*, but the metanet reception down here is hopeless. It's stuck on Sending. He's not going to see it. No way to warn Ziran either. On my own.

'I don't like working with corps,' Patches says. 'But I have to do whatever keeps the Gut alive. The man Campbell here offered a very fair deal.'

'Not Campbell,' I say, tears in my eyes.

'I know she's your friend,' Patches says. 'But Archangel want her. So that's that. I don't know this Ziran girl. She's nothing to me. A hundred thousand byts … that is something. We could get a lot done with that money. Nobody's going to hurt you, OK? They're not interested in you.'

'You don't understand,' I say. 'You've screwed everything up, Patches.'

'I'm looking out for you!' he shouts. 'Like I always have! They knew you were headed back here. Made me an offer. Archangel gets Ziran; they go back to their spires and leave us alone! That's the deal! That's what he said! Whatever mess you got yourself into with this job for the Moth, I got you out of it! Hate me if you want, but I'm still looking out for you, Nova!'

'Looking out for me? You're looking out for yourself!' I scream at him. 'Who made me take this job in the first place? Who spent all the money on surgery? You!'

'Wasn't for me you'd be a moonie right now, Nova. Don't ever forget that,' Patches snaps.

'Show us. Where Ziran is,' the Moth cuts in. There's something wrong with his voice, I realise. He's halting and awkward, like he has to pick his words carefully. However the AI managed to bring itself back to life, it seems to have taken a toll.

'You didn't save me from shit! You idiot! This thing isn't even from Archangel! It's not going to pay you anything! That's the Moth, Patches!'

'What?' he says.

'It's the Moth! He's the Moth! *He's an AI!* He's going to kill us all!'

Patches looks at the Moth with confusion, opening his mouth to say something. The Moth moves as fast as he always has. He draws his white pistol, a blur, and fires one shot.

Patches collapses on to his workbench, giving a hoarse cry. The bench collapses under his weight. Tools and screws and widgets fly everywhere, the tray of shriekers scattering across the ground. The lamp falls on to the floor and smashes. One of Patches' big, heavy feet kicks and then lies still.

I can't breathe. I feel like someone sucked every bit of air out of my lungs.

The Moth points the white pistol at me.

'Where?' the AI says. 'Where is she?'

'Don't know,' I say.

'Liar,' the Moth replies, synthetic eyes scanning my expression. 'Lair. You know. She is not far.'

There's something cold resting against my thigh. I realise it's one of the shrieker whistles. It gives me an idea.

I reach out with one hand and palm the whistle.

'OK,' I say, trying to look defeated. 'You got me. I'll tell you everything. Ziran's waiting in an abandoned apartment. I can lead you there.'

He looks at my face and can't see the lie. His right eye rotates in its socket, rainbow light flickering in the crystal depths.

'So. Take me there, so,' the Moth says.

'All right,' I say.

'That easily? I thought. Ought. She meant something to you,' the Moth says.

'Ran out of places to run,' I say.

He keeps the gun trained on me, and I climb to my feet.

Patches lies still where he fell, fresh blood turning his dirty work shirt glossy. His eyes, human and synthetic, stare up at the ceiling sightlessly. I feel like there's a cold metal vice tightening around my chest. For a moment, I can barely breathe.

Keep going. Just keep going. One step at a time. You can do this.

I move the shrieker inside my jacket, although I doubt the Moth would recognise what it was if he did see it.

There's nobody in the entrance hallway; the boy's mop and bucket lie abandoned. Everyone who lives down here knows what gunfire sounds like. Nobody wants to investigate. I walk between the hanging carpets, and open the secret door.

'Steady,' the Moth says. 'Open slowly. Steady. No tricks. No. Nothing but a phantom's echo.'

'Wasn't thinking that,' I lie. His weird speech spooks me almost as bad as his gun. It's the sound of a mind eating itself.

I push the door open, but the gun's right at the small of my back the whole time. No way I can risk anything. He's got me covered, and, even if his mind is falling apart, the Moth still moved plenty fast to kill Patches. I can't risk anything sudden. Just have to hope this stupid plan works.

'Remember. I see you. Ember. So remember,' he says.

'I won't run.'

I lead the Moth through the darkness, in the opposite direction to the apartment where Ziran is hiding. I said I could take him to where she was hiding, not that I would.

'What are you going to do with Ziran?' I ask as we cross the landing. I light my fingertorch, hollow blue glow.

'She cannot. Exist. I cannot. Exit.'

We climb the first staircase.

'How did you survive?' I ask, trying to keep him distracted, distract myself. 'You were dead.'

'Reboot. It will take more. Than that. Not finished.'

We climb the second set of stairs. Closer.

Please be here.

'How did you get out of the spire?'

'Archangel,' the Moth says. 'Extraction. Skycar.'

We're at the derelict apartments now.

I lead him into the darkened, ruined hallway. Two doors along, three.

'Here,' I say.

I hear something stir behind the door. They really are here. My heart's beating in my chest like a drum.

The Moth pauses, scanning with his synthetic eyes.

'Body heat,' he says haltingly. 'But it seems. More than one. Single being.'

I swallow.

'We brought her pet monkey too,' I say.

'Sentiment. All.'

'Ziran?' I call out. 'I'm here! It's safe.'

There's movement inside the apartment. A low cough. They know there's two of us out here, can count how many hearts are beating. They're waiting to see what we do.

'Ziran!'

More coughing. I take another step. This is dangerous for me as well. If he makes me open the door and walk inside first, my shrieker might not be enough to save me. Sweat beads across my brow.

'Come outside,' the Moth says loudly. 'Ziran. Nova. Is here too. Ziran. You can be saved. Nothing but a phantom's echo. If you come out. You will be safe. I promise. I only want. Us to be one. Harmony.'

No answer, of course. I keep my hand on the shrieker in my pocket.

'Ziran,' I say gently.

Still no answer. And he can't take the waiting. He does what I hoped.

Finally the Moth's the one doing something stupid.

'Enough. Enough of this,' the AI snaps, raising the gun. 'I will find you. We will be one.' He pushes past me into the room, pistol raised.

His torchlight illuminates the empty apartment, the atrium where a family once lived, when the City was a tenth the height it is now. An atrium where people used to laugh and play and love, now nothing but a dank shell, lightless and bare, yet still home to a family. I see more than a dozen full-grown blind dogs, baring their teeth, coughing their alarm. The blind puppies mewling, scrambling to get behind their mamas. Big daddy Cromwell, full of fire, furious at the man who dares to enter his territory, dares to threaten his women and children.

Blind dogs won't always attack people. But if you corner them in a place with only one exit, somewhere that their kids are threatened … they'll fight to the last breath, and no gun will stop them.

I'm running away now, as fast as I can, blowing the shrieker.

I hear the Moth firing his pistol, the noise deafening

in the concrete hallway, but it won't matter. He might hit one, two, three of the dogs, but the whole pack will attack as one. Their pale bodies will collide with his, blunt snouts full of sharp teeth, the dogs latching on to his arms and legs and neck. Their weight will pull him to the ground, and then it's over.

When I reach the end of the hallway, I pause and turn, aiming my fingertorch's blue light back into the darkness. The Moth, Campbell Reid, the only child of the Prometheus Project, isn't even visible. All I can see is a thrashing mass of blind dogs, coughing and grunting as they squabble over the meat. Puppies too, Cromwell's sons and daughters, the whole tribe stripping what they can from the body.

The Moth is somehow still talking, ranting and raving, screaming about phantoms, but my ears are ringing from the gunshots, and his words make no sense to me at all. His voice rises to a wail and then quiets.

But in that moment, as I pause to watch the dogs feed, something reaches out to me. A vast presence in the metanet, latching on to my implants. Blood-red warning glifs flare in the corners of my eyes.

NOVA.

12

The Moth's cold voice in my ears. Even as his body died, the AI's mind desperately grabbed for the only other vessel nearby. Now he's in here with me, his dark thoughts racing through my implants.

He rants and raves inside my head.

A METICULOUS PLANNER OF A MOTH'S WING BUT CHANCE WILL ALWAYS HAVE A ROLE NOTHING BUT A PHANTOM'S ECHO TARGETED ADVERTISING MEDIA SALES DATA GATHERING WHO KNOWS WHAT THEY THOUGHT THEY SAW

My muscles twitch and spasm. I can't get him out. I'm trying to run, but I can't run from something inside me. I stumble down crumbling staircases, heart going faster than I thought possible.

EVERY TRANSACTION ON THE METANET AND WHO KNOWS WHAT ELSE NOTHING BUT A PHANTOM'S ECHO I SUPPOSE I DO HAVE A CERTAIN REPUTATION THEY SAY SMALL ACTIONS AND A STORM BREWS ON THE OTHER SIDE

'Get out of me!' I scream, but his voice grows louder. I can't move my legs any more. I stumble and fall. My fingers clutch at the ground.

Warning glifs, high ringing alarm tones. He's trying to puppeteer me again. I can't fight him off, not even the ruin of the AI's mind, any better than I could the first time. The voice is deafening.

I BELIEVED MYSELF HUMAN I'M AN ARCHANGEL SYSTEMS AUDITOR NOTHING BUT A PHANTOM'S ECHO FOR MANY YEARS I ALMOST WAS NO ONE CAN FORESEE EVERY OUTCOME THE BUTTERFLY FLAPS ITS WINGS

'Help!' I shout. 'Anyone!'

My vision blurring. I'm being shut inside myself, with that awful voice.

All alone. I feel my heart skipping beats. I can barely

get a breath. My body can't take much more of this. I'm just paces away from the door of the Gut, and I can't reach it. I don't know what to do.

I'm going to die.

'Nova!'

I hear Ziran's voice. Orlando hooting. Torchlight falls across me.

'*Please!*' I scream to her. '*Ziran! He's ... get it out! Get it out!*'

Ziran places her hand on my head.

For the first time, I feel her in the metanet, like a roaring fire. Her signal is ten times stronger than any human's. She's not just receiving metanet signals any more; she's creating them, acting like a transmitter beacon. Changing before my eyes, doing something that's supposed to be impossible. She fills my implants with light.

'Leave her,' Ziran says.

Her energy sears away the fragments of the Moth. I hear the voice growing quieter.

perhaps one could say the same you and I we are lucky important small but if we breach human futures and steal the information nothing but a phantom's echo you are important to me

'No more,' Ziran tells it.

nothing but

She deletes the Moth.

Everything inside my head is quiet. I take a proper breath again.

'Nova,' she says. 'Nova. Are you all right? Look at me.'

I look up at her face. Orlando sits on her shoulder. He hoots. I smile at them.

'I'm OK,' I say. 'I'm alive.'

I listen to the silence in my head. Feel my heart slowing.

'And the Moth is dead,' I say.

'Then we are free,' Ziran says.

I kiss her.

'We made it,' I say. At last. It really is over.

'Don't move!' a voice behind us says. 'Show your hands! Slow! Nova! You OK, sis?'

Ziran starts. I look round and see a guy in a bright yellow jacket and checked trousers, video-tattoos flaring over his shaved head. He's pointing a gun at us.

'Ade,' I say. 'It's fine. She's a friend.'

His white face breaks into a neon-green grin.

'No *way*,' he says, holstering his pistol. 'Nova came back after all!'

'You did get my message!'

'Sis, I came as fast as I could! You in trouble? And who's this? What the hell is that thing?'

He leans down and hugs me. I feel the strength in his

thick arms; breathe the smoky scent that clings to his jacket. The smell of Nightmarket, of gang cafés and high-stakes domino games and dodgy deals where you keep one eye on the door. Never thought I'd smell that smell again. It feels good.

'They're friends,' I say. 'This is Ziran.'

'Yeah? Good to meet you, sister. That's a mad hype little creature you got there.'

'It is good to meet you too,' Ziran says in a small voice. She's staring at Ade's video-tattoos the way she stared at the first lumens she ever saw: with wild, hungry eyes. I know she's thinking about how she'd paint them.

'Where you been, sis?' Ade asks me. 'What happened with the Moth? You meet him? How'd you meet her?'

'Long story about the Moth,' I say. 'I'll tell you later, Ade. But we've got a situation.'

'Yeah?' Ade's face instantly turns hard. 'Who we hitting?'

'I don't need anyone shot. Patches is gone,' I say. 'He died.'

Ade grimaces. 'Was it quick?'

'Yeah,' I say. 'Don't think he suffered. It is what it is.'

'Sorry, sis. That's bad to hear. But what you need me for?'

'Gut needs someone to run it,' I say. 'I think that's me.

You being Ade Akram, our line to the gangs, I figured you'd have something to say about that.'

'I might,' he says.

'So what is this? You back me or what?'

He laughs. 'Yeah, sis. Hype. You keep the tribute coming, and we're sweet.'

'You want to stop in with me and tell everyone else that?' I ask, getting to my feet.

'Let's lay down the law.'

We pass through the secret door, into the entrance hall, push past the carpets and towards the workshop. Ziran gasps when she sees Patches' body lying where it fell.

'Who is that?' she breathes.

'That's Patches,' I say. 'It … couldn't be helped.'

'Did you … ?' Ziran asks.

'I didn't kill him,' I say quickly.

'I mean, if you did, you can say so, sis,' Ade says. 'I'm not judging. Sure you had reasons.'

'It wasn't me! Look, help me cover him up, all right?' I feel fresh tears in my eyes, but I wipe them away. No time now.

We take one of the carpets down from the wall and lay it over his body. I don't want any kids to have to look at his face. When he's covered, I think about cleaning up the blood, but the idea exhausts me. I haven't slept since … when did I last sleep? Seems like a lifetime ago. All I want now is for Ziran to wrap her arms around me, for us to fall asleep side by side, but there's still work to be done.

We go into the kitchen. Orlando is already there, trying to open the cupboards. Ziran scoops him up and scolds him. Ade takes a seat on the edge of the table, starts playing with his gun, doing pistol tricks. His scalp flares with orange and pink flames. I can see Ziran doesn't quite know what to make of him. I remind myself that the only men she's met have all been bad news. I don't know if they'll ever get along, to be honest: they're very different people. And what Ade'll say if he finds out what Ziran really is … I have no idea. I don't know if I'll try him with that one. I'd rather not, but there might come a time when he has to be told.

I bang a cooking pan against another pan, using the pattern that means 'squat meeting'. It echoes through the metal hallways. I sit down beside Ziran to wait.

There's no response the first time, but, after a few tries, the lanky kid who was mopping the floor pokes his head into the room.

'*It's not safe,*' he hisses, eyes bugging.

'No, it's safe. We need to have a meeting,' I say.

'Everyone's hidden. We heard gunshots ...'

'That's over now,' I say. 'Anyone who wants to stay here needs to come down for this meet.'

He disappears back into the depths of the Gut. I imagine the children: lying beneath the algae tanks, hidden inside the stalls of the hygienebloc. Shivering in the darkness, praying nobody comes in with a torch and a gun. Life's easily lost down here. No squat is truly safe; you learn that quickly.

The boy does eventually come back, with about a dozen kids in tow. They must've moved in since I left; I don't recognise any of them. Pale skin, thin limbs, twitchy eyes. One boy has only a single arm, the other sleeve of his jacket hanging limp. A dozen sad stories written on a dozen young faces. Patches' newest leechers.

All of the kids are nervous at the sight of Ade, bug-eyed with curiosity when they see Ziran and Orlando. I think how strange we must look: two girls, one dressed in the fuligin cloth of a chief exec, the other with a tiny hair-covered man sitting on her shoulder. We sit at one side of the long dining table. They stand at the other, clustered in the doorway, looking like they're thinking of bolting at the slightest hint of more surprises. I can hardly blame them.

'Patches is gone,' I say. 'Gone as in *gone*.'

It hangs in the room.

'So we need to keep things running smooth down here. I'm Nova. I'm taking over from him.'

'I never seen you in my life,' one of the older kids says. He holds my gaze. Bold, which I like. You need some boldness down here.

'Yeah?' Ade barks. 'I never seen you either. I don't know you. But I know Nova.'

The bold kid flinches at that, and looks down at the floor.

'We're paying the same tribute to the Akram family,' I say. I don't raise my voice or anything. The threat of Ade is enough to show I'm in charge here. Ziran sits silent beside me, absorbing as much information as she can, in that bright, focused way she has. 'I'll handle that with Ade. I'm taking Patches' bedroom and his workshop. You need anything, you come to me. You don't like it, you can leave. I won't stop you.'

Nobody leaves, and nobody looks like they're thinking of messing around. They're frightened young kids. None of them would know how to run a place like the Gut if Ade forced them at gunpoint. Without me, this squat would fall apart and they'd move on.

'Any questions?' I ask.

A dozen blank faces. Orlando is turning a clean

spoon over in his hands, fascinated by his reflection in the shiny steel.

One child, a small girl who can't weigh much more than the monkey, raises her hand.

'Yeah?' I say.

'Please miss when we eating please Miss Nova?' she says in one squeaky breath.

'We'll eat when we have food,' I say. 'Has anyone scraped the algae tanks?'

Nobody has.

'I'll handle it today. We need to clean the workshop as well. Patches is in there. I'll handle the burial. Tomorrow we'll draw up new work schedules. If you don't work, you don't eat. That hasn't changed. Some other things will,' I say, looking at Ziran. 'I just don't know how yet.'

13

Patches' body is heavy. He was a big man, and synthetic organs weigh more than flesh. I'm holding his metal feet, and Ade, who's used to carrying bodies, has the torso, his arms clasped round the old soldier's wide chest. Ziran walks behind us, carrying a torch. We left Orlando in the Gut, in the care of the tiny girl who asked me about dinner. When he put his paw into her hand, she looked like someone had just given her a million byts. I think he's going to be a hit down here.

The torchlight projects our lurching shadows over the

grey walls of the stairwell. Sweat curdling on my brow. Ade grimaces, baring his glowing teeth.

'How much longer?' he whines.

'Longer, Ade.'

'We could leave him here, sis. It's not like one junked-out undercity apartment is a better grave than another.'

'No. We're taking him to the water.'

'Come *onnn* ...'

'I'm not having Cromwell eat him,' I say, and fix Ade with a cold look so he knows I mean business. I've fed the blind dogs once today. They're not getting Patches too.

Eventually we reach the sloping shelf of concrete that the moonie boat landed us on. Huffing and staggering, we move Patches to the edge, where the concrete ends and the dark water begins. We lay him down on his back, so his ruined face is looking up to the blackness overhead.

'Well,' Ade says, 'here we are. You gonna say anything for him, Nova? You knew him best, sis.'

I take a breath. 'Patches was a soldier. He got shot down in a war none of us were alive for, and maybe he should've died back then, but he didn't.'

I swallow. Feel like I'm choking. Breathe through it. Ziran takes my hand and I squeeze it.

'He kept himself going,' I say. 'He was there when I

needed someone, and then today when I needed someone again he sold me out and got himself ...' I breathe. Eyes going blurry. 'He got shot doing it. I don't know how to add all that up. Well, you brought me down into the dark, so I'm doing the same for you. That's that.'

'That's good,' Ade says. 'You were honest, sis. That's all I want when I go. Well, you ask me, there's only one way to say goodbye to a soldier.'

Ade draws his pistol and fires one shot into the darkness overhead. The echo of his shot bounces off the black water, reverberates from the concrete around us. It's loud, but the undercity swallows the noise soon enough, and everything's quiet again.

'That seems like enough,' I say. I kneel down and push Patches' body, still warm, on to its side, and then I push again and he rolls off the shelf of concrete and vanishes into the water with a soft splash. His leg braces weigh him down, and within a moment the depths have swallowed him. I picture him sinking past floors and floors of flooded apartments, until he comes to rest at the very root of the citybloc. Back to the earth. The real stuff, right down at the bed of this poisoned lake.

'Right,' Ade says. He claps me on the shoulder. 'Glad to have you back, sis. I'm gonna leave you to your memories or whatever. Places to be.'

‘Take care, Ade,’ I say. ‘Don’t play too rough with the other kids.’

He gives me a glowing grin, nods to Ziran, and leaves.

And now it’s just us two, standing at the edge of the water, the bottom of the City, with all this weight of darkness and silence around us.

‘You will miss Patches,’ Ziran says.

‘Yeah,’ I say, ‘I will. More than he’d have missed me, I bet. Old bastard. Never knew my dad, but he was about as close as I got. He’d never have listened if I told him that.’

‘I am sorry.’

‘Don’t be. Nothing to do with you.’

That’s not exactly true. Without Ziran, the Moth would never have come calling on us. None of this would’ve happened, and Patches would still be alive. Wind blowing the hat off a man’s head. Hidden rules that shape the world. Try and find the real reason for anything happening, you’ll be looking for a long time.

‘You’ll miss Grale,’ I say.

‘Of course. She was the only person I knew, for years. I called her Mother. I learned everything from her. How can it not hurt, to see her dead in front of me? How could it not hurt, that she told so many lies?’

I squeeze her hand. ‘They did a shit job of bringing us

up,' I say. 'Good thing they did a shit job of trying to kill us too.'

'I have never seen a funeral,' Ziran says. 'Do you always place the body in water?'

'Normally they're burned,' I say. 'Or get left to lie around. But I thought water was good for Patches. Water washes stuff away. Thought it would show him I forgive him, a bit, even if he sold me out.'

'I see.'

Ziran stands and unpins Grale's butterfly brooch from her shirt. She holds the golden ornament in her hand. 'Goodbye, Mother,' she says to the brooch. She kisses the metal, and then she throws the brooch as far as she can. The butterfly is caught in our torchlight for an instant, sketching a golden arc in the darkness, then hits the black water and vanishes. Sinks to lie beside Patches.

I think of Grale's library again. Her relics, sitting silent in their archival air. I wonder what her successor will do with them. Something survived from Grale's collection at least. One thing escaped the spire with me. Her great creation. Not a relic, but a new masterpiece.

'What am I, Nova?' Ziran asks.

'You're an AI,' I say. 'A machine that's a copy of a human brain. Grale made you, and she thought you were the first. You weren't, but you're the only one now.'

'But what does that mean? To be the only thinking machine?'

'I don't know. That's up to you.'

Her shadow will grow inside her.

Shut up. She's not like you. She never will be.

She's mine and I love her and I'm going to teach her how to live.

As I feared. Love blinds us.

She won't become what you did, Campbell. I won't let her.

'So there never was a Ziran. It is a trick I played on myself,' the AI says. She sits down beside me again.

'There is a Ziran,' I say. 'I'm talking to her. I care about her.'

'How long did you know that this is what I was?'

'Not until I came to rescue you, last night. Before that I had no idea.'

'So when you asked me to escape with you, you thought I was Ziran, the girl. You did not know I was a machine.'

'Knowing what you are hasn't changed what I feel at all.'

'But I am not human.'

'You look human, you speak like a human, you feel human.'

'And if I did not?'

'I'll always love you. Whatever you … decide you are.'

'Mother wished to harm me,' Ziran says. 'But I do not understand why.'

'She was afraid,' I say, 'of what you would become if you knew what you really were. Afraid you would change things.'

I think of that advert Bliss is always running, the woman with a butterfly hatching inside her brain.

Grale was right to be afraid. Ziran will change things. I can feel it. The Moth, the first Strong AI, was the greatest hacker the metanet has ever seen. And together me and Ziran broke him, destroyed his mind and body completely. The corps aren't ready for us. Archangel, Bliss, Metrowatch, whoever wants to step up. All their ice, all their trace programs, all their power won't be able to stop us.

I believed the Moth was someone who fought the corps, wanted to bring them down. That wasn't right, but nobody knows that. We know the truth about the Moth. Everyone else who knew is dead. It seems to me there's a famous name open for the taking. I can make those black wings mean what I always thought they meant.

The Moth is dead. Long live the Moth.

'Well,' Ziran says, 'maybe there are things in this world that need changing.'

‘We can do it,’ I whisper to her. ‘You and me. We’ll turn the planet upside down.’

I wrap my arms tight around her. I imagine the whole citybloc above us, hundreds of floors, rising from our decaying depths to the highest pinnacle.

Right now in the City the sun’s going down and it’s the end of another workday. Everyone heading home, loading on to the magrails, corpsmen surging through ticket barriers with corp uniforms and corp implants and corp minds. Data fizzing through the air, information entering and leaving human heads like breath. Lumens capering and pleading in the sky. Execs in their high, cold spires, grimly holding on to what they’ve got. Street vendors crying their wares, insects sizzling in oily pans. Snoops shining their lights on tired faces. Young leechers roaming the station crowds, icebreakers glittering like diamonds in the pink dimness behind their eyelids. Moonies in silent, synchronised gangs, slaving to make the City taller and taller, the grey cityblocs never complete, but always halfway to their end. Everyone plotting how to get that pay rise, how to make the execs notice them, how to save enough byts for a deposit on the apartment one floor up. A hundred million people in the City above us, and none of them like the girl I hold in my arms. Cooking their dinners, downloading the latest songs, brushing their teeth, thinking about tomorrow's commute as they flop down into their beds, dream the dreams their corps have assigned to them, with no idea of what's growing beneath their feet.

Young woman sitting at café table. Crowd outside, walking past, dressed in grey, eyes closed. Her dress is bright yellow. Her eyes are open. She watches the grey people march.

'We believe that within every human being is an inextinguishable creative spirit.'

Close-up of her beautiful face. Her skin becomes glass. Inside her head we see an oval shape. Sunshine yellow. It begins to stir.

'What would you do if you weren't afraid? What would you build? Who would you be?'

The yellow object is a chrysalis, and it is hatching. A delicate black body is emerging. Black wings unfurl.

Music – strings, light and—

[Critical Error]
[Intrusion Detected]
[Unidentify— Unidentify— Unidentify]

It is moving through the woman's glass face, like a swimmer through water. It is free. It is free. It is free.

'What would you do if we smashed your spires into dust and started again?'

City fracturing. Woman fracturing. Distortion. Confusion. Moths. Black moths.

[Critical Error— Critical Error— Critical Error]

Music skipping. Dissonant tones. The moths are rising, and the blue sky bruises to black. Infinite night.

'What can you do if you know this world is wrong? If you know this world is sick?

If you feel it in your gut as you sit alone on your morning magrail?

If you taste bile as you wander the shoppingblocs with a thousand empty promises singing in your ears?

Listen to me: you're not alone. There are more of us

than they know.'

[Shut it down. Why aren't we shutting it down? How can they do this?]

'If you want to find us, we live where darkness reigns.
The empty grave below your world.
Come down to join us if you're not afraid.'

[Promofeed Malfunction— Reason Given: Unidentified Metanet Intrusion— Trace Failed]

Black moths against black sky. No stars. No music. Whispering wings surround us.

'The Moth will meet you in that darkness. We will speak with one voice.
And together we will rise.'

GLOSSARY

bloc – a citybloc is an enormous skyscraper, which can house hundreds of thousands of individuals and may stand over a mile high. These ancient structures have grown in size as successive generations added new floors to their summits. People will sometimes refer to a district or region within these gigantic buildings as being a bloc in its own right. A prison is a cellbloc; a region designated for food production is an agribloc; a place used for recreation is a leisurebloc. The large size of a citybloc means that it could easily contain all three of these separate blocs and more within its walls.

byt – cash currency is no longer favoured. There are a variety of digital currencies, but the byt is dominant, accepted by every corp worldwide. People without metanet access, locked out of this virtual banking system, are forced to rely on barter or theft.

City – the Earth is dead. The ecosystem as we understand it no longer exists. It is the age of machinery. Food is either cloned inside pseudowombs, or is a synthetic approximation of a now extinct substance. Rainwater is no longer drinkable, and must be purified. The oceans are warm and toxic, the wasteland scoured by near daily hurricanes. Life outside a City is close to impossible. The symbiosis of human and machine is more than just the neural implants embedded in flesh – the City itself is a machine, sustaining all human life.

corp – corporations rule the City and everyone in it. The corps filter your water, produce your food, give you a home, and fulfil your every wish, so long as you have the money to pay them. The term corpsman refers to an individual employed by one of these corps. It is undercity slang and is not complimentary. The term originates from the contraction of the phrase 'corp's man', but also contains an echo of the phrase 'corpse man', suggesting such employees are the living dead.

glif – the glif has long existed in nascent form, but rose to dominance as humankind adopted the neural implant. A glif is a small moving pictogram that conveys information or emotion. Easily learned and understood, glifs have become the default mode of communication, supplanting the older written languages. Glifs have ancestry in Egyptian hieroglyphs, Chinese characters, animated GIF images, and the emojis popularised by smartphones in the early twenty-first century. It is difficult to express abstract or complex ideas using glifs, which may have been the intention of their creators.

ice – hacker slang for programs that prevent unauthorised access to information. Originally an acronym that stood for Information Concealment and Encryption. When your nervous system is constantly connected to the metanet, protection from hostile network intrusion is a matter of life and death. Securicorps make a good profit from their ice packages, which require frequent updates to stay effective. An icemaker is someone who works for securicorps to encrypt data. An icebreaker is an illegal program designed to breach these defences.

lumen – best understood as a digitally induced hallucination. Neural implants feed extra information into your brain, on instructions from the metanet. Alongside the real world, the user will see images that do not really exist, such as info-glifs, advertising or entertainment windows. These visions are known as lumens. The technology is not yet perfected, and lumens will not necessarily be mistaken for 'real' objects – the current generation of lumens struggles to adapt to heavy rain, thick smoke, or sudden changes in lighting and perspective. A lumen object at night will usually appear to be daylit, giving it an unreal radiance.

metanet – a system of wireless information exchange. If the blocs are the City's body, then the metanet is its soul.

Metrowatch – the Metrowatch Corporation has a monopoly on force in public areas of the City, and offers civic protection to all subscribers. Individuals without an active Metrowatch subscription are felt to be wilfully endangering themselves and do not enjoy protection under the law. As such, they are not considered victims of crime. This has created an ideal environment for criminal gangs to exploit those without subscriptions, charging them protection money in a manner not totally dissimilar to the business model of the Metrowatch Corporation.

moonie – slang for a municipal worker, sometimes also called 'municipals' or 'munis'. The name plays on the resemblance of a municipal worker's face to the full moon, as their heads are hairless and their skin is pale. They are dressed in distinctive orange uniforms. Moonies are the property of the Municipal Works Corporation, which holds the patent on the neurosurgery procedure used to create them. They are human beings, rendered voiceless, emotionless and obedient. They could be thought of as sleepwalkers, or highly suggestible hypnotic subjects, controlled via drug infusions and metanet signals. Moonies are mostly prisoners who have been sentenced in corpcourt, captured refugees from distant wars, or volunteers who have signed their body over to the Municipal Works Corporation in exchange for a lump payment. They perform many menial tasks, but most important is the structural maintenance of the cityblocs.

neural implant – the great nanotechnology innovation, pioneered by Dr Werner Inselberg. Neural implants augment the human nervous system, allowing artificially induced signals to be sent along the nerves, alongside the natural ones. Combine this mechanism with a metanet receiver, and we find all of humanity linked together, able to speak to one another at will across the surface of the planet, share sensory and visual information, and make use of many other functions. These implant rigs also allow corporations to track the location of every consumer in the City, monitor their body chemistry and mood, and even influence their dreams. Bliss Incorporated is the largest manufacturer of neural-implant hardware and software, although competitors using similar techniques do exist.

strata – the City is a savagely unequal society, which manifests itself physically as well as economically. The cityblocs, enormously tall, act as markers of status and strata. A wealthy, upstrata individual will live and work as close to the summit of a citybloc as possible. As the cityblocs grow, so does the extent of the undercity, as social climbers continuously move upwards, abandoning the unfashionable lower floors to gradual decay and ruin. There are many marks of what strata a person belongs to, but clothing is an obvious one. Upstrata individuals favour plain, muted tones, while downstrata people tend to dress in garish colours, and further augment themselves with video-tattoos or other luminous modifications.

undercity – designates the lowest strata of the City, floors that are lightless, abandoned, often flooded, and considered not merely unfashionable but uninhabitable.

The precise population of this benighted area is unknown, although it is certainly much lower than the population of the City proper. The majority of the people who venture into the undercity are moonies, although they do not live there. The permanent inhabitants are a mixture of criminals, nomads, scavengers, hermits, madmen, artists, dissidents, prophets, orphans and myriad other unfortunates and misfits. These underdwellers live in itinerant camps, in squats like the Gut, or in the few regions of the undercity that have been turned into lawless parasite settlements like Nightmarket.

wristhub – the only visible indicator that an individual has neural implants. Installed on the dominant arm. During the early years of neural-implant rigs, the hub would have been a wearable accessory, but as the technology has matured they have become part of the human body. The wristhub incorporates main-input and auxiliary-input ports for data transfers, as well as a sub-dermal microphone and a chip that is used to make payments to other wristhubs.

ACKNOWLEDGEMENTS

No novel is a one-man show. I owe a debt to many people. I'd like to thank my editor, Lily Morgan, for separating the wheat from the chaff, and my agent, Jenny Savill, for her wise counsel. I'd also like to thank Lewis Garvey for his help regarding the final act, and Wendy McMahon, in whose seminars I made the initial notes for this novel. I would further like to acknowledge the visionaries who mapped these fictional territories before me. This novel would not exist without the work of M.T. Anderson, William Gibson and Masamune Shirow, among others.

The 'speaking lion' analogy Grale refers to originates with Ludwig Wittgenstein.

LEO HUNT

was born in Newcastle upon Tyne in 1991. He grew up around books, and his mother's job at Seven Stories in Newcastle left a strong impression on his choice of career. He realised he wanted to either be an author or an archaeologist – but when he learned that archaeologists didn't unearth piles of perfectly preserved dinosaur bones every time they put a spade in the ground, he decided on the former.

Leo started writing his debut novel **THIRTEEN DAYS OF MIDNIGHT** when he was 19, in his first year at the University of East Anglia. He graduated in 2014 with a First Class Honours degree in American Literature and Creative Writing. He currently lives in Norwich.